THE GREEN FEATHERS

THE GREEN FEATHERS

MIKE KINGDOM THRILLERS
BOOK 5

DAVID JARVIS

This edition produced in Great Britain in 2025

by Hobeck Books Limited, Unit 14, Sugnall Business Centre, Sugnall, Stafford, Staffordshire, ST21 6NF

www.hobeck.net

A CIP catalogue for this book is available from the British Library.

ISBN 978-1-915-817-89-1 (pbk)

ISBN 978-1-915-817-88-4 (ebook)

Cover design by Jem Butcher

www.jembutcherdesign.co.uk

Printed and bound in Great Britain

ARE YOU A THRILLER SEEKER?

Hobeck Books is an independent publisher of crime, thrillers and suspense fiction and we have one aim – to bring you the books you want to read.

For more details about our books, our authors and our plans, plus the chance to download free novellas, sign up for our newsletter at **www.hobeck.net**.

You can also find us on Bluesky @**hobeckbooks**, Twitter/X @**hobeckbooks** or Facebook **www.facebook.com/hobeck books10**.

PROLOGUE

It would be confirmed later that two shots had been fired.

In the sky, there were several drones and two police heli-copters, but in the galvanised ventilation shaft, he could barely hear any of them over the noise from the street below, where most of the crowd were cheering and waving flags. A significant minority, however, was demonstrating angrily while being corralled by the police; the government was treading a very fine line, and security levels in the country were inevitably high. On top of this, all the proceedings were being recorded and broad-cast by the world's media, who were contained behind metal barriers immediately opposite the main entrance.

For security reasons, the fast-food restaurant beneath him had been closed, as had the other shops in the street. The army had taken up position at key points, and, to his right, there were marksmen from the special forces, wholly dressed in black, on the top of the two main buildings across from the Mahaica Convention Centre. They were visible to everyone in the street but not to him.

He was part of a team that had been planning this for three months, right down to installing a new ventilation system in the restaurant – ostensibly to take away the smells of cooking burgers and fries – although the old shaft had strategically been left in place and sealed off. To the uninitiated, the whole extraction system read as a whole. This substantial work had been done so a man could lie prostrate in what felt like a tight metal coffin. His sole purpose was to gain a direct line of sight 200 yards down the street to the convention centre's steps and main entrance.

He'd been in the roof space for nearly thirty-six hours, only moving into the shaft when tipped off by his colleagues that the police were checking the building before closing it and sealing the doors. It had been incredibly hot and humid, and his only company was a fat rat with the best supply of food in Georgetown.

Once he fired his shots, he would leave the rifle behind in the shaft. There were no markings on it or fingerprints, and the make had specifically been chosen to incriminate others. He would pass through a storeroom to exit the upper floor before descending a flight of stairs to the back of the restaurant. There was no need for him to worry about alarms because the system had already been turned off. After heading out past the waste bins, he would emerge onto a side street and make his way along a narrow alleyway. Here, he would blend into the background, being dressed in a black suit and tie over a white shirt, just another attendee at the biggest event in Guyana's history since its independence from the UK in 1966.

Once across a car park, he would get into a silver Mercedes with blacked-out windows, from the embassy and be driven off southwards out of Georgetown. The car wouldn't attract attention in its short journey to a nondescript bungalow on the banks of the muddy Demerara River. The chauffeur would barely stop before driving back to the embassy compound at 3 Public Road, Kitty.

A waiting tender moored on a wooden jetty would take the

sniper downriver, out into the estuary, and across to one of the many superyachts and motor cruisers moored here for the meeting and conference. The crew would be waiting, and the tender would be lifted on davits to its storage position. By the time the aft doors were closing, the superyacht would be beginning to manoeuvre out into the Atlantic Ocean, heading for the Azores and the Straits of Gibraltar. This was all planned for Tuesday, 25th March, and four weeks later, it would be moored in the marina at Cannes in the south of France.

———

On that fateful Tuesday, the British King had landed at Cheddi Jagan airport, from which he would arrive outside the Mahaica Convention Centre in Georgetown ninety minutes later. He was scheduled to speak at the opening ceremony of the Commonwealth Heads of Government biennial meeting, known as CHOGM. It was the first such event to be held on the mainland of South America, which wasn't surprising as Guyana was the only English-speaking country on the continent. There couldn't be a bigger contrast to a previous gathering on the islands of Samoa, surrounded by the Pacific Ocean – an expanse representing a third of the earth's surface.

The previous day, the King had flown in from London to Saint Lucia on an Airbus A330 from RAF Brize Norton in Oxfordshire.

The presidents, prime ministers and chiefs of fifty-six countries from across the globe were represented in the audience at CHOGM. Together with their entourages, VIPs and the media, there were 1,600 people waiting to hear the King open the conference and set the tone. Reparation for slavery was the hot topic, given Guyana's past as a British colony providing sugar and rum from over 200 estates and farms. Although the country is actually located on the north Atlantic coast of South America, it's culturally aligned with the Caribbean, whose attendees made up a fifth of the audience, and this was the subject at the top of their agenda.

Tensions were high even before the shots were fired on that sweltering March day.

Guyana was the second poorest country in South America, with a population of only 1 million, but it had recently discovered a substantial oil and gas field offshore, so it was – unsurprisingly – the focus of the world from China to Russia and the USA. The Guyana Finance Minister had already awarded every citizen a one-off payment of $300 as the first dividend from a bonanza that would soon give Guyana the wealth of Qatar or the United Arab Emirates. The GDP growth of Guyana had been the largest in the world for the last two years.

The presence of the King and the PM at CHOGM had been a nightmare for the British secret services; the Foreign, Commonwealth and Development Office (FCDO); and so many departments and government organisations in London. For weeks, there had been intelligence and rumours that terrorist groups were intending to target the event.

Both the British PM and the King had insisted they must make the trip, despite several separate meetings at which they or their representatives had been briefed by the head of the Secret Intelligent Service, MI6, about the risks.

The race to identify the threat and eliminate it had gained pace. The burden of this task lay firmly at the door of Gordon Overton, a controller within MI6, who had sent one of his agents to Guyana and nearby Trinidad and Tobago a month earlier to liaise with the high commissioners and various contacts in the area.

———

Sadly, despite everyone's best endeavours – including those of the CIA in London – the terrorists appeared to have succeeded in firing two shots.

Outside the convention centre, a body sprawled on the steps, hidden from view by a bunch of secret service agents and police. The TV cameras from the world's media continued to roll as two black Range Rovers and a Discovery reversed before eventually turning and roaring away back to the British High Commission a few blocks away.

Within the main hall, news of what was happening outside came from multiple phone conversations. Was it safer to stay in the hall and perhaps lie on the floor between the seats, or to begin to leave by the fire exits? The noise generated by many hundreds of frightened guests was becoming deafening. The master of ceremonies, in a black suit and tie, came to the microphone on the stage and asked everyone to stay calm and to stay put while the police and emergency services dealt with the incident on the front steps. He repeated that there was no threat to anyone inside, but his source of this information wasn't revealed.

The British delegation was standing near the front of the room in a huddle. Everyone had a phone pressed to an ear. There was much waving of hands, and voices were gradually being raised.

The Commonwealth Secretary-General walked out onto the stage, wearing a colourful dress and headscarf. She looked calm and lowered the microphone on its stand. The noise in the room reduced considerably as she informed everyone that the incident was now under control. An ambulance was on its way to the hospital. There was no cause for alarm. She asked everyone to stay in the hall while the police swept the area and added, rather unnecessarily, that the morning session would be cancelled. Over lunch, everyone would be updated with the new programme. She stressed that threats to the Commonwealth would not prevail and the meetings over the next few days would continue as close to the planned timetable as was possible.

The sound of sirens could be heard all over the city as an ambulance headed for Georgetown Public Hospital. It was in a convoy of police cars racing away at high speed.

This was unnecessary. The patient was dead.

PART ONE

CHAPTER ONE

The acting head of station for the CIA (aka the Agency) in London had thanked everyone for coming. Such an unexpected death had come as a shock to the entire office. He had called an impromptu gathering, both to celebrate a life of service and to reassure the workforce that all was well in the world.

The staff members were solemnly filing out of the large meeting room to return to their desks and workstations; many had tears in their eyes, and there was a respectful silence. While most were sad or indifferent, one member of staff was angry.

Michaela 'Mike' Kingdom chose to take the stairs down to her office rather than the lifts, in order to avoid human interaction; her fingers were digging into the palms of her hands.

"Total BS," she whispered under her breath while replaying over and over in her mind the words she had just heard.

Brent – the new head honcho – was tall, thin and wore crisp, dark suits. He was from Massachusetts, and his irritating voice emanated from high up inside his nasal passages. He was about as different from his predecessor, Leonard de Vries, as it was possible to conceive. The eulogy, if that's what he had delivered, reeked of sanctimonious cliché and appeared to blame everyone apart from the Agency for what had happened.

"God, I hate you," she said, although whether this was directed at Brent, God or some other person wasn't made clear. The list of human beings that she disliked was famously extensive.

Everybody on her floor knew better than engage Mike in any conversation today; her temper was short at the best of times, and her lack of tolerance to injustice was evident to all.

"She wears her fuse on her sleeve," Morag, who sat at a desk near Mike, had once said appropriately – or perhaps mal-appropriately.

It was Friday afternoon and almost the end of the working week. Everybody was distracted, and there was a fair amount of clock-watching. Mike signed out of her system and went down to Security to collect her bag and phone. A weekend away from all this loomed and might be what everyone needed.

Unfortunately, Wazz had flown back to Warsaw in Poland for his mother's funeral. He and Mike weren't officially boyfriend and girlfriend, perhaps most people would say *not yet*, but their lives seemed inextricably linked, and there was an inevitability about the way forwards. After a disturbed adolescence and some unfortunate events, Wazz had pulled himself up to the point that he was buying a flat in West London. This was where she would usually go after the one day a week she spent in the Agency office – but today, when she really needed him, he was away.

Not all was doom and gloom, however. After a series of incidents in the preceding year that had changed her life, she had sold up everything apart from her motorbike and bought a small house in Wiltshire. She was an analyst and could work from home, or at least she was able to under Leonard de Vries, who'd treated her like a gifted daughter. What was going to happen now under Brent Cromer was anyone's guess. In her mind, she couldn't see her new boss as anything other than a stuffy Pilgrim Father who had gone across on the *Mayflower* and was unlikely to treat her in such a relaxed fashion. But this was a problem for next week – maybe.

There was another reason why travelling to her new home might improve her mood: her friend Tina was coming to stay.

————

A few days earlier, Tina Persad had been looking down at the Caribbean Sea out of a plane window, but she wasn't arriving for a holiday; she had been flying the sixty-five miles from Tobago to its larger sister island, Trinidad, having completed her meeting. After a tiring and difficult assignment, she had hoped to have only a few days of work before returning to London.

Nor had she been on a scheduled flight; rather, Tina had been sitting in the small back seat of a Bombardier Challenger plane belonging to the Trinidadian Coastguard, which was used to track drug smugglers trying to make the crossing from South America, a mere seven miles away to the south and west. In the narrow cabin, there was only one seat on either side of the aisle, and in front of her had been three men wearing headphones and sitting at keyboards and screens – two on the left side and one on the right. Her forward view had been limited by the computer equipment that stretched up to where the overhead lockers would have been if this were configured as a commercial plane. The fact that she'd been hot and uncomfortable hadn't mattered, as she'd only been hitching a ride on the very short flight.

On arriving at Piarco airport, the captain had left the engines to idle as she had walked across the apron towards the terminal. Before she had entered the building, he was ready to taxi out to the runway, annoyed that, yet again, he was being used as a bus service by the ministry.

With her laptop bag in one hand and the other shielding her eyes from the sun, Tina had entered a dedicated door that avoided most airport formalities except the need to pass through a security scanner. A tall, young man called Everton, in trousers just a tad too short, had loped over to her and shook her hand. She had followed him through some corridors, out into the sunshine and across to his car, which had been parked in the shade of a casuarina tree.

Christina Franklin Persad was born near Maidstone in Kent to a British mother of Pakistani descent and a father originally from Roseau, the capital of Dominica, which is a tiny country in the Windward Islands. He was a chemist, and his wife was a doctor. Their thirty-five-year-old daughter was a spy.

Obtaining a degree in biochemistry wasn't the usual route into the secret-squirrel world, but her work on identifying the source of illegal narcotics for the police had led in a circuitous way to MI6 and, for a short secondment, to Five Eyes in Chiswick. It was while working there with other English-speaking colleagues from the USA, UK, Canada, Australia and New Zealand that she had met Mike Kingdom, who was from Portland in Oregon and had been on secondment from the Agency. At that time, Five Eyes in London had been headed by an American, Leonard de Vries.

After spending two weeks in Guyana, as well as Trinidad and Tobago, she was soon to fly home. A stay with her friend Mike had been tantalisingly close, and she could already taste that glass of Pinot Grigio.

———

The Green Feathers had been a drinking establishment for 350 years and was still standing despite many attempts to demolish it or put the building to another use. While the rest of the main street of the Wiltshire village of Rodbourne had been gentrified, mostly by Londoners who were tempted by the railway station a mile away, The Green Feathers had been left to decay like a bad tooth.

The saying "a creaking door hangs the longest" didn't apply here, as even the old pub sign could no longer be bothered to squeak on its rusty support. It was so faded that any words were illegible, and it was impossible to tell if the painting was of a bird (perhaps a green woodpecker on a tree) or a mythical man with leaves in his hair performing some rite of spring involving a local virgin.

Whatever the reason for the pub's name, this was usually the second question that most visitors asked. The first was "Where's the bar?"

The Green Feathers had never had one, and this made it very unusual. Stepping through the studded oak door, a visitor was confronted not by a cheery landlord behind a row of beer pumps but by about a dozen tables in a large but dingy lounge where everyone stopped talking the moment the old brass bell tinkled above the entrance. In the back wall was a door hidden behind a thick curtain made of a length of heavy, faded tapestry that was crudely extended to the stone floor by a piece of dark-red velvet. From this, a woman often emerged. She had thinning, white hair smeared over a brown scalp and almost always wore a thick, mousey-coloured cardigan with deep, distorted pockets over what looked like a white nightdress. Her name was Jess.

Men who were 'something in the city' rather enjoyed coming here. Whether this was because they weren't paying £400 for a bottle of fizz in a Docklands brasserie or because they gained some masochistic pleasure by being totally ignored by Jess if they in any way tried to demand attention, it didn't matter. She was an equal opportunities abuser – a not-so-distant relative of the King came here precisely for this experience. It reminded him of his preparatory school.

When and, more importantly, *if* Jess asked whether you'd like to order, she'd disappear back behind the curtain to return with a tray of filled glasses. There was no food menu, and whether it was midday or early evening, the meal on offer consisted of what was essentially a ploughman's lunch: local cheddar cheese from a farm outside Wedmore and bread she had baked that morning in the oven built into the lounge wall, where it sat to the side of a long-dead games machine on which stood a stuffed green woodpecker in a tall glass dome. Which had died first – the machine or the woodpecker – was the subject of ongoing debate. Her pickled onions could be found in jars on shelves around the back room, and the piccalilli chutney was to a recipe that her uncle had brought back from the Indian subcontinent, where he had been an engineer on the railways, but it consisted mostly of vinegar, grated turmeric and cauliflower that grew out in her vegetable garden.

It was 9.30pm on that dark Friday evening in early March when Mike walked into the pub with her friend Tina. In The Green Feathers, the weekend was well underway.

Mike had recently moved to a brick-and-flint terraced house in Rodbourne after her cabin in Oxfordshire had been destroyed in a fire. The insurance payout and the sale of one surprisingly valuable gift from her benefactors, the Murchison brothers, had enabled her to afford to buy 3 Church Lane without a mortgage.

To the locals, she was another rich escapee from London in her thirties who had moved to the area or bought a second home, pushing up the property prices. Apart from the facts that she was American, always wore a hat or scarf on her bald head, and her boyfriend's Polish surname was unpronounceable, she had warranted little attention.

Having both had long and mentally exhausting weeks, Mike and Tina were in desperate need of a drink.

The brass bell tinkled, but it could hardly be heard. They stepped down into the lounge to be confronted by thirty or so people laughing and chatting around a dozen tables or standing next to the defunct games machine, using it as a shelf. A few people nodded and said hello.

As if by magic, Jess came out from beyond the curtain and asked them what they wanted to drink. Mike ordered a beer, and Tina had a large white wine. They sat on a padded bench where a group of young farmers had shuffled along to make space. Two attractive young women were a welcome addition to their party, although it didn't take long for them to realise that the girls were more interested in talking to each other. One of the farmers had also met Wazz in the pub before and didn't wish to get involved with someone who looked as if he could snap most people in two.

Mike was wearing a tight, red, knitted skull cap and her usual sweatshirt and jeans. Tina, who was a little shorter, had her thick, glossy, black hair tied back and was in a lumberjack shirt and dark trousers.

"Right, tell me about the trip." Mike was wasting no time, even if the conversation would have to be conducted in a coded way.

"Well, I must tell you about a strange meeting I had with our friend. He chose to meet me on the Pitch Lake in La Brea."

"Really? Why there? And what do you mean by 'on'?"

"No idea, but it was empty when we walked out onto the tar at that time of the morning."

"What? What are you talking about?"

"Yes, you can walk out onto the tar ... it's like grey elephant skin. You're OK as long as you don't stand still for more than a minute or two, otherwise you start to sink. It's fine, except you have to navigate all the oily pools and puddles."

"Couldn't you have met in a bar or hotel, like normal people?"

"It's a sort of tourist place down south in Trinidad. It's pretty big, a hundred acres, and was private ... well, it was until this other guy turned up."

Mike was transfixed and subconsciously reached for her non-existent drink on the table. "Who was he?"

"A local man who likes to wander about and talk to visitors. He'd probably been smoking ganja, and I should no doubt mention that he was very tall and very naked."

"Tina!"

The young farmers stood up to leave, having had a long day sowing spring barley.

"He wasn't completely naked. He had a piercing: three Carib beer bottle caps hanging on his foreskin,"

"Oooh!" On hearing this, one of the farmers with curly, blond hair reached for his groin in a protective way and frowned. "Excuse me, ladies."

The farmers walked around the table and made for the door, nodding to Jess, who was coming out from behind the curtain with a tray. Mike and Tina moved along the bench and pushed the men's empty beer glasses to one side of the table, ready to receive their drinks.

"No Wazz?" Jess asked in a rich West Country accent as she put the beer in front of Mike.

"Still in Poland. This is my friend Tina."

"Hi," Jess and Tina said in unison. They both had very pale eyes. Tina's were a hypnotic amber colour, emphasised by her dark-brown skin, both inherited from her mother, and Jess's were a weak blue-grey, washed out from old age.

Mike paid by tapping her card on the machine proffered by Jess, who then walked back between the other tables.

"Where was I? Oh yes, standing out on the Pitch Lake talking to Sheldon with a naked man showing me his piercings."

"How did you get rid of him?"

"I memorised the address and agreed to meet his contact in Tobago two days later." Tina was relaxing.

"Not Sheldon; I meant the naked guy?"

"I gave him $5 and asked him to go and get a bottle of Carib for me."

"You're mad. I would've been scared shitless and said something rude."

"Mike, you stick to the analysis, and I'll do the fieldwork. Staying calm and in control is a prerequisite."

"You're so right. I lose it in my office when they run out of paper coffee cups, so what hope is there out in the field?"

Tina sipped her wine and looked around the pub at the odd cross-section of society brought together by geography and the need to have a drink. There was no one near and plenty of background noise; therefore, they could speak more freely. "It was unfortunate timing – this trip, I mean – but unavoidable. It clashed with Carnival, everything was booked, and I couldn't get a flight to Tobago and back. They let me take a ride on a government plane."

"Carnival is my idea of hell; there are too many people."

"I didn't get to see Carnival this year, and you don't get much sleep for about a week before. The steel bands practice into the early hours of the morning all over Trinidad and especially in Port of Spain. I used earplugs and slept under the covers."

Having a friend to stay was an unusual occurrence for Mike, principally because she didn't really have any friends. However, from the first time she'd met Tina at the Five Eyes office in Chiswick, they had clicked. In many ways, they were similar, even if they came from different countries and backgrounds. They had worked together on the same drug-smuggling project that had necessitated Tina spending time in the Caribbean. For the whole time Tina was there, Mike had tried to give her the best back-up, but Mike had constantly worried about her.

"What was Sheldon's new contact like?"

"Initially, I didn't like him much, but I have a feeling he might be useful. We met outside a building right next to the

TEMA building; you know, the Tobago Emergency Management Agency on Bacolet Street in Scarborough. No idea why."

"Weren't you scared?"

"No, if he were going to kill me, he wouldn't have chosen a place like that. There were government employees and police coming and going all the time."

Mike looked upwards as if this was all beyond her.

CHAPTER TWO

In The Green Feathers, Tina had ordered another round of drinks and finished updating Mike on her Caribbean trip. Jess had brought the wine and beer over on a tray, together with a little bowl of chopped gherkins; the latter weren't explained.

"Right, enough about me; how was your week?" Tina asked.

"Pretty shit. My project has ground to a halt, which is pretty annoying as I've put in the hard yards. I need to find some new line of attack for Monday."

"Is it about the usual?"

"Yes, I spend my life tracking the cartels around Central America and Europe. They're moving on to meth production at industrial scales."

"Which country? Can you say?"

"This week, I've been checking out Costa Rica. Have you been there?"

"No, sorry, can't help you, but I've heard it's a nice, safe place."

"It's why the characters I'm after live there, I suspect."

"It's only the size of Belgium, I think."

"What is it with you Brits? You use Belgium for area, London buses for length and Nelson's column for height."

"Or football pitches; we like to use football pitches."

They both picked up their glasses to drink.

"Today wasn't great either." Mike's mind had wandered back to earlier in the afternoon. "Brent Cromer held a sort of memorial service on the top floor. God, I hate him. Makes me appreciate Leonard, and that's not something I thought I'd ever say."

"Was it for a member of staff?"

"An analyst called Zara; I don't think you've met her."

Tina put down her wine glass and stared at Mike. "You're joking. I didn't know. Nobody told me." Tina let it sink in. This sort of thing often happened in their world, where everyone worked in silos. "She's part of the team working on my project. What happened?"

"She was knocked down while she was out running three days ago. Never regained consciousness."

"What? They sent me some of her intel last week while I was in Port of Spain. Did they get the driver?"

"No, not that I've heard. She was a great kid ... came from Philly."

Tina reflected for a minute. "She was really sharp. The stuff she sent was spot on. That's sad news. How long have you got to put up with this Brent guy?"

"Hopefully, only for another week, but it could be longer. Leonard's having an operation in the US of A and should be back soon. I sure hope so."

"Is Leonard all right?"

"With him, it's always questionable; I know his health isn't good, but I'd rather the devil I know. I have no idea what Brent's done before in the Agency. He's from Rent-A-Manager, if you know what I mean? And he's religious."

"Oh dear," Tina commiserated, but her mind was clearly elsewhere to the point that she choked by absent-mindedly eating a few bits of vinegary gherkin. She took a swig of wine. "This place is decidedly weird. Who serves gherkins?"

"I think they're left over from the ploughman's lunch. If you're really unlucky, she puts pickled onions out."

They finished their drinks.

"Time to go?" Mike suggested.

They both stood up.

Jess half pulled back the heavy curtain and watched them walk to the door, with several people mouthing various goodbyes.

As they stepped out into the cool night air, Mike could sense Tina had gone into work mode, looking up and down the empty village High Street illuminated by its three lonely street lamps.

"What's up?"

"Nothing," Tina replied, "I'm still on edge from the trip. It takes me a few days to calm down."

"You can relax; we're a hundred miles from London in the middle of nowhere. It's one of the reasons I chose to live here. Let's get a good night's sleep."

Above them, as they walked along and into the dark of Church Lane, the International Space Station shone brightly like a star. It was only 250 miles from earth. How deceptive distance can be.

———

"When are you coming back?" Mike was asking on her phone. It was Sunday morning.

"It may be the end of the week; my grandfather isn't well, and the authorities are requiring some more paperwork regarding my mother." Wazz was still in Warsaw, having to deal with the complications following an unexpected death.

"Things here are shit." There was no recognition from Mike of the difficulties he was facing.

"I'm sorry; what's happened? Can you tell me over the phone?"

"Not really. I'll try to come up to London and stay later this week."

"Perfect; we can listen to each other's moans and groans."

"Ha! You should be so lucky."

Wazz knew she would laugh. He was the only person who made her calm down and breathe normally.

She walked back into her kitchen to join Tina, who was pouring milk from a carton onto muesli for her breakfast.

"That was Wazz. He hopes to come back on Friday. I'll go up and stay for a couple of nights."

"Why don't you move in together?"

"I know what you're asking, but, no, I couldn't take that last step, and coming here wasn't about Wazz; it was about me. He'll be in London for a few months; after that, who knows?"

"You've bought a great place here. Don't get me wrong, I loved your old cabin, but it was too remote for me. Do you miss it?"

"Yes, I do, but I wanted a change; something different. I thought I'd give a small village a try."

"... with a pub."

"Yes, I never thought I'd like a British pub, but I do. It's slightly anarchic, which floats my boat."

"Trust me, that isn't a typical British pub, but I think being near Salisbury is fantastic."

"I didn't even factor that into the equation."

―――

The previous day, they had driven to Salisbury to play at being tourists. Mike had wanted to get to know her nearest adopted city, and Tina had wanted to do something mindless that wasn't connected to work and, specifically, didn't involve the Caribbean.

They had wandered around the cathedral and found a restaurant for lunch, over which they chatted about the poisoning of Sergei and Yulia Skripal in March 2018 by two Russian nationals. There was a certain irony that Mike and Tina, an American and a British spy, were sitting very close to where their opponents had carried out such a bold attack a handful of years before.

They had done more touristy things and, afterwards, bought some ready meals and a bottle of red wine for their dinner; a ploughman's – with or without gherkins – at The Green Feathers didn't appeal. It was only a short drive home along the Wylye valley with its soft, rolling chalk downland on either side.

Once back in Rodbourne, the red-brick-and-flint inserts of Mike's thatched terrace had come into view, and Tina had parked the car on the street, alongside a ditch flowing with water. Their hunger was such that they had eaten immediately when back in the house, demolishing the bottle of Shiraz while chatting into the evening. They had gone to bed about 10.00pm, both as distracted from their workday problems as they could be.

A series of storms had been forecast overnight, but these didn't materialise.

———

With absolutely no reason for either of them to wake early on a Sunday morning, that's exactly what they did, and they met up in the kitchen with one of them needing coffee and, in Tina's case, tea.

"Mike, I know this is a bit odd, but can I use your laptop for a few minutes to check something out? It's been bothering me all night. I don't want to use my phone."

"No problem; let me set it up for you. There's not much interesting on there anyway. Clear the search history when you've finished."

Mike gave Tina access and went upstairs to shower and finish dressing. This took fifteen minutes. "Success?" she asked when she came back into the kitchen.

"Sort of ... thanks." Spies in the field like Tina are actors, and she kept her face from betraying anything about what she had just discovered. It was inconclusive but odd enough to give her plenty to think about on the journey home.

"What's up?"

Tina explained that she couldn't say, but there was something separate that she wanted to pass on to Mike. "Something's not right. When I met my new contact in Tobago, he gave me a name that could be relevant to your project, I'm guessing. I passed it back to my boss, and he appears to have kicked it into the long grass. Why? Why not pass it on to you and everyone via Five Eyes?"

"What name?"

"Eric Fournier."

An almost three-hour drive to London, up the A303 past Stonehenge and then on the M3, was looming large, so after breakfast, Tina washed and packed her bag. She didn't fancy catching the Sunday afternoon traffic heading back up to the capital. In addition, although she had successfully hidden it, something was ever-more preying on her mind.

Mike was sad to see her leave. Tina was the only woman with whom she had developed a bond in recent years – if she were honest, for decades. She felt odd standing next to the car, waving her off. There was something bothering Mike as well, but the two of them weren't yet close enough to confide fully in each other.

Mike walked the few steps to the High Street to watch Tina drive past The Green Feathers and off in the direction of London.

———

The cottage wasn't large but after Tina had left, it felt very empty. After hours of wasted effort on her project, Mike had spent a long Sunday night tossing and turning. This was ironic because it was quieter at night in the village than it had been in her cabin in the woods where owls, foxes and muntjac deer hooted, barked or shrieked. She hadn't got used to the silence. Wazz's flat in Ickenham was even noisier from the sounds of the London suburbs: the police sirens, the bin lorries and the occasional drunken revellers at 2am.

After breakfast on Monday, she felt revived and immediately checked out Eric Fournier, but she found nothing of interest. Tina must have been wrong, but this was nothing new – agents in the field often passed back new leads enthusiastically, only for them to prove to be of little value. Instead, Mike looked forward to spending a couple of days trying to find new connections between South American drug producers and their European and US distributors. This involved listening to hours of taped conversations in Spanish that had been forwarded to her after they'd been selected and ranked by a sophisticated AI program. If something piqued her interest, she would follow the thread of calls, contacts and locations back in time. It was laborious, but it suited her on a day like this where she needed to be kept occupied. If she stopped, dwelt on the private thoughts in her head or, worst of all, interacted with another human being – whether friend or foe – she would become moody and irritable. It was best that she was on her own for two days.

By Monday afternoon, she was getting nowhere. She decided to take a break and go for a walk around the village. After grabbing a packet of bird seed and two slices of bread, she opened the glass-panelled kitchen door and stepped into her back garden. Two great tits flew away, but only as far as a hawthorn tree from which they watched her fill up the mesh holder. She wandered back towards the house, going past her motorbike under its silvery cover, and opened the gate that allowed her to walk down a tunnel under her bedroom, which gave rear access to the houses in the terrace. When back out in the daylight, she was faced by a short footbridge over a narrow ditch that ran along Church Lane. Two feral Muscovy ducks swam towards her in single file, waiting for the pieces of bread, which she duly dispensed. They were the size of geese, and black and white with red faces, though what they had to do with Moscow was lost on Mike. Where they slept was also anyone's guess, but they'd been around for years apparently. In The Green Feathers, they were called Philby and Burgess.

It took her twenty minutes to walk around the village and back to the thatched terrace. By then, the two ducks had made their way along the ditch towards the church at the far end. Another couple of hours listening to intercepted phone calls awaited her. Ready to attack the task in hand again, she turned down the passageway to her back gate, lifted the latch and headed back into the house.

She had barely settled at her work desk when she heard a firm rat-a-tat-tat.

Her front door was made of substantial, white-painted wooden planks with a diamond of opaque glass that served no useful purpose – neither providing light to the sitting room nor identifying who was outside. There appeared to be two faces outside, but she could make out no detail. She approached expectantly as visitors were a rare, almost non-existent occurrence.

On opening the door, she was confronted by two men, both dressed casually without ties but wearing jackets. They looked as if they were about to tell her about Jesus and hand her a leaflet.

"Mike Kingdom?" asked the taller man, who wore black-framed glasses and was carrying a large briefcase.

"Yes. Who are you?"

"We're from your office. May we come in rather than speak out here?"

"No, you can't. I have no idea who you are."

He didn't reply or show any identification as if expecting that response. The other man had his phone in his hand and pressed a button, saying nothing.

"We'll wait here while you take a call on your phone."

"What call?" At which point, she could hear a ringtone in her kitchen.

She closed the front door, leaving them outside, and walked back through the sitting room. Her phone was on the work surface near the sink. She picked it up. "Hello?"

"Please wait, I have Director Cromer for you."

It was a very long wait, during which the temptation to end the call mounted.

"Miss Kingdom, this is Director Cromer. I've sent two of my officers to your house. Please do as they ask without question. Their instructions come directly from me. Do you understand?"

Mike was caught off guard and her normal 'attack is the best form of defence' mechanism didn't seem appropriate. "I don't understand."

"Come into my office tomorrow at 10.00am, and we'll discuss all this in detail. Do as they say without question."

"Discuss all what?"

"Tomorrow."

"How do I know this call is genuine?"

He gave the unique four-figure code that was for her to use if she was ever threatened.

"OK," she said.

He rang off.

Mike couldn't process what was happening, but while she was thinking it through, she walked over to the back door and locked it. In years to come, she would often reflect on whether it would have been better for her to have crept out the back and hopped over the fence at the end. She could have made her way to the rear of The Green Feathers, where Jess would have hidden her.

Her decision needed to be made in seconds. Trying to think logically, she dialled her office number asking for Cromer. His PA listened and passed on her message while she stayed on the line. "Yes, it was Director Cromer. He says he'll see you tomorrow at 10.00am. Have a nice day."

Trying to calm her breathing, she rationalised it all by breaking it down into simple points: she'd done nothing wrong, the two men were CIA officers, they couldn't arrest her or force her to leave the house, and Director Cromer had asked her to go into the office tomorrow morning.

With her face set in a frown, she returned to the front door and opened it. "I've spoken to Cromer. He wants to see me tomorrow in London. Thank you for coming."

She went to close the door, but the shorter man put his foot over the threshold. "We need to collect some Agency property and then we'll be gone."

"What property?" She realised that resistance was useless and stepped back, allowing them to enter.

"Your Agency phone, your laptop with the gizmos and your ID card."

"What? Why? What have I done?"

"Sorry, ma'am, we've been told nothing. You know the drill. We're here to collect Agency property and to offer you a lift to London."

"No, thanks; I'm staying here."

"Your choice."

They followed her into the kitchen, where she made sure she was logged out of the laptop and closed its lid.

"We need to take this, sorry." The taller man lifted the briefcase onto the worktop and put the laptop and her connected gizmos inside. "And your phone?"

She handed it over.

"ID card?"

"It's upstairs; wait here."

She ran up the stairs to her bedroom and grabbed it. On her return, they were still standing in the same place, but she was suspicious they'd been prying or had attached a microphone somewhere. She would check later.

"Here." She handed over the ID card with its thumbprint image. "How am I going to get into the office tomorrow?"

"Ask at the desk. They'll be expecting you."

"Any other Agency property that you have here?" the shorter man asked.

"No."

"Sure you don't want a lift? It seems convenient."

"No ... thank you."

"... and thank you, ma'am. We'll take our leave."

CHAPTER THREE

What had just happened?

Mike was back in her kitchen with a coffee. She felt violated, although the two officers had been civil; so civil in fact that it made her contemplate what would have happened if this had taken place in her home state of Oregon. CIA officers have no powers of arrest – it would be the FBI who did that – but they had no jurisdiction in the UK. She was reassured that the British police weren't involved, which meant that, whatever this was, it was an internal Agency matter.

By the time she had swallowed the last mouthful from the mug, her emotional response had changed from fear to anger.

How dare they! What did they think she'd done? Because she was struggling to think of anything. As the rage welled up, she did her best to control it, well aware that she could do something stupid and make matters ten times worse. Perhaps this was something simple, and the temporary recovery of Agency property was standard protocol while they investigated.

It was probably best that she didn't try to contact anyone until she knew what this was all about – especially if it were all a misunderstanding. The two people she most wanted to phone were out of the country. Wazz wasn't back until Friday and Leonard ... Well, this would never have happened under Leonard. He was in Washington or Alabama or wherever he was recovering from surgery.

Her eyes roved around the kitchen shelves, not entirely without an ulterior motive. They stopped on a white tin with "Sugar" written on it in blue. She hopped down from her stool and wandered across. Tina; there was always Tina.

Before making the coffee, Mike had checked around the kitchen, looking for bugs or cameras. None were apparent, but this didn't stop her from lifting down the tin, taking out a phone from inside and attaching it to a battery pack. She walked to the far end of the garden before turning it on and, despite the low battery, calling Tina's personal number. She kicked at the remains of a compost heap left by the previous owner while she waited.

It went to voicemail, so she left a message: "Tina, I've just had a visit from two men. They were from my company and took all my kit with them. They want me to see the boss tomorrow at 10.00am up at HQ. I have no idea what's happening, and I have no one to call." She had chosen her words very carefully.

She returned to the house, and once back inside, she locked the back door, left the phone on charge and went upstairs. On the landing outside her bedroom, she used a pole with a hook to open the roof access and pull down an integral ladder. She began to climb it, and halfway up, she stretched inside, avoiding the sooty cobwebs, to turn on the single light bulb. Only part of the roof space was boarded, and she was careful where she walked. At the far end, she reached under the planks and pulled out some orange fibreglass insulation. She fumbled around, trying to find some equipment, which she retrieved before replacing the insulation. With a laptop, charger and cable in her left hand, she retraced her steps to the kitchen, but not before making a diversion into her bedroom, where she collected a memory stick from a ledge inside the built-in wardrobe.

With the laptop on charge alongside the phone, she went back upstairs to pack her rucksack. It would be a 5.00am start tomorrow if she was going to make it into the office by 10.00am.

———

It was still dark the next morning when Mike locked the back door and pushed her bike through the tunnel to the front of the house. Dressed all in black, she was wearing her leathers, matt helmet and gloves, plus carrying a large rucksack on her back. The village was silent, and she wheeled the bike the few yards to the High Street, where she started it. The street lamps had turned off hours ago, and there were no signs of life in any of the houses. When would she return?

The previous afternoon, Mike had checked over the bike in case a tracker had been attached to it, and she'd tied the silver cover back on so any interference overnight would be obvious.

She was careful as she rode, but it would be very difficult to physically follow a motorbike travelling up the A303 at 5.30am when the traffic consisted of mostly lorries and vans. Stonehenge was passed unseen, and the glow on the horizon began about an hour later. The M3 and M25 motorways were navigated in a blur of thoughts, and a little before 8.00am, she found herself pulling the bike onto its stand at the back of Wazz's flat in Ickenham, a village now engulfed by London's western expansion.

It was an ugly, modern block of flats, but it served its purpose and was handy for Heathrow. She struggled up the stairs as her left leg ached after the long journey. Taking off the rucksack was a huge relief, and her back was wet under the leather jacket. On entering the flat and shutting the door behind her, she could smell Wazz's aftershave; the flat was as clean and tidy as he always left it.

There was only time for a piece of toast using frozen bread with peanut butter and a coffee from his mini espresso machine. While eating and drinking, she wrote a note and left it on the table in case things didn't go according to plan - that's if there were a plan. After clearing her private phone's history, she left it by the bed. Today, Mike wouldn't take anything to the office apart from her credit card, although being without a phone would seem very strange. Sometimes, she rode her bike to work, and other times, she took the London Underground. Today, she decided to catch the latter. With an uneasy feeling in her stomach, she walked to Ickenham station.

———

The train ride was surprisingly soothing, principally because of the rhythmical click-clack and the gentle rocking. It helped her, and she was a little calmer by the time she arrived at work.

On entering the office building, Mike couldn't follow her usual route through Security, but she instead had to join a queue before being asked to take a seat while someone came down. She was issued with a visitor's badge. Time dragged, and she grew tired of nodding in strange ways at vaguely familiar staff who were unaware why she was sitting outside the barriers and body scanner.

A bored-looking middle-aged woman in uniform came down to escort her up to a meeting room adjoining the director's office. She knew it well, but it would feel very different sitting opposite Brent Cromer rather than Leonard, with whom she could speak frankly. The security guard made it clear that she would wait outside the door in case Mike should need the bathroom or for when she left the room, as she couldn't walk around unescorted. Mike tapped the door and was called inside.

Around a polished table, there sat no one she recognised: a broad-shouldered man with a red tie, who introduced himself as

Scott; a fierce woman with a face like an eagle, called Kathryn – that's Kathryn with a K and a Y she had stressed; and, finally, another woman from Human Resources, who smelled of soap or cheap perfume. Mike was asked to take a seat as Director Cromer would be along presently. The room was stuffy, and there was no small talk, which worried Mike. Her bald head under the paisley bandana was beginning to itch.

The adjoining door opened, and in walked Brent Cromer wearing a black suit, white shirt and silk tie. There was a Stars and Stripes pin in his lapel. He told everyone not to get up. To do so hadn't crossed Mike's mind.

"Thank you for coming," he addressed his visitor.

"I didn't appear to have a choice." She was about to launch into a tirade, but she thought better of it. The temperature in the room seemed to have dropped.

"What we've done is precautionary. I hope that, by the end of this, you'll see its necessity." His nasal twang was at its most irritating, but he hadn't finished speaking: "Tell me about your relationship with Christina Persad."

Mike was weighing up every word before saying anything; Wazz would have been impressed. "We worked together when she and I were seconded to Five Eyes under Leonard de Vries. The project was successful." Mike bit her tongue to prevent herself rambling on about the mistakes Tina had made on that project until she knew what was happening.

"Have you seen her since that time?" Brent Cromer was sitting stiff-backed as if he had a broom handle up his jacket.

"Yes, a few times privately." There was no point denying the obvious.

"The most recent meeting?"

"She came and stayed overnight with me on Friday and Saturday night. She left about 8.30am on Sunday morning."

"Did you discuss work?"

"No." If Mike said yes, it would open up a can of worms.

The director digested this. "Not her recent trip?"

"She said she'd been in the Caribbean recently, but that's as far as it went. We're both operatives. We both know the rules."

"I thought you were an analyst?"

Mike had reached her limit; it hadn't taken long. She pulled off her bandana and threw it down on the desk in front of her. "This doesn't happen sitting at a computer screen, does it?" She'd added the last words with venom while pointing at her shiny, bald head, a consequence of a horrific accident out in the field that had killed Dylan, her husband.

He swallowed and avoided looking at her. If he thought her outburst was over, he was wrong.

"Why don't you tell me straight what's happened instead of pussyfooting around?" She was now glaring at him with her dark, almost-black eyes.

He slowly regained his composure, having come to a decision. "That's not how I expect my staff to speak to me, Miss Kingdom. I was hoping we could have a civil discussion about a serious problem that has arisen. Your cooperation would be beneficial."

"I'm happy to help. Let me have my phone, laptop and ID back, and we'll pretend it never happened."

The other three around the table were silent, as if watching a chess tournament.

"Sadly, that's not going to be possible until you've been eliminated from our enquiries."

"What enquiries? Am I being arrested? Do I need a lawyer?"

"The Agency has no powers of arrest, and here in the UK, we'd need to involve the police, which I wish to avoid at all costs." He reflected for a moment. "Christina Persad works for British Intelligence, so it all becomes complicated."

"What has she done?"

"I can't tell you that right now."

"Then how can I help you?" It was her turn to pause. "Why can't you trust me? If you need a reference, ask Leonard."

"As you know, Director de Vries is back in the USA for medical reasons. He may not return."

"I asked you why you can't trust me."

"Because of the evidence I've been shown."

"What evidence?"

"You know the world in which we operate. I cannot tell you."

"Either accuse me of something or let me get back to work."

"This isn't easy, but I can't let you work until this is resolved. I'd like to suggest that I leave you here with these good people, and they'll explain what I'm offering you. You'll be suspended on full pay, and you'll go on garden leave for as long as it takes to sort it out. In that time, you'll contact no one from the Agency or related agencies. Please consider it carefully." This was a man who had patently not read Mike's file.

She had reached the end of her tether. "No, I've had enough of this BS. I resign ... with immediate effect. I'm taking it that you don't want me to work out my notice period?"

Nobody spoke.

"I'll take that as a no. You have my pass and all my equipment. Anything else?"

"If you want my advice, what you're doing isn't helpful. I pray this works out for you."

"Don't bother praying for me."

She stood up, grabbed her bandana and left the room without saying goodbye.

The security guard escorted her from the building, and like when she had left her cottage, she wondered if it was the last time she would ever set foot in it.

———

The Tube journey back to Ickenham was difficult for her. She couldn't distract herself by reading on her phone, listening to music or messaging anyone. It felt strange.

Even stranger was the realisation that she was unemployed.

The train was soon overground, and the landscape outside the carriage window was disappearing backwards into the distance – a bit like her career. Running the last few days over and over in her mind provided no answers and didn't help her to calm down. She was on a knife edge, but, thankfully, no one near her tried to engage. This was one of the benefits of the Tube, where everyone studiously avoided eye contact.

Reading the advertisements above the passengers' heads opposite didn't delay her for long, and she went back to two basic questions: What had she done innocently to trigger this? And how was Tina connected?

The first one was baffling. She could think of nothing, unless one included the occasional massaging of the rules by Leonard, but why would this interest Cromer? He was only meant to be the acting head of station for a month or two, so why would he choose to rake over the past? Obviously, he was a sanctimonious asshole and a stickler for rules, but didn't he have bigger fish to fry? Maybe he had spotted something to do with Leonard, and she was being dragged into it.

As for Tina, their one project at Five Eyes – where they'd been part of a huge multinational, multi-agency team – had been very successful in the end. Nobody had broken any rules, certainly not her, and while Tina had misjudged someone in the field, she had come good in the end.

Mike was staring at the various shades of chewing gum on the floor, ranging from beige to black, while replaying the weekend visit to Rodbourne and trying to think of what Tina had said or done.

Later, while walking towards the flat, past the semi-detached houses hiding behind the closeboard fences and the brick walls, she felt a tinge of regret. Should she have accepted the offer of garden leave? Would this have been better? Luckily for her, the salary was largely irrelevant; it was the freedom to do what she wanted that mattered to Mike. When Cromer had said she wouldn't be able to contact her colleagues, her mind had been made up.

It was Tuesday and almost 1.00pm as she hauled herself up the concrete steps to the front door.

CHAPTER FOUR

Thirty-eight miles away as the crow flies, a man who had been christened Johnny Boswell was unfastening his seat belt, having landed at Stanstead airport in a Dassault private jet. This was one of what he called his '*official* visits'. He absolutely adored England, but he had an overriding problem: he didn't like paying any tax. This had given him a dilemma because he had wanted to spend a lot longer in Essex than the ninety-one days that the British tax authority, HMRC, allowed for non-residents like him.

He had paid millions to accountants and lawyers to find ways around the problem, and while they had saved him even more hundreds of millions in tax through legal mechanisms, they couldn't find a way around the ninety-one-day rule. His business affairs should be relatively simple, but he'd had it up to his back teeth trying to keep track of his many companies registered in the British Virgin Islands, the Turks and Caicos islands, Trinidad and Tobago, and Antigua. He was sick of talking to his paid advisers about it. All this made him more money, but it gave him no more days in the UK. When the lawyers added twenty per cent VAT to their extortionate bill for giving him advice on how to save tax, he had suffered enough.

He was never embarrassed by his heritage. He still had the genes and that instinct to make money and to crack problems, but despite going to private school, he had craved respectability for all his forty-one years. Applying everything, he had found several ways to live in Essex while ostensibly living in Monaco.

His grandfather, Rex Boswell, was part Romany and part, well, a bit of everything. He was uneducated and said that he only understood two words: 'topsoil' and 'cash'. In the 1970s, Rex bought every cubic yard of soil he was offered around London and sold it on to developers and builders at a handsome profit. He had almost achieved a monopoly in the South East and could insist he was paid in cash, even though this made difficulties for the limited companies and authorities with whom he dealt. He had a simple trick to ensure the system worked: he wasn't greedy and left them no alternative. It was them who had to sort out the tax liabilities. He didn't care if they had to use middlemen or simply paid the tax – that was their problem. *Never renege on a deal and be cheaper than anyone else.* It never failed, and he spent his days being driven in a dirty, dark-green Aston Martin around the dodgiest parts of London and the suburbs, where he met buyers and sellers of what he said was "the nearest thing to gold you'll find in Hillingdon or Redbridge".

Duke Boswell, his son, had an unusual problem when his father died in 1998 – what to do with all the cash. They found £4.5 million in a strongroom deep within the brick mansion Rex had built outside Chelmsford. Apart from always having a chauffeur because he hated driving, regularly buying second-hand Aston Martins and never being seen without a thick gold chain around his neck, Rex never spent any money on himself, and, most of the time, he slept in his vardo, a traditional caravan, inside the walls of the four-acre garden.

Unfortunately, Duke had none of his father's natural business nous and never built on the foundations Rex had established. He did, however, decide that his son – Johnny, as he was then known

– should be privately educated. This worked – well, half-worked – as when he left school at eighteen, he at least knew considerably more words than 'topsoil' and 'cash'.

Johnny Boswell was fifteen when his grandfather died; he loved the man and was heartbroken. The genes had obviously skipped a generation and not just in terms of the business acumen: they looked the same. Tall with swarthy skin, smiling eyes and shoulder-length, black hair that was divided in a central parting. At school, he was nicknamed 'Tonto' after the Native American sidekick to the Lone Ranger. It never bothered him in the slightest.

It continued not to bother him. He was worth almost £1 billion.

———

However, Johnny Boswell wasn't the name in his passport.

Early on, he had realised that someone else should superficially assume his identity. His idea was simple. There was no need to pay millions to lawyers and accountants or hundreds of millions in taxes; he could work out how to solve it himself. His cousin Darren should unofficially adopt the name, and it should be his photograph in the passport.

It was Darren who would fly in and out of the UK, but on pain of death if he even thought about breaking the fiscal rules of any country, especially the UK. In fact, he would live the life of Reilly in Trinidad and Tobago, paid handsomely by the real Johnny, who was holed up in his Monégasque penthouse or Cannes villa.

The real Johnny possessed a very expensive passport in the name of Peter Swift, who was registered as a care worker living in a trailer park just outside Brightlingsea on the Essex coast, north of the Thames estuary – a person of no interest to HMRC. Ironically, Peter was technically still at his erstwhile address: he was buried six feet under the caravan. The whole site was owned and managed by the Boswell family.

Johnny and Darren looked enough like each other that they might be mistaken across the street, but not in a way that would fool a Border Force officer or an AI program analysing CCTV; however, this didn't matter.

Two or three times a year, Peter Swift would fly first-class into Ireland, where he would spend an enjoyable night before catching the Dublin to Holyhead ferry. The next day, he would be in Essex, where he would spend as long as he liked. He would return to Monaco via a similar ferry route, perhaps Newhaven to Dieppe or Harwich to Hook of Holland. This was all overcautious, but the financial consequences and even time in prison didn't bear thinking about.

While in Essex, he was scrupulously careful not to use anything traceable in the UK: phones, credit cards or anything similar. This wasn't a problem for someone brought up on cash. His close friends and family did the actual paying for everything, and they were rewarded five-fold in other ways.

His empire worked perfectly and grew in scale. The business model, however, never changed, being based on two immutable concepts: family and fear. It was also uncomplicated. 'Keep it simple, stupid' was his mantra. KISS!

The system had worked for six years, and there was no need to change it until one day when his life was turned upside down and time suddenly became of the essence. Now he had no choice: Peter Swift needed to fly direct to Stanstead in Essex. There was no time to take the scenic route, as he called it.

He didn't care that it was a family member who had betrayed him; they would pay dearly. Greed: it was always when people got greedy that the train went off the rails.

———

So it was that he had been aboard a Dassault private jet, which he had rented in Nice. It had landed through cloudy skies.

Carrying only a laptop and accompanied by his PA, Louise, he walked out of the terminal at Stanstead and dived straight into a brand-new Aston Martin DB12, which was driven by an uncle. This obsession was a homage to his grandfather. It's no longer possible to pay in cash for a £200,000 car from a UK showroom, as money laundering checks prevent this, but this didn't stop Peter Swift. Jimmy, an uncle, bought it legitimately and received twice the price, paid into a foreign bank account. His nephew, whom he struggled to call Peter for his usual two-month visits, sat in the passenger seat, still fuming.

The one-hour journey to the eastern part of Essex was awkward. This wasn't because Peter had any beef with his uncle Jimmy, far from it; this had more to do with the almost uncontrollable anger that was raging inside him. There were long stretches of silence peppered by quick outbursts or random thoughts that he might ask Louise to note down. Neither Uncle Jimmy nor Louise dared initiate any conversation.

As they drove along the A120, they passed the outskirts of Braintree, and his mood lightened slightly, perhaps connected to his deep love of the county. Monaco was sterile, Nice was an industrial port, and Dubai was a rich Disney theme park. They were all great, and he was happy to spend a few days in any of them, but they weren't Essex. He had a tattoo of the county symbol – three notched cutlasses – on his right forearm.

There was still half an hour to go as they drove around Colchester and headed towards Brightlingsea, which is a small harbour town on the estuary of the River Colne. His mood darkened again – he really wasn't in a good place mentally – and he began wittering on about the *Mignonette*, a yacht built in Brightlingsea in 1867.

It was famous in English law for establishing one common legal principle. The yacht had run aground on its way to

Australia, and four of the shipwrecked crew had grown desperate. Three of them had murdered and eaten the sickest member: the seventeen-year-old cabin boy named Richard Parker. The resultant trial established a key common law principle, namely that necessity isn't a valid defence against a charge of murder.

Peter Swift was having black thoughts.

———

While trying to fall asleep in Wazz's double bed that night, Mike regretted only one thing: that she had called Tina using her own secret personal phone. If the Agency and others were suspicious of Tina, they would see the missed call and the message she had left. They would now know Mike's number – although, of course, getting another burner phone wasn't a problem.

She had already factored in that the Agency was bound to break into her house looking for evidence of whatever she was meant to have done. This didn't bother her unduly, as she had brought everything important in her life, such as her passport, in her rucksack up to the flat.

Agency analysts spend their lives hiding their virtual/online tracks, and Mike knew she had to avoid searching on her laptop for anything that might draw attention to her, but she didn't know where to start looking anyway. If only Tina would ring back or make contact.

Sleep came fitfully. At some godforsaken hour early in the morning, she gave up and left the bed. She was only wearing her pyjama bottoms and was rubbing the smooth top of her shaved head. Despite the earthquake that had just happened in her life, she had only one thing on her mind: coffee from Wazz's mini espresso machine. Deep inside, she felt every staccato thump as it pushed the water through the capsule. A cup of coffee would cure all ills.

At the ridiculously small kitchen table, she was musing on

where she should begin to look. This was no different from her normal life at work, except that now it all centred on her.

Where was Wazz when she needed to shout at someone or something? Lasting until he returned without going mad would take an enormous amount of effort.

Her focus turned to Leonard. He was someone else she could, on occasion, shout at. Where was he? Cromer had said he might not return. What did that mean? Perhaps his surgery had gone wrong, and he was leaving on medical grounds. Dare she try ringing him? She had both his work cell phone numbers, but she was worried that his calls might be put through to Cromer or his cronies. The thought of being unable to contact Leonard and maybe never seeing him again struck home.

A sense of helplessness began to grow.

She put another capsule in the machine, but she wasn't paying attention. After pressing the button, it began spraying brown liquid all over the work surface as steam came out of every orifice, while hissing loudly to confirm that the gods were displeased.

Mike put her head in her hands.

At least cleaning up the mess gave her something to do. She grabbed a dishcloth and began wiping and rinsing it out into the sink. Two pieces of kitchen roll took care of the last smears and drips. The flat must be perfect for when Wazz returned, although the smell of coffee may take some time to dissipate. She might need to empty the bin and change the liner.

At this low point, her phone rang, but the name of the caller was withheld. No one had this number.

"Hello," she said, "Who is it?"

"Mike Kingdom?" asked a soft male voice, probably British.

"Yes, who is it?"

"You tried to call Tina Persad's phone on Monday. I'm Oscar, a friend of hers."

"With access to her phone?" Mike wasn't in the mood for games.

"Yes, obviously. May I ask you a few questions?"

"No."

This response derailed him. "Are you alone?"

"That's a question. I said no questions."

"Ah, true, and so is 'I'd love to talk to you privately about what happened to Tina, so where can we meet?'"

"Are you British or American?"

"British."

"Do you know who I work for and my current status?" She almost used the wrong tense.

"I can guess who you work for, but I'm not sure what you mean by your 'current status'."

The fact he had said, "what happened to Tina," in the past tense was bothering her. "Why would I possibly want to meet a random male caller?"

"I'm guessing because we both care about Tina, but may I make it easy? You choose the time, place and any rules. All of which I'll accept." His words were unhurried and delivered in a gentle and unthreatening tone; if this was a pitch, it was unconventional.

She imagined him with glasses halfway down his nose, which he constantly needed to push up onto the bridge. "London?" came out of her mouth, with no forethought.

"No problem."

"Tomorrow?"

"Fine."

"I'll send two friends to check you out first. Is that a problem?"

"No."

Mike was making this up as she went along, with her enthusiasm overriding any professional caution. "I'll meet you in front of The Shard at 11.00am tomorrow, Thursday. How will my colleagues recognise you?"

"Shall I carry a *Financial Times* under my arm?" There was a gently mischievous tone to his voice.

"Why not?"

"Until tomorrow."

CHAPTER FIVE

It was a bright but bitterly cold March day as Mike emerged from London Bridge Tube station in Southwark and walked along Borough High Street. The doorway of a vacant shop provided a vantage point. She was taking a huge risk, but finding what had happened to Tina was a priority. Discussing this with anyone she trusted wasn't an option as Wazz didn't come back until Friday and Leonard was under the surgeon's knife across the Pond. There was, however, a voice in her ear. Dylan, her late husband, was urging her to think what he would do. He'd been an experienced CIA case officer, and she tried to apply some of his tradecraft.

At the appointed time, she telephoned Oscar, whom she presumed was standing outside The Shard – the tallest building in the UK – awaiting her arrival.

"Can you go along St Thomas Street? And I'll meet you outside London Bridge Tube station on Borough High Street. We'll go on a short trip."

He asked no questions, simply said yes, walked for a couple of minutes until he reached the busy junction and turned left.

She spotted him immediately, and when he was outside the

station entrance, she rang again. "Keep walking along Borough High Street. I'll tell you when to stop."

He didn't reply, but he looked around searching for her.

Mike wasn't concentrating on him; she was looking out for anyone following him – an individual or team who would now be panicking that he was going to get on the Tube. This technique might, just might, flush them out as they hurried to get to a position where they could catch any train. Nobody appeared interested, and so she assumed he was alone.

As he reached Lloyds Bank, she telephoned for a third time. "Whoa! Turn left into The George. Order me a Peroni or similar at the bar. I'll be sitting outside."

Next to the bank, there was a very narrow passage under a metal arch that gave access to the oldest pub in London with a galleried courtyard. Mike had met Leonard here twice before, and they had sat at the wooden picnic tables, avoiding the internal rooms.

After one last check, both up and down the street, she crossed it and entered the tight alleyway. At that time of the morning, it wasn't busy; it had just opened, and any people were inside on such a cold day. She chose a table under a furled green umbrella that gave her a view back out to the street through the only access point. Dylan would have been proud of her, but if she was honest, it was Leonard who had explained the advantage of being able to watch everyone coming and going from the street. He had also pointed out that it was a dead end, so it wasn't a good place if you were expecting violence or unfriendly people. She had ignored the last bit.

A man in a thin, beige windcheater jacket with a pink newspaper folded under his arm came out of a door, carrying a tray with two pints of beer, a large bottle of sparkling water, two glasses and some packets of crisps. Mike gently raised her hand, but he had already decided she was the person he was looking for. She was in her black leather jacket and a baseball cap.

He was as nondescript as it was possible to be – surely an advantage in his job. Brown hair, hazel eyes and a soft, clipped beard that was at the high-street end of 'designer'.

He put the tray on the table and performed the complicated routine of trying to slide onto the seat while lifting his legs over the wooden supports. He didn't bother to offer a handshake.

"Oscar," he said, handing one of the beers to her, "Oscar Smith. Thanks for meeting me. What's your name?"

"Mike Kingdom, which is my real name, unlike yours. Who do you work for?"

He didn't exude confidence. "The same sort of organisation as you, I'm guessing, from the subterfuge involved in meeting here."

"Quite likely. How do you know Tina professionally?"

"We work in the same department. Are you Canadian?"

"A bit further south, although there may not be a distinction for much longer if our latest President gets his way."

They were engaged in a delicate dance. However he tried to suppress it, he was the most keen and got straight to the point. "OK, whoever you are, Tina has gone" – he took a deep breath – "missing, and I'm worried. You were the only person who's tried to contact her."

"You have her phone?"

"I have access to her phone records." He let this sink in.

After a moment, she asked, "Are you MI6?"

He gave up on any more obfuscation. "Something like that. I heard your message. Are you at the US Embassy?"

"Something like that."

"You're obviously close to Tina, and you sounded, well, anxious in your message."

"She's a friend, and we've worked together in the past. She stayed with me at the weekend after her recent trip."

He lifted the tall beer glass to his lips and took a very long, slow drink while he was weighing up the options. He made up his mind to trust her. "Look, I'm new to all this, and I'm personally going crazy. I'm her support." He looked dejected, but he carried on, "I was her liaison while she was on her trip, as you call it. On Monday, she was meant to come into the office up here." He nodded in a direction that meant nothing in an enclosed courtyard with only the towering glass pyramid of The Shard above them providing any orientation. "She didn't turn up and has gone missing. My bosses have gone all defensive. They think she's run off with the family silver. My name really is Oscar, by the way, but not Smith. I'm not trained for any of this. I sit at a desk all day."

"So do I. This is new to me too."

In the next half-hour, alone in the courtyard, they began to confide in each other.

"I don't know how operatives or case officers – whatever they're called at your place – cope with this madness. I'm an analyst. I'm happy at my desk." He had both hands on the beer glass as if it might topple over.

"So am I." Mike was warming to him. If he was a foreign agent, then she had no hope of ever grasping the subtleties of being in the field.

"I'm so worried about Tina."

"Me too."

"Was she all right when she left you on Sunday? Had she said anything?"

"She was a bit nervous, in retrospect. She drove off about 8.30am, heading back up here."

"I don't think she made it. What makes you think she was nervous?"

"Look, Oscar, Tina and I are friends; we worked together at" – she looked around – "Five Eyes. She and I probably shouldn't talk about work, but we do ... a bit. You know how it is."

He nodded.

She finished her recollection: "We had a great chat in the pub until I mentioned someone from my office had died last week. She said she knew them, and it seemed to bother her."

"This is Zara, I'm guessing."

"You know about her?"

"She was your – by which, I mean your company's – analyst on our project. She and I were providing the intel to Tina out in the Caribbean. When I heard she'd been knocked down, I got nervous as well. Now do you see why I phoned you?"

Mike was frustrated. She didn't know what Tina was working on. "Oscar, what have you found so far?"

"Apart from the message you left her, I've found nothing. Her phone disappeared off the radar not long after she set off from wherever you were together in Wiltshire. She hasn't used her credit card, you know, or any of the usual things we check."

"She told me she didn't like the contact she met on Tobago. The one Sheldon gave her. You know about that presumably?"

"You know about Sheldon?"

"It was me who discovered him two years ago."

"Oh. As to her new contact, I only have a brief one-paragraph report that she sent back while out there. The team was meant to be updated by her on Monday."

"There's something else you need to know. I resigned yesterday."

He reached for a packet of crisps and opened them, which was clearly a displacement activity. "Oh, that's a shame."

"I couldn't hack it any more, but I might have been a bit premature. I no longer have access." She didn't bother to mention that this had been removed from her whether she stayed or left.

"Is that your personal phone?" He nodded at the one on the table before her.

"Yes, but I think it won't be private for long."

"How do we stay in contact?"

They were discussing this when a woman sat down at the

table next to them; her partner had dived inside to the bar to order. Mike had watched them enter from the road, walking under the metal arch with its central lamp. Why sit next to them and not on one of the other vacant tables?

Mike glared at her, craving privacy for the last bit of her chat with Oscar. The woman didn't look across once, even with the dark-brown eyes of a woman in a baseball cap boring into her.

Odd that, Mike had thought as she limped down the Tube on the way back to Ickenham.

———

When Mike stepped onto the pavement outside Ickenham Tube station, she purposely loitered and watched the other passengers who had got off the train with her. Nobody acted suspiciously, nobody looked at her and nobody hung around. Reassured, she walked off towards the flat. There was no other human in sight.

When she reached the landing at the top of the stairs, she unlocked the door and could immediately smell something.

Fortunately, it was the aftershave she had grown accustomed to over the last year.

"Honey, is that you? How was your day?" Wazz asked in a mock American accent. This was all part of an oft-repeated routine they had developed, based on some generic soap opera, but today, there was no sarcastic reply about the traffic jams or Sandra in Accounts being pregnant.

"Oh, thank God; you're back." She ran into the kitchen, threw her arms around him and kissed him. "I thought you were coming back tomorrow?" The baseball cap had fallen off her head, and she bent down to put it on the table with her bag.

"Everything is either sorted or I've left it with a solicitor. No point staying any longer."

"Did it go OK? Well, you know, as OK as it could go."

"Catholics sure know how to drag out a funeral. They make

you feel guilty for surviving, but no matter; it's done. I'm glad to be home. How was your weekend with Tina?"

Mike burst into tears. This was one of the few times she'd done this in front of him, and he grasped that things were bad – *very* bad.

"OK, tell me all about it."

They pulled out chairs and sat down.

He could smell the alcohol on her breath, but he thought it better not to make any jokes. Instead, he said he needed a beer and took two bottles from the fridge. "Right, off you go. Start from the top. I'm sure it's not as bad as you think."

"I've resigned and Tina's gone missing."

"Oh great." Wazz dropped his head, breathed slowly and tried to think of something else to say. "I was only away six days. Couldn't you go to the office, file your nails, come home and watch Netflix like the rest of the population?"

"I ... no, I couldn't ... and you weren't here."

"I'm sorry, but if it helps, my father's long dead and I've just buried my mother, so I think you're safe that this won't happen again. Tell me what I've missed."

While drinking, she recounted what had taken place at the weekend, avoiding many of the operational details of Tina's Caribbean trip. "... and then I mentioned that Zara in the office had died last week, and she became a bit twitchy. She drove off on Sunday morning as planned. She hasn't been heard of since."

"I'm so sorry. I hope she turns up soon. It's only Thursday." He could always see the positive side.

"While I was at Rodbourne, I had a visit from two Agency men. They took my phone, card and laptop. I appear to be suspected of something."

"Really?"

"They told me to come into the office on Tuesday where the boss ..." She stopped and looked into his eyes. "Where the boss was going to suspend me and put me on garden leave. I got pissed and resigned. Don't say anything; I know, I know."

"Mike—"

"I know, I know. I have no idea what they think I've done."

"So what are you going to do?"

"I think I've already done it."

He frowned.

"I met somebody this morning who's also concerned about Tina."

"I'm going to take a wild guess that you really, really shouldn't have met this person?"

"You're so negative."

"That'll be a yes, then?"

"He works for MI6. He's the analyst who's been supporting her on her project."

"These three things – your suspension, Zara's death and Tina going missing for a few days –aren't necessarily connected."

"True, but in my world, we don't do coincidences."

"What did Leonard say?"

"He's having an operation in the USA, and I can't risk trying to ring him; my call will get transferred to the new boss. Whom I hate with a vengeance, by the way."

"That was taken as read."

She drank from the bottle while Wazz offered her his great idea: "I suppose I could call Leonard, or you could borrow my phone and call him?"

"It'd still end up with the douchebag here ... but you've given me an idea. I'll get to him via his daughter; she's a chef in Alabama."

CHAPTER SIX

It was mid-afternoon, and Wazz was in the kitchen, having put a load of washing into his machine. It was filling with water and swishing back and forth.

Mike was searching on her laptop. "You know he's never mentioned his wife or daughter to me?"

"No, but then do you talk about personal matters at work?"

"Given what I've been through with Leonard, he might have said something. All I know about him personally is that he loves food and basketball."

Over three or four jobs, none of which had completely gone according to plan, Leonard and Mike had developed a love-hate, father-daughter relationship that was completely at odds with his position as the CIA head of station in London. It suddenly dawned on her that, after six or seven years, he was no longer her boss. "Damn you, Leonard."

The machine started its wash cycle.

It was on her last overseas trip for him that Chuck, a work colleague, had casually mentioned that he'd overheard Leonard speaking to his daughter, who was a chef in Montgomery, Alabama. How hard would it be to find her?

It took twelve minutes for Mike to have all the details she needed, including his daughter's phone number.

"What time's it in Montgomery now? Hey, it's 10.00am. Perfect." She was talking mostly to herself.

"Whoa! Slow down. Why not use my phone? Won't they search your history once they know your private number?"

"Good thinking, Superspook."

He raised his arms and flexed his not inconsiderable muscles in a bodybuilder's pose, testing the short sleeves of his white tee shirt. He handed over his phone. "Do you need my passcode?"

"I know it, thanks." She smiled sheepishly. "What? Relax, it's my job. I'll go into the lounge."

The washing machine had begun its first spin.

Wazz was spreading some butter on toast as, through the open door, he watched her tap in the numbers and wait. As she spoke, he heard just one side of the conversation, punctuated by long silences.

"Hi, is that Diana? I'm Mike. I'm a friend of your ... father. How is he doing after his operation?

"... Gee, that's great news. When's he back in London?

"... I've worked with him for years ... Yes ... No ... mostly about food, you're right.

"... Diana, can I ask a favour? I have a new phone number, so will you pass it on to Leonard? Can you see it on your screen? Great ... No, great ... Thanks.

"... That's interesting.

"... Ask him to call me please ... if he's recovering, he'll be glad of the distraction ... Tell him I need to update him on the basketball over here urgently.

"... That's kind ... You too ... Bye ... Bye, Diana."

Wazz appeared at the door, taking the last bite of his toast.

"She sounds just like him, but that's not surprising, I suppose." Mike began walking back to the kitchen.

"No problem getting him to phone?"

"I'm hoping he will. She said she's been ringing him every day since he's been in hospital. Can I hang on to your phone for the rest of today? You can use mine if you like?"

"Very kind."

"I've thought of something else: Chuck. If necessary, I could go around to Chuck's house. He owes me a few favours." Mike didn't need to elaborate why this was so. Wazz had been involved in the whole episode a year ago in Spain that involved her work colleague Chuck, but she said, "You know what I mean, if I need access to the Agency systems."

"Why don't you wait to hear from Leonard first? He might know the answers already or solve everything for you by making a couple of calls."

"OK, OK, I'll wait ... a bit." But at least she now had a smile on her lips.

He lifted a washing basket onto the work surface. "I'm not going back to work until tomorrow evening. We can have a bit of quiet time together." He was a bouncer at a strip club in Paddington, as a temporary job to pay the bills while he finished his degree.

She made a noise halfway between a laugh and a snort. Obviously, she thought this was unlikely. "I wonder when Leonard will phone?"

"It's been two minutes. You don't do patience, do you?"

————

Wazz was in the lounge listening to music on his newly bought and very expensive headphones, and Mike was at the kitchen table, scrolling through websites on her laptop. They were both relaxing – or at least trying to relax – after a fraught week. It was almost 9.00pm.

A phone buzzed. It was on the table next to Mike. She saw

the country code immediately and a wave of relief swept over her.

On picking it up, she heard an American voice: "Hey, I knew I'd convert you to basketball. How are the Surrey Scorchers doing?"

"On fire? Burnt out? I have no idea. I could ask Wazz, if you're really interested? "

"Nah, don't bother."

"This is his phone by the way. Sorry for ringing your daughter; I couldn't think of another way of getting hold of you. How are you?" She was letting it all pour out as she always did in situations like this. There was no off button.

"I'm doing good. I've been at home for a few days."

"When are you coming back over here?"

"Are you missing me?"

"Don't flatter yourself."

"What's up?"

"I resigned yesterday."

"*Holy cow!* Why?"

"I don't see eye to eye with your replacement, and he was going to suspend me."

"What have you done?"

"No idea. He wouldn't tell me; he just confiscated my phone, laptop and card."

"Oh great. Leave it with me, and I'll find out."

"You know that Zara was knocked down and killed last week while out running?"

"I heard."

"But you may not have heard that ..." Mike hesitated, trying to pick the right words to use on an open line. "You remember that Brit who worked with me and you at the other place? She's gone missing as well."

"Shit, what's happening? I've only been gone five weeks."

"I'm worried about her. She was with me at the weekend."

"I know what she and Zara were working on. Be careful."

"That's why I'm using Wazz's phone. I don't know what's happening or who to trust."

"Great way to be. I'll make an operative of you yet."

"I've just posted my resignation, remember?"

"Nah, there'll be a clerical error, I expect. The office is really crap at filing and letters get lost all the time."

———

It was a sunny Friday afternoon.

Mike had taken a bag of rubbish down to put in the wheelie bin around the back in the parking area while Wazz was shopping at the local Tesco Express for their evening meal. He had left his phone behind in the kitchen as there was a chance Leonard might call it. In fact, while she was putting a new white liner in the bin, it was Mike's own phone that rang. She didn't recognise the number, but she answered it anyway.

"Mike? It's Oscar. I'm ringing from a different phone. I have no idea who's listening to what."

"Me neither. What's happening? Any news of Tina?"

"Yes ... well, no. Nothing that's useful, I'm afraid. She turned her phone off quite soon after she left you in Wiltshire, and it hasn't been back on since, but her car has been tracked. She followed the obvious route back to London, but then she went around the M25 clockwise and bought petrol at South Mimms services, paying with cash. After that, she drove around to Junction 28 and disappeared somewhere near Brentwood. She didn't drive along any of the obvious roads, such as the A12. They're still checking. I've been going through the hotels, but no luck so far."

"Why would she not go straight home? Is Brentwood relevant to your project? You don't have to answer that, by the way. I know the rules."

"No idea why she didn't go home, and I'm not aware of any connection between her project and Brentwood."

"No problem. But she hasn't used her cards?"

"No, not to my knowledge. She paid cash at the services. It was number-plate recognition that led to my colleagues spotting her route."

"And her car's not left the Brentwood area?"

"Well, no one's found it yet."

"How big is Brentwood?"

"Quite big. I don't know – a bit less than 100,000 people. I don't really know."

"I'm really worried about her."

"Me too. I'll keep you updated. See you later. Bye."

She turned and saw Wazz was standing at the door with a bag of groceries.

"Was that Leonard?"

"No, that was my new friend Oscar. Tina never went home from Wiltshire. She drove to Brentwood, wherever that is. She's disappeared."

"I know Brentwood. It's about forty-five minutes from another strip club in the chain, the one in East London." Wazz worked principally in Paddington, which was much nearer to his flat.

"Oscar couldn't tell me everything, but he gave me something to get my teeth into, which I'm going to spend all afternoon checking. What are we eating tonight?" Her thoughts, like Leonard's, were never far away from food.

Wazz smiled, but he hadn't even said anything when she asked, "Actually, what are we eating now?"

"You haven't eaten lunch?"

She checked the time on her phone. "I got distracted."

He smiled in resignation. "Would you like me to make you a sandwich? Cheese and tomato?"

"Yes, please."

With that, she opened her laptop on the kitchen table to begin looking more deeply at the connection made tentatively following the call, which had led to a whole series of possibilities. She was miles away, staring at the strip light on the ceiling, when the sound of the plate being put in front of her broke the spell.

"Thank you," she said without truly registering the food Wazz had prepared.

What had Zara in her own office been working on? This would be very useful to know.

Unfortunately, Oscar wasn't in a position to reveal what Zara and Tina had been working on. The world was crazy. Mike and Oscar were both surreptitiously trying to find Tina, but they were both working for different secret organisations with limits on what they could tell each other about operational matters. Suddenly and separately, it dawned on Mike again that, technically, she wasn't actually working for the Agency any longer. This thought frustrated her, but that didn't matter; her right of access to the Agency network, data and staff had already been removed before she had resigned.

So she had no route in to where she wanted to search via the British and no route in via the Agency. Time to go it alone.

The cheese-and-tomato sandwich had chutney in it, her favourite.

"*Thank you,*" she shouted out, not having seen him leave the kitchen.

———

Sheldon Douglas was in California, close to the sea.

Unfortunately, it wasn't as glamorous as it sounded; this was a residential district behind the port of Point Lisas on the west coast of Trinidad, somewhere between Pitch Lake in the south and Port of Spain, the capital, in the north. Point Lisas was part of the largest industrial area to be found on the island.

He was on the balcony of a two-storey house painted turquoise; the metal security grilles on the French windows were folded back to give him access, but the wrought-iron bars across the balcony were permanent. The sky behind the tangle of perhaps twenty telephone and power lines filtering his view was a dark purple as the daily thunderstorm built up.

A couple of *Adonidia merrillii* Christmas palms, in the grass of the small front garden, competed with the telegraph poles to obscure the view further. Perhaps this was a good thing as, in the near distance, all that could be seen were the backs of industrial warehouses and the higher elements of the ammonia production plants. There was a constant smell of gas in the air.

He sat back down on a white plastic picnic chair and played with his phone. One of his contacts would meet him here soon. Appointment times were plus or minus an hour if they involved travel along the Sir Solomon Hochoy Highway.

Earlier, he had broken the monotony by walking seawards to watch the *Esprit de Bordeaux* leave port, heading for France on its nine-day journey; it was laden with 9,000 tonnes of anhydrous ammonia that was destined to be used across the arable fields of Picardy in Hauts-de-France or Les Landes in Nouvelle-Aquitaine.

Sheldon had done well for himself, given his background of poverty on the streets of Chaguanas. He grew up sleeping under a sheet of plastic draped between an electricity substation and the boundary wall of a cemetery. There were three of them who had called this home for a few years, and they had looked after each other. He'd done so well for himself compared to his friends that he had to be careful, or they may begin to suspect. He now owned his own bungalow, which he had built in fits and starts whenever he had money or materials or free labour.

A few years previously, his life had changed. He'd been recruited by the Agency to provide them with intelligence on several matters of importance in Trinidad and Tobago. 'Blackmailed' might be a better word than 'recruited', but it added up to the same thing. At first, he had railed against it, but he had gradually realised that the regular income and occasional bonuses were a lot easier than working in a shop in Port of Spain or moving drugs around the island for the gangs. He never knew it was Mike Kingdom who had identified him and his involvement in the drug trade; she had passed his details on to someone else.

Then, he'd been transferred to a British handler, but he didn't know why or how this had happened. He had never heard of Five Eyes. The TT dollars kept flowing into his bank account, and that was all that mattered. He thanked the god who had looked after him.

Two weeks earlier, he had met an acquaintance at the Pitch Lake to pass on the name of a contact, together with a meeting time and place on Tobago. He had met her five or six times before and found her attractive. The meeting had gone well. He couldn't work out if she was a Trini or a Brit or a bit of both. When the local space cadet had come over, his dreadlocks in a colourful beanie hat but wearing nothing else, she wasn't fazed at all.

It was the easiest money he had ever earnt.

There was always the need to be careful. Each one of the million people in Trinidad and Tobago was connected by family, work, sport, church or community; secrets were hard to keep, and with more than one murder every day, by bullet or machete, it was worth keeping your wits about you.

The huge, black clouds towered above him, and the heavy rain started. The sound of the drops on the rusty, corrugated tin roofs was deafening. His guest would be even later if the local roads became flooded, which was a near certainty.

There was an almighty crack of thunder, and the rat's nest of telephone wires in front of the house fizzed. None of this seemed to bode well.

CHAPTER SEVEN

At the flat in Ickenham, the weekend had consisted of Wazz attempting to distract Mike. In this, he had failed dismally as she had spent most of it at her laptop, tapping away, regularly throwing her hands up in the air and cursing a long list of things in the world – this included everything animate and inanimate.

Not having access to either the CIA or British systems, she was having to work in isolation as a private citizen. Annoyingly, this meant having to repeat searches she had undertaken previously.

Over the weekend, Mike had become more and more tense, frightened and fractious; she was worried sick about her friend. Wherever her mind wandered, it always returned to Guyana, together with Trinidad and Tobago – surely this area held the key? It was one of the locations of the project on which Mike and Tina had met. Although Mike didn't know the details, Tina's latest case was obviously centred there, and she had only just returned from the trip there before she disappeared. What had happened or what had she stirred up while she was out in the Caribbean? And what was the connection to the UK?

Mike could only think of one starting point: Sheldon

Douglas. The irony wasn't lost on her. She had found him in the first place, and now she needed to find him again.

This didn't take long, but now she had resigned, she couldn't risk contacting him, and this frustrated her. Everything would have to be done at arm's length and not leaving any trace. While she might start with Sheldon, her main objective was to find the person he had introduced to Tina and whom she had met outside TEMA's offices in Tobago. Who was he? He was obviously a nasty piece of work.

At her Agency office in London, it would have taken Mike minutes to look through Sheldon's phone and other records, but as it was, it took her most of the weekend. Firstly, she had to download the illegal software that was necessary for her to hack into his phone and social media accounts. Secondly, she had to find his numbers and addresses. Only then was she ready to look at his contacts. By Sunday evening, she still hadn't found anything that might lead her to this mystery man, and there was a huge sense of disappointment.

Wazz took the brunt of her frustration and suffered as a consequence. They went to bed on the Sunday night sleeping back to back, even though it hurt her to stay on her left side for too long.

———

Wazz didn't work on Monday and Tuesday; therefore, he thought they might go somewhere together to clear the air. He suggested visiting the National Portrait Gallery in St Martin's Place and so, by 11.00am on a grey but dry Monday, they found themselves staring at slightly disturbing works by Francis Bacon. Wazz had hoped she might be drawn to more-saccharine, calming pictures, but this was unlikely to happen.

Not long afterwards, they were standing in front of a seemingly anodyne eighteenth-century painting of Benjamin Hoadly, the Bishop of Winchester. Mike was in a world of her own, reading the notes, when she stopped. He'd been the leader of the Feathers Tavern Petitioners – a controversial group. It took her back to The Green Feathers and the exact words Tina had used in their conversation.

Mike was evidently distracted as they made their way through the rooms.

Two hours later, they were in the Audrey Green café, eating lemon cake with cups of strong coffee. The inspired idea of going to an art gallery appeared to have worked, and she was chatting away about the paintings when her phone rang.

"You're late for work." There was no introduction, but she didn't know many middle-aged men who spoke with an Alabaman accent.

"I'm unemployed, remember?" She stood up and began walking out of the café.

"That's a shame. Are you looking for work?"

"No, I'm actually busy on a project at the moment."

"Looking at paintings doesn't count as work."

"What?" She digested this. "Are you tracking my phone?"

"That's illegal. Anyway, I don't have the skills, but I know someone who does. Actually, I employ quite a few of them. Talking of employment, I'm recruiting."

"I'm not coming back to the USA."

"No, it's London based. I'm interviewing at the moment."

"Go easy on the poor bastards. Not everyone likes basketball."

"I'll have to put that down as a black mark, but otherwise you're doing well."

"Leonard, what are you talking about?"

"This interview. It's going well. In fact, I'm happy to offer you the job."

"What job?"

"Your old job."

"What?" She was flummoxed.

"Can we discuss it?" He sounded almost reasonable.

"Um ... yes, I suppose so."

"OK, I'll join you for a coffee. Order me a big slice of cake."

She pivoted around looking for him, gave up and walked back to join Wazz. "That was Leonard. He's joining us for coffee."

"Really? He can use my chair. I'll leave you to it." Wazz wasn't a good actor.

"You knew! Did you set this up, or was it Leonard?"

He was standing and unsure whether to keep a straight face or to smile. The resultant odd grimace was rendered irrelevant as an overweight man with thinning ginger hair walked up and shook his hand.

"You must be Wazz. Thanks for everything. Great work. I'd offer you a job, but the only vacancy I've got has just been filled." Leonard sat down, preoccupied with the empty side plates and cups. "You ordered yet?"

———

Johnny Boswell would often say he hadn't developed his grandfather's ideas very far. He would joke that his focus remained on cash and topsoil.

It was true that he himself no longer dealt in *cash*. It was more likely to be Bitcoin or asset swaps, but the principle was the same: it was mostly untraceable. As to the *topsoil*, he had moved more into what was added by way of fertiliser and on a global scale. He was one of the largest producers, transporters and traders in anhydrous ammonia, a commodity in unquench-able demand by China and Russia. Every country required fertiliser to sustain and maximise the returns from its agricul-ture. The world's population was growing, and Johnny was someone who stood to benefit from the increasing demand.

The answer was either using mined phosphates from places

such as the USA and Morocco or manufactured anhydrous ammonia from countries that had natural gas and a pragmatic approach to environmental impact.

One such place was Trinidad and Tobago. Located in part of the Venezuelan oil and gas fields, it was in the perfect position to use a percentage of its gas to make ammonia, although production on the Caribbean island had suffered over the past few years due to a decrease in natural gas output. This meant the gas supply to the eleven production sites in Trinidad had now limited ammonia production capacity to 5.2 million metric tonnes per year. Some of these facilities might close or need massive reinvestment to produce ammonia and hydrogen in cleaner ways that were more socially and environmentally acceptable.

From his Monaco base, or wherever he was that week, Johnny would buy and sell what he called his 'topsoil', moving it around the globe. Like his grandfather, he kept it simple. He didn't diversify or spread into new areas, neither did he do anything to attract attention to himself. This was a golden rule and the key to his success. No one outside his close family and a very small coterie even knew his name. Sometimes, he forgot he was Peter Swift.

Whatever his name, he hated greed, which was slightly odd given his multimillion-dollar business, but he had clear lines that he wouldn't cross, and he demanded loyalty.

———

His cousin Darren played a critical part in all of this. He masqueraded as Johnny as far as the UK tax man was concerned and lived a relatively exotic life in a villa on Tobago near to Rainbow Reef in Mount Irvine Bay. He paid all his taxes on time and, equally, didn't draw attention to himself unnecessarily.

While in the Caribbean, he thought of himself as Johnny

Boswell, having played the role for so long, but this didn't bother him – he was richly rewarded. His less-than-arduous task was to liaise with the management of the ammonia plant on Trinidad, a very short flight away, and be his cousin's eyes and ears. Two or three times a year, he flew back to Essex, but never exceeding the ninety-one days and always keeping a low profile.

For six years, this had gone well.

Unfortunately, he didn't share his cousin's self-discipline to the same degree, and over the previous year, he had been slowly intrigued by Eric, a friend in Tobago who had made his own fortune importing fire extinguishers and fire-detection systems into the Caribbean. It was over barbecues at his bougainvillea-covered villa, or drinking rum on his friend's motor cruiser, that Darren learnt of other money-making possibilities.

It began after a special trip to the north of Tobago for his twelve-year-old son, Patrick, to see the white-tailed frigate birds and red-footed boobies on Little Tobago, which is a tiny island bird reserve off the coast. His friend had a son of the same age, and the journey in the boat across Tyrrell's Bay had been great fun. While the two boys were off birdwatching, the conversation had wandered to other uses for natural gas and, in particular, other uses of ammonia.

Nothing more had been said until they were sailing past the Nylon Pool on another trip weeks later. This was a natural area of sea with a sandy bottom about three feet deep, created by a sandbar. It resembled a swimming pool and was a tourist destination that had grown in popularity ever since Princess Margaret had swum there on her honeymoon in 1962, when she had said it was as clear as her nylon stockings. The name had stuck. It was now said to have mystical and healing properties, which is a sure sign that the tourist board needed to boost visitor numbers. It's the most visited spot on Tobago, and at peak times, it resembles a marina when all the boats from Pigeon Point and Store Bay drop anchor while people splash about in the water, taking selfies and wondering what nylon stockings were like in the 1960s.

Darren was more restless and more inquisitive than his cousin. New ideas tempted him. The seagrass was always greener on the other side of the reef.

Inauspiciously, it was while he was sitting on a sunbed, trying to extract a piece of sharp coral from his foot, that he made the decision to give the new idea a try. It was perhaps the worst decision of his life.

———

It felt odd for Mike to be arriving at her offices on Tuesday morning and having to hand over her passport and wait for Kathryn, with a K and a Y, from Human Resources to come down. There was no need to take her fingerprints – these were on file – but her old ID card had been destroyed. She was given a temporary visitor's card; her new ID would be delivered later.

Reinstated, she could now proceed through Security and collect her new work laptop, gizmos and phone. After this, it was back up in the lifts to her room, where everybody smiled and welcomed her back. She hadn't even logged in when Leonard appeared at the door and nodded in the direction of his office. The next few minutes would be interesting. She headed towards his office.

He called her in immediately on hearing her knock.

"Welcome back," she said.

"Yeah, and welcome back to you ... but it's like you never left."

"What's happening, Leonard?"

They hadn't discussed anything contentious or secret at the brief meeting over a coffee and cake at the Portrait Gallery the day before.

"Don't blame Brent; it was an automatic trigger. He had no choice. I know it was a bummer, but he's a stickler for the rules."

"Tell me about it. What was the trigger?"

"Consorting with the enemy."

"*What?* Who?"

"Tina Persad. She was being tracked and ended up at your house. That was enough to trigger the system."

"She's on our side. She's a friend. Why is she being suspected?"

"Heck, I'm already telling you more than I probably should. What did she say when she was with you? Anything that might sound suspicious?"

"No. Nothing."

"Think about that for a bit longer and tell me tomorrow."

"Have they found her yet? I'm worried, especially after what happened to Zara."

"That was an accident."

"I know you don't believe that. You're more cynical than me, and that's pretty cynical."

He smiled. Only some dark bags under his eyes hinted at the trauma he had just been through, up to and including the operation. Leonard was weighing something up. "Just for a second, are you able to imagine that Tina may, you know, have gone bad?"

"Well ... um, yes ... but I don't believe it."

"What if I asked you to leave it to the Brits to find her?"

"Do you really think she's gone bad and that's why she didn't drive home?" She instantly regretted saying this.

He leant back and smiled again. "Now, how would you know that?"

"She's a friend. Before you came back, I was doing what friends do - looking out for her."

"Talking to the Brits?" He was testing her, and she knew it.

"I talked to one guy I know. I was worried."

"Who was that?"

"His name's Oscar; he's an analyst at MI6. He works with Tina."

"I've heard his name. He was working with Zara supporting Tina. What'd he say?"

"That he was worried about her too. We said we'd stay in touch," she added quickly, "but this was before I knew you were coming back."

"It's the Brits who tipped us off about you and your weekend with Tina. They tracked her to your place, then she disappeared. She's a Brit, so perhaps we should leave it to the Brits."

"But Zara was American. Don't you think we should investigate?"

"The British police are investigating."

"But they think it's a typical hit-and-run. They don't know what she was working on ... nor do I, by the way."

Leonard didn't speak, but he shifted his considerable weight in the chair to get more comfortable.

"Who took over Zara's role on this project?" She needed to know.

He mulled something over. "No one. There's no longer a role. It's now entirely run by the Brits."

"What was Tina working on?"

He had obviously changed his mind. "Threats to CHOGM in Guyana."

"What's CHOGM?"

"The Commonwealth Heads of Government Meeting."

"Really? What's that got to do with the USA? And what was Zara doing?"

"Some of the characters involved might be US citizens."

"Oh great."

CHAPTER EIGHT

As to when the conversation on how to make the illegal drug methamphetamine had first come up, Darren couldn't remember. He was certainly alone with Eric, his good friend, and probably having a drink at one of their villas while their sons played in the swimming pool or flew kites from the corner of a patio.

Then it came back to him: they had been talking about how fires started, and this had led to the subject of safety matches, with Eric explaining about red phosphorus and its properties and uses. He had gone on to describe that it could be one of the key ingredients in the production of meth, as methamphetamine is known, together with some chemical found in typical cold remedies. The conversation had ended, and Darren had thought no more about it.

Weeks later, the subject had come up again. Eric – who was half French, half English – often spoke about a farm he had bought in France near where he had grown up and his plans for it. While talking about the poor grain harvest, he had moaned about the cost of fertiliser and joked that he should be given a discount by his friend's company, which was the biggest importer of anhydrous ammonia into France via the industrial port at Le

Havre. He had then explained it was one of the other key elements that could be used in the production of meth.

Eric had joked that they should start producing it themselves, as meth was apparently everywhere in the USA and Asia, but not Europe, where the market was growing and unfulfilled. Over some rum punches, they had discussed hypothetically whether it would be better to produce it on the farm in France or at a unit near Darren's company facility on Trinidad.

From such alcohol-fuelled discussions, the idea had developed.

Production of meth differs from most other drugs. It can be produced in small amounts by amateurs who steal some agricultural fertiliser and set up local labs in sheds and abandoned vehicles. The crude technique had been around for over a hundred years, and videos of how to make it were readily available on YouTube. The drug authorities around the world had tried to keep pace with this by placing restrictions on the legal pharmaceutical preparations sold as cough medicine, and they were beginning to insist that ammonia fertiliser had small amounts of calcium nitrate added. This had no effect on the agricultural application, but it reduced the output from any illegal drug lab by a factor of fifty, rendering it an unattractive proposition.

These small, temporary labs produce toxic waste. However, this isn't a problem to these itinerant manufacturers, who move on frequently and don't care about the immediate area or the environment in general.

Eric and Darren had been musing on how meth could be produced on a more industrial scale; this was beginning to happen in Mexico and Burma. There were now 35 million users worldwide, and this was a tempting market, given how hard it was to give up meth or 'ice', as its crystallised form was known.

Darren was unaware that his friendship, the fishing trips and the random discussions about subjects such as drugs had been thoroughly planned and orchestrated.

It was during a torrential storm one afternoon that Eric had announced he had rented a small industrial unit and warehouse in Point Lisas, right next to the ammonia production plant belonging to Darren's company, and he was importing all the necessary equipment to produce meth. However, he had told Darren that he could relax, all he had to do was supply unadulterated anhydrous ammonia in relatively small quantities to the unit next door. There was nothing illegal in this, he was told. For this, he would be paid handsomely by whatever financial mechanism he chose into his personal bank accounts.

Darren had been hooked.

Nine weeks later, the equipment was in place and a new sign on the industrial unit wall proudly displayed "Pyrandox", the name of a company making fire extinguishers, fire-fighting equipment and other related equipment; this would be the cover for this small but sophisticated operation. Eric imported both full and some empty fire extinguishers, which would be filled with meth and then shipped from Port of Spain to Europe and the USA.

A chemist from French-speaking Martinique had been recruited to oversee production, and the handful of local Trinis who made up the workforce were none the wiser.

Twice a week, a lorry would arrive to take the hazardous waste to the large landfill site outside Port of Spain where, having completed all the appropriate paperwork, it was disposed of legally into rubber-lined areas of domestic waste that helped to filter and dilute it.

The fire extinguishers filled with meth were wrapped in plastic film, palletised and loaded into containers that were driven to the capital to be hoisted by giant gantries onto the cargo ships.

This operation was tightly run by Eric, with Darren benefitting personally to the tune of $10,000 a month.

———

Unusually, Mike was back in the office for a second day in a row. Although it was a Wednesday and Wiltshire was very tempting, she wanted to have access to everything the Agency and its sister services could offer. It was forecast to be showery, but she had decided to come in on her bike in preference to catching the Tube. The weather forecasters had got it right.

The previous evening, Oscar had phoned to say he'd officially been told that Mike had been reinstated by Leonard. He was free to contact Mike using the usual route and within the normal limits; they no longer needed to do anything clandestinely and had agreed to speak through the official channels before lunch the following day.

At her desk, Mike started straightaway with Zara. The police had made no progress identifying the car that had killed her and driven off. They were at a dead end until new evidence emerged. There was nothing Mike could do that hadn't already been done by the police; they'd been through any CCTV footage – none of which was directly of the incident. They knew the exact time it happened and so had begun the laborious task, aided by a computer program, of checking a long list of vehicles that were using the road nearby at that time. Mike guessed this search would throw up the names of some low-life criminals and people on various databases, but not the real culprits, who'd have hidden their tracks well; however, anything was possible – people make mistakes, and luck may play its part.

It was what Zara had discovered and passed on to Tina via Oscar that excited Mike. Tina had said that the intel was "good stuff". She was also intrigued by any feedback that Tina had sent Oscar and Zara.

Zara had been checking up firstly on Sheldon Douglas, picking up where Mike had left off a couple of years before. Contacts, informants and go-betweens like Sheldon aren't static entities: they change, they evolve. This is sometimes for the better and sometimes not. It looked as if he had remained loyal and productive. Zara had been searching through his calls and listening to his messages, including on his second phone. She had collated and cross-checked everyone mentioned so that, when Tina had met him at the Pitch Lake, she already knew who he was going to suggest she see in Tobago and exactly who this new contact was.

His name was Hector Candelo.

Zara had established that he was a chancer trying to join the big leagues. A man with a wide selection of business cards to fit any occasion. Hector was from Guyana, according to his passport, and thirty-three years old. On various of the documents Zara had found, he had put down his profession as 'realtor'; she had discovered that his self-avowed specialism was selling very small Caribbean islands for private or leisure use by international hotel chains – although she hadn't found one successful real estate transaction. He didn't have a criminal record and wasn't on any watch list.

Among Sheldon's messages, there was one referring to an enquiry to buy an uninhabited island that was perfect for industrial uses, and this had led to him getting in touch with Hector. There was a message immediately after, from Sheldon to another friend, in which he had said that he had ended up paying for the drinks when they met and that Hector was a hustler. Tina said she didn't like Hector, but she obviously didn't have a problem with him and had flown back to Trinidad and then back to London. What had they been discussing?

Mike looked next at the short, redacted report – if it could be called that – from Tina back to Oscar and her controller. It was timed and dated at 18.34pm local time on Wednesday, 5th March, two days before they had met in The Green Feathers and, coincidentally, the last day of Carnival. This was what she had mentioned to Mike when she said she had missed Carnival completely and that the noise below her around Queen's Park Savannah, the central park in Port of Spain, was deafening. In the dispatch she listed Hector's requirements before he would release the information he was touting; these included $10,000 paid into his Georgetown bank account, British citizenship and a passport. When Tina had said nothing would happen until he gave some proof of the quality of his information, he had become slightly aggressive and had said he would wait until she needed it, when the price would have doubled. Eventually, he had given a name, but, unfortunately, this was redacted in the text available to Mike.

It was perhaps obvious why he hadn't sold any islands.

————

As agreed, Oscar contacted Mike at 12.30pm.

"Any news on Zara?" he asked.

"No, I've left that to the police. No news on Tina, I'm guessing?"

"No," he replied, "and there's a specialist police team scouring Brentwood. They're having to trawl through door-camera footage and the like to follow her route through, around and out of the town – or whatever she did."

"Her car can't simply have disappeared."

"It could be in a garage, parked around the back of an estate or have been put through a car crusher. Your guess is as good as mine."

"Why Brentwood?"

"I have no idea. Honestly."

"It's been ten days, Oscar; it's not looking good, is it?"

"Sadly not. I've prepared myself for the worst."

"Have you asked Sheldon Douglas whether he knows what's going on and whether he's heard from her and this new contact, or potential contact, Hector Candelo? What's the latest?"

"Sheldon has heard nothing, but he's acting a bit strange. This is one reason my bosses are beginning to smell a rat. They thought she might make contact with him. As you well know, Sheldon has been our and your main source in Trinidad and Tobago for years. I have to say, however, that he seems not only to lead a charmed life but also to have nine of them." Oscar hesitated before returning to Mike's second question: "As to Hector, Sheldon heard he was bragging about something he knew, and so Sheldon gently cultivated him. He asked whether Hector wanted to meet someone from our outfit and said he could dictate the terms of the meeting. This Hector had accepted. We've checked him out thoroughly, and we believe he overheard something in a bar and thinks he now owns the Crown Jewels. He's basically a bottom feeder."

"Do you think that, for all his aggression, he's frightened, and that's why he chose somewhere not on Trinidad and outside a government building with security and emergency services people all around?"

"Could be. Unfortunately, we don't know if it really is connected to our project. He gave her some names and some ideas, but he's probably a time-waster."

"He didn't, or couldn't, even pay for the drinks when he met Sheldon."

"True."

"We ought to avoid doing the same research. What are you looking at next?"

"My controller wants me to track Hector's phone and build up a map of his movements and contact points. What about you?"

"Because I don't have access to Sheldon or Hector, I'm going to concentrate on Tina, starting at Brentwood. It's a luxury for once to have a place of interest that's only an hour away; normally, they're halfway around the world. I want to know whom she met and what she did."

"I'll send over the details from Tina's phone. It won't add much to the rough route of her journey back from your house until the phone disappears in Brentwood."

Oscar was in some difficulty because he'd been told by his controller not to release some specific information to Mike or the Americans. However, this was commonplace.

Their chat was over. She leant back to stretch her left leg, and this reminded her that she needed to walk. Sitting in one place for too long wasn't good for her. She got up and went to get a drink.

Alone at the refreshment dispenser, she stood waiting for her coffee to finish squirting into the paper cup. There was no point replaying the conversations she'd had with Tina over that fateful weekend; she'd done this too many times. Instead, as she stood there drinking her coffee, she tried to visualise Tina's trip back to London. What had changed her mind? Mike was convinced that, when Tina left, she was heading back to her flat and something, or some thought, had made her change her plans.

By the time she got back to her workstation, Oscar would have sent over the log of Tina's phone locations and CCTV footage, which would add some flesh to the bones of her three- or four-hour car journey. Something while at Rodbourne, or while driving, had altered her mood or changed her priorities.

She leant back, tipped the last mouthful of coffee into her mouth and dropped the cup into the recycling bin.

CHAPTER NINE

Having something real to get her teeth into was exactly what Mike needed. It was now lunchtime, but, while her colleagues came and went, she stayed at her workstation, completely absorbed.

She had the route Tina had taken driving east from Rodbourne and also the last time and location that her car had been spotted. This was as she entered Brentwood and appeared to be at a hotel – or what would have been called a motel in years past – on the road into the town. Did she meet someone here?

However emotional and random Mike was in her private life, she was clinically methodical and objective when in work mode. She was trying to piece together Tina's movements, knowing there was no guarantee that she had made it to Brentwood. All that Mike knew for certain was that her car did, but it may have been driven there by someone else.

She called up a map of the Brentwood area and scrolled around it, trying to form a mental picture of the place. It was while zooming in that she saw the village of Featherstone. This was a lightbulb moment.

While in The Green Feathers, Tina was asking about the

name of the pub and had mentioned casually that her sister lived in a village called Featherstone. *How many villages have that name?* Mike wondered. She found a handful, but given Tina's family were from Kent, it was very likely that her sister lived in the South East, somewhere near London. It would make sense that, for whatever the reason Tina had decided not to go home, she would go somewhere safe. She also wouldn't need to call; she could simply turn up.

Tina was nervous and hiding her tracks from everyone – so nervous that she had to disappear completely off the radar. What was frightening her, and where was she now?

The next few minutes were spent finding her sister's details. Her name was Janet, and she was married to a successful electrician. They had two children and lived in a four-bedroomed house with a double garage that had last sold for £800,000 two years previously. From an initial search, it looked like it was only a few miles on minor roads from the location of the hotel.

Mike realised she was sweating under the thin scarf wrapped around her head. She gave her scalp a good scratch as the circumstances of Tina's disappearance began to crystallise in her mind.

Something had worried Tina on her trip to the Caribbean, and the mention of Zara's death when they'd been in The Green Feathers had made her even more twitchy. So twitchy in fact that she'd said nothing to Mike. Was this Tina's way of protecting Mike by not getting her involved? Essentially, from the moment she left Rodbourne, Tina had intended to disappear without leaving a trace. She had made no calls and hadn't turned on her phone in Featherstone. She had presumably arrived unannounced and hidden her car at her sister's, perhaps borrowing her sister's car. She had, in all likelihood, acquired a new phone and ...

And what?

Before phoning Janet, Mike wanted to make sure she had

checked everything. A new thought came into her mind: *Why didn't Tina confide in anyone at work? Was she suspicious of them or worried they would stop her doing something?* This meant Oscar was out of the loop. It was also unlikely that he would make the connection between Brentwood and her sister.

Mike buzzed Leonard's PA and asked to see him after lunch; she knew better than to disturb him while he was eating. She would ask his permission to take the afternoon off, not telling him that she intended to visit Janet in person.

———

Twenty minutes later, she was sitting opposite Leonard's big desk with the room smelling of pork fat and French fries.

"Is that OK?"

He wiped his mouth with the back of his hand. "Sure, if you want some time off. But, Mike, please don't get involved in anything. Something's not right, I know, but it's a problem for the Brits now." Leonard suspected that Mike was up to something. He knew her of old.

"Anything new on the CHOGM threat connection?" she asked as innocently as possible.

"Not that I've heard, and nothing on Zara from the police. I don't think they know where to look next. You concentrate on your Costa Rican project, but make sure you phone me real quick if Tina gets in touch – and I mean *real* quick."

"OK." She stood up to leave. "I'll leave you to digest your lunch."

"Don't worry, it goes straight through me since the operation."

"That's way too much information."

"You can never have too much information. It's too little information that's the bummer."

———

The journey to Featherstone would take about forty-five minutes.

Mike left Central London with fluffy, white clouds above her scudding along towards the horizon. It was a new route to her after the M25, and she headed along the A12 towards Brentwood. Instead of tearing along, she paid extra attention to the vehicles following her, but nothing caught her eye.

A few miles of lanes took her past the perimeter of a golf course and Featherstone Country Park until she reached a line of poplars that marked the edge of the village. It didn't take long to locate the cul-de-sac of five newish houses where Janet and her family lived. Mike pulled up slowly outside number two and dismounted.

As she was approaching the front door, she had to be prepared for several scenarios. There was a possibility Tina was inside, but it was more likely that she had gone off to some other safe haven. Outside a porch filled with wellington boots of various colours and sizes, she pressed the bell.

If Tina had inherited her skin colour and features from their Asian mother, Janet had the black skin and curly hair of their father. She opened the door wearing dungarees, hooped gold earrings and yellow rubber gloves, to be confronted by Mike in a bandana and motorbike leathers, with her helmet under one arm. Janet thought she was a courier, but she wasn't expecting any deliveries.

"Hello, Janet? I'm Mike. I'm Tina's friend."

"Hello, how can I help?" Her accent was slightly more 'estuary' than her sister, having spent most of her life in Essex.

Mike didn't want to alarm Janet or betray any secrets about Tina's real line of work. "Janet, I'm trying to get hold of Tina; do you know where she is?" Mike hoped this would reveal – at least on Janet's face – what she knew.

Unfortunately, Janet's intelligent eyes betrayed nothing, and the door remained firmly in her right hand. "Sorry, I don't."

Mike was unaware that she must look like a cross between a Hell's Angel and a pirate, which – along with her penetrating, almost-black eyes – didn't instantly disarm people she had just met. "Tina was with me last weekend in Wiltshire before she came up here to see you."

Janet didn't move, but there was a slight recognition in her eyes. "She travels a lot. We never know where she is."

"That's the nature of her job ... and my job. We work together." Mike had come prepared. "Can I give you this?" She handed over a piece of paper with her burner phone number on it. "Please ask her to call me. Tell her that there's lots to catch up on."

Janet took the piece of paper, folded it and put it into the pocket at the front of her dungarees. "It's a long way back to Wiltshire," she said, nodding towards the bike.

"It is; I couldn't use your restroom, could I?"

Janet pulled open the door and released her hold of it. "The toilet's in there." She indicated a door almost immediately behind her.

Mike walked into the hallway, trying to absorb every detail as if she would be tested on it later. Once in the toilet, Mike was immediately aware of the dark-blue-framed cartoon of the jetty at Pigeon Point in Tobago with its random hand-painted signs proclaiming "Don't be a litterbug" and "This jetty is reserved for paying guests only". Was this a present brought back by Tina? She flushed, washed her hands and rejoined Janet.

What should she say in parting? "Thank you for speaking to me, Janet. I know this visit was a bit out of left field. The next time Tina phones, please tell her I rode over to see her, and please give her my telephone number."

Janet did well to bottle up all the questions and all the emotions. She must have been concerned and perhaps confused as to why her sister had disappeared off the scene and strangers were turning up asking questions. "I will, but I don't see her very often." She looked as if she were about to say something more, but she stopped herself. Her last reply seemed to indicate that Tina wasn't around or wasn't anywhere local.

With that, Mike took her leave.

Although it was a boring route, Mike decided to ride all the way around the M25 anticlockwise to Junction 16, where she joined the A40 towards Ickenham, rather than riding through London. With so many thoughts to process, the trip passed quickly.

———

It was Thursday, 20th March, and Johnny Boswell was in southern France, on his way back to Monaco, enjoying a cold glass of Château d'Esclans rosé wine from Provence.

He was sitting in one of the tented bars on the beach that are reserved for guests of the most expensive hotels on La Croisette, the stylish promenade in Cannes. In front of him, across the beach, was the gently lapping Mediterranean Sea, and behind him were the palm trees blocking his view of the Hotel Carlton. His photochromatic glasses had gone very dark in the late March sunshine.

A 'friend' was sitting next to him; she was wearing an expensive see-through beach dress over a white bikini. Her name was Stroma, and she provided escort services to the wealthy along the coast from Nice to Cap Ferrat. She had grown up in Sussex with her Australian mother and her English father. Nursing had always been her vocation, and at twenty-five, she had started a job looking after medical emergencies being flown back to the UK, mainly from Europe. She flew back and forth on small jets once a day. Somehow, she had acquired a taste for the more expensive things in life and had morphed from nurse to escort rather easily after the first man had propositioned her, despite him being in no fit medical condition to do anything about it.

Johnny was too much of a control freak to share his life permanently with anyone and was horrified at the thought that they might lay claim to half of his fortune. He preferred to live a happy, carefree life doing what he wanted, when he wanted.

He was in a reflective mood, sipping his wine, and Stroma recognised that he didn't want or need to talk. She scrolled through her phone while he looked at a couple of girls doing yoga on the beach.

In fact, he was miles away: Brightlingsea to be exact.

He'd been faced with a dilemma when he flew back home. What was he to do about his cousin? After he had received a tip-off from a contact that Darren was supplying anhydrous ammonia to a drug concern in Point Lisas, he needed to nip it in the bud. Things, however, weren't straightforward. His immediate thought was to recall him, cut him into little pieces and dispose of him in a landfill site. He would find someone else to babysit the Caribbean end of the operations.

But two things stopped him from chopping up his cousin. Firstly, he was close family, and this would have repercussions among his aunts and uncles, nieces and nephews. Secondly, to all intents and purposes, he *was* Johnny Boswell. He would be killing off himself.

In one way, this could be a good thing – laying 'Johnny Boswell' to rest, that is. There would be no further interest in him from the tax authorities, and he could continue living as Peter Swift when necessary. However, something stopped him from going through with it; instead, he gave his cousin the dressing-down of his life and laid out what he had to do: go back to Tobago; stop providing ammonia to the drug producer; terminate any individuals who might use knowledge of the connection with the Boswell family; and, finally, never to wander from the straight and narrow again – or it would be the end for him.

Hopefully, the idiot had put most of these into action by now as he'd been back in the Caribbean for four or five days. Communications between Monaco and the Caribbean must always be kept to a minimum. If anyone checked, there must be no direct link between 'Johnny Boswell' and 'Peter Swift' in Monaco. This meant they had to use the family in Essex as intermediaries, which delayed matters.

A waiter dressed in black and white approached and asked *madame* if she would like a fresh chilled glass; wine warmed so quickly outside in the heat.

Stroma pushed her sunglasses up into her blonde hair and answered in French: "Yes, please. Peter, are you having another glass? Shall we have another bottle or look at the menu first?"

"Another bottle and a look at the lunch menu. Actually, do you have the *moules*?"

"Yes."

"In that case, another bottle, and I'll have the *moules*."

"They're too messy for me. I'll look at the menu, please."

The waiter smiled and disappeared off to the kitchen nearby. The restaurant wasn't overly busy, which it had been during the Porn Festival and the Property Festival. It was still a few weeks to the Film Festival.

"I might disappear a day earlier,"

"Oh, that's a shame." Stroma was thinking of the lost income. Her mother would never know that calling her daughter Stroma, which she rather romantically thought was an uninhabited Scottish island, would be so apposite – in Latin, it meant 'bedspread', on which she spent so much of her life. "You'll stay tonight, won't you?"

"I will. I want to listen to the piano in the Hotel Martinez bar tonight."

Where she ranked in his arrangements wasn't evident. It paid her to have a thick skin.

CHAPTER TEN

Did Tina stay the night at Janet's house, or longer? Of course, she could still be there or nearby.

This was the question that had been bugging Mike all the way back to the flat. Annoyingly, she couldn't bounce ideas off Wazz because he had left for his late shift at the strip club. An evening and night alone lay ahead of her; therefore, as a poor substitute, she began asking herself questions. Perhaps vocalising the answers to them might help.

Why not drive straight home?

"Because she was too scared," she answered herself.

Why go all the way to her sister's house?

"Because it was safe, and no one would find her."

Why not stay for a few days while she sorted out the problem or whatever it was?

"Tina might have stayed for a few days, but she probably left because she was going on to somewhere else."

But why go to her sister's house in the first place?

"To pick something up."

She sat down in an armchair to mull this over while removing her bandana. Perhaps Tina had left a survival kit with Janet in case of emergencies?

"*Her passport!*" she shouted to the empty lounge.

For work, Tina would use a false passport in the name of her alias; this would be standard procedure for a case officer. Perhaps she'd left her own with Janet for safe keeping?

Mike pulled the laptop from its bag and linked it to the pieces of hardware known in her office as 'gizmos'. It was time to find out where Tina had gone if she had indeed flown somewhere using her own passport. There was a chance she was using another alias, which would completely stymie Mike. While she was searching, the question of why she needed to conceal this from her work colleagues came to the fore. Was what she was doing illegal? Did her controller not want her to take some risk? Or was there another reason?

After three hours, it was time for a break. She stepped out onto the tiny balcony and, in the dark, lit a cigarette; she needed one and it was a reward to herself for getting this far. Across the road, the floodlights of a golf driving range lit up the balls like shooting stars as they curved away into the distance. There was the sound of a generator coming from a nearby building, but there was no logical reason for it being used at that time of the evening while there was no power cut. She now needed a beer after the smoking. The cigarette butt followed its own curving trajectory as it headed down towards the bins below, and she went back inside to resume her illegal hacking.

With a bottle of cold beer opened before her, she marshalled her thoughts. Which airport? Which airline? Which destination? What date? It was all a daunting prospect. She needed to be systematic. Where should she check first?

Janet lived half an hour from Stanstead airport, and this was the reason Mike began her enquiries there by looking at a list of airlines and destinations. Nothing grabbed her eye, so the laborious searching continued, but to no avail. It took a very special type of mind and discipline to persevere. To most people, looking for a needle in a haystack is beyond their comprehension, but Mike was looking for a needle in a field of haystacks, not knowing if there even was a needle in the first place or if it was the right field. For all she knew, Tina could have taken a taxi to the station and caught a train to Scotland.

Mike couldn't let thoughts like that weaken her resolve, and for the next two hours, she targeted flights from Heathrow – one of the busiest airports on the planet. It was past midnight when she gave up this line of attack. Perhaps her idea was crazy, and Tina's actions had nothing to do with passports.

She remembered that Tina came from Maidstone in Kent; therefore, she began looking at flights from Gatwick forty miles away. It was now 2am, and Wazz would be back soon; the fact that she was still up and working wouldn't surprise him in the slightest.

It was while checking flights from Gatwick that she finally had some success. Tina had booked a single ticket through Air France from Gatwick to Charles De Gaulle airport in Paris.

Did she actually catch the plane? Mike searched and found that Tina had indeed checked in her bag and boarded the plane at London Gatwick.

What did she do when she arrived in Paris? Which hotel did she stay in? Questions; there were too many questions.

It was, however, unfortunate that Tina had chosen Air France, which wasn't linked to the various US and British airlines in an alliance. An hour later, Mike had moved on to the immigration system at Charles de Gaulle airport to see whether Tina had actually arrived.

Mike knocked off her bandana as she flung her arms back above her head. There on her screen were the details showing Tina passing through the airport system. Mike was exhilarated and jumped up to do a celebratory dance. Mike was so out of sync with her sleeping and eating patterns that she was desperately hungry, and she grabbed the easiest thing available to her – some taramasalata on digestive biscuits. She was still dancing while trying to eat.

This was what confronted Wazz when he came through the door at 3.30am. "Have I missed the party or is it just beginning?"

"You won't believe what I've found."

"That's an absolute and total certainty. Everything about your world is beyond my comprehension. Let me wash my hands, and I'll join you." The need to do this was partly psychological after working a shift at the club, and he walked into the bathroom only to reappear a short while after. He hugged her, kissed her and sat down in an armchair. There was no way they would be going to bed any time soon.

"I've found Tina; well, I've found out where she went after she left me and what she did next" – there was a pause for dramatic effect – "she flew to Paris."

"Panic over. She's gone back to work on her project." Wazz had a knack of reducing anything to its bare minimum and defusing situations, although he had no idea if Paris was relevant to Tina or anybody's projects.

"Huh? She hasn't told me or anyone – especially anyone at her work. She flew using her own passport, not her work one."

Wazz was confused. "But they'll know ... they'll find out like you did."

"Huh!" she said again. This wasn't how she thought this conversation would go. "Possibly, but they think she's in Brentwood, which she hasn't been for a week, I think."

"Surely the British secret services, or whatever they're called, have more resources than you and can check airports and flights in minutes?"

Mike had now brought both of her hands to her waist, so she was standing in front of him, arms akimbo. "They'd only check if they suspected she had flown somewhere or left the country. I only worked that out because I went to see her sister near Brentwood and realised Tina kept her real passport there as a safety measure."

"Why doesn't she want people at her work to know what she's doing?"

"I'm on to that next" – her voice was becoming more aggressive – "and where she's been staying for the last, I don't know, ten days under the radar."

A whole bunch of questions were jostling for position in his head, but he was tired from standing on his feet outside in the cold for eight hours. Wazz knew he was skating on thin ice. "You've done really well ... no, really. I'm sure you'll find her and make sure she's not in trouble."

There was a third, "*Huh!*" but expressed with less venom.

He went to bed. She wouldn't sleep; she needed to investigate further.

––––––

The next hour was challenging as she concentrated on why Tina had flown to Paris.

Mike was intrigued and excited in equal amounts, but, right at the start, she began by rechecking all the flight details.

She stood up and walked across the room. After quietly sliding the door back, she stepped out onto the balcony, both to have another cigarette as a reward for making even more progress and also to clear her head. The night air was on the cool side of pleasant, but this didn't deter her. She leant on the solid metal rail and looked up at the stars. She wondered where Tina was at that very moment. Was she looking at the moon and the stars from a hotel balcony? Mike hoped so.

The feeling that Tina was in deep trouble hadn't left Mike since she had first met Oscar. In the stillness of the night, nothing dissuaded her from these deeply unsettling thoughts. Tina was clearly hiding what she was doing from her British bosses, and this was serious – very serious. Concealing her movements and flying to France hinted at the need to distract from what she was actually doing. Why had she felt the need to keep Oscar and his colleagues in the dark?

"Because you don't trust any of them" – Mike actually said this out loud, but in a whisper, and then she prepared to go back inside – "and you don't trust me enough to confide any of this." The latter disturbed her. Was this private, personal or embarrassing? Why not mention or even hint at it?

Once back at her laptop, Mike spent another hour allowing herself to drift aimlessly wherever her searches took her, which was Paris and its hinterland. Sitting on the small sofa, she promptly fell asleep, her energy all used up.

———

Wazz came out of his bedroom at almost 11.00am, weighing up if his urge to use the toilet outweighed his need for strong coffee. Decision made, he turned left and pulled the cord triggering the light and extractor fan. He was staring at a poster for a bullfight with his name crudely printed on it in bold, black lettering while counting down from fifty. How long until his first shot of caffeine?

Mike was still fast asleep and spreadeagled across the cushions. She was fully dressed and oblivious to the world, her bald head partially hidden by the tartan car rug that had slipped down from the back of the sofa.

He crept into the kitchen and pulled the door towards him.

The staccato thumping noise from the espresso machine woke her up.

"What time is it?" She appeared in the doorway rubbing her eyes.

"Gone 11.00am."

"Shit, I need to be in work." She turned and disappeared without saying anything else.

He had eaten his cereal and was on his second cup of coffee when she returned to the kitchen, fully dressed and wearing a red bandana.

"Good morning," he said, smiling.

"Sorry, I got carried away ... again. I need to see Leonard and use the system at work."

"No problem." He stood up and kissed her goodbye. "See you when I see you."

She looked at him as if he was speaking in Swahili. "Bye." She closed the door and headed downstairs.

CHAPTER ELEVEN

"You need to tell the Brits." Leonard was tapping his pen on his desk while giving his reaction to her update. Mike was back in his office.

"Why? She obviously didn't want them to know."

"So what? How many agents go rogue or screw up or find themselves up shit creek? I've seen it a hundred times. She's had enough time to do whatever she wanted to do. How many days has she been out of contact?"

"It's nine or ten days, but she's probably alive. She flew on the Thursday ... the 13th."

"That's too long. Call Oscar and tell them what you've discovered."

"But she went to a lot of trouble to lay a false trail."

"Tough. She's had enough time. Let the Brits wind her back in."

"I'll work for a few more hours and then phone Oscar."

"She may have gone on holiday with a secret lover; who knows? Give her a break."

Mike's face left no interpretation other than this was not an option.

Leonard made it quite clear: "Phone Oscar or I will."

She went back down to her office via the vending machine, where she bought as much chocolate and drinks as she could carry. It might be a long evening, and she would soon begin to flag without a sugar rush.

Whatever Leonard had said, she wanted to find Tina before telling Oscar. There must be a reason she had gone to so much trouble to hide her tracks. After eating a Mars bar, Mike began with checking the hotels, but there were over 1,500 of them in Paris and that didn't include Airbnb or other short stay rentals. As if this weren't enough, she might have stayed with a friend or any number of other options. It was becoming impossible. She had reached a dead end. All she knew for certain was that Tina had flown to France. That was it. As Gilbert and Sullivan didn't write, "An analyst's lot is not a happy one."

It was 6.00pm, and tiredness began to creep over her, exacerbating the feeling of abject failure. She set off back to the flat, where she would sleep on it before ringing Oscar in the morning. Probably.

Not falling asleep on the Tube and missing her stop at Ickenham was a top priority; everything else was secondary. She made it, but it had been a close-run thing. The cold, fresh air as she walked home from the station in the dark had kept her awake, but an empty flat awaited her as Wazz would have already left for work.

It was perhaps for the best that she was alone, because she sat at the kitchen table and burst into tears. It was the culmination of the pressure on her over the last ten days, which had become overwhelming. She knew her friend was in trouble – probably big trouble – but Mike had failed utterly and miserably to find her, to help her or even to discover the source of any threat. Mike was finally admitting to herself that, despite all her natural gifts and experience, she'd been defeated. The searches had revealed nothing except that Tina had flown to France and disappeared. So what?

She was overtired and hungry, which wasn't helping her to cope. An early night in the small box room beckoned; that way, Wazz wouldn't disturb her when he came in at 3.30am. She would leave him a note so he didn't think it was because of something he had said or done.

"Tomorrow is another day," she said while preparing a quick snack before bed, but no cliché was likely to have any effect. It's hard to fool yourself.

The food perked her up for about half an hour while doing the washing up and vacuuming the flat. The distractions were helping. When washed and undressed, she collapsed into the single bed and, before falling into a deep sleep, asked herself the simple question: *Where are you, Tina?*

Hopefully, her subconscious would solve the mystery while she was asleep; otherwise, she would have to telephone Oscar in the morning and lose control of the search.

———

The box room was on a different side of the flat from the main bedroom. This meant that the light shining through the white curtains in the morning woke her from a long, undisturbed sleep. She crept out to the bathroom and washed as quietly as possible, avoiding using the shower, which was noisy and next to where Wazz slept. The face in the mirror displayed the toll of the recent past, although the stark light over the basin wasn't helping matters. She dressed while the toaster and coffee machine were doing their jobs. On the table was her note to Wazz, on which she had scribbled "We really should stop meeting like this XXX". He had crossed out the word "meeting" and written "missing".

She decided it was a khaki-cap day and packed it into the rucksack before putting on her helmet and setting off.

Riding the motorbike was also intended to blow away the cobwebs and give her something physical to do, rather than festering on the Tube; it worked. With her mind and body back in some sort of equilibrium, she entered her offices at least partially reinvigorated. Mike had finally made her decision over breakfast, and her first task would be to ring Oscar and tell him her news.

To make sensitive calls like this, there were two dedicated rooms at CIA HQ, both about the size of the box room in which she had spent the night. The empty walls, tables and chairs were several shades of cool grey; they were designed for privacy, not with aesthetics in mind – although the floor-to-ceiling panels of graphite-grey noise-absorbent rubber added something to the décor.

Before booking the small room, Mike had messaged Oscar from her office to let him know she would call at 10.30am. He had replied with a thumbs-up emoji.

Half an hour later, she was in the grey, padded cell, checking the time on her new work phone and dialling.

There was no reply. She dialled again with the same outcome and waited five minutes. There was no reply, but she did receive a message from him that said, "Please call my controller, Gordon Overton, immediately." It provided a London landline number and an extension.

Now what? Mike composed herself and dialled. A female voice put her through to extension 127.

"Overton."

"Hello, Mr Overton, I've been told to phone you. I'm Mike Kingdom from the CIA here in London."

"Thanks for calling, Miss Kingdom," he began in a voice and tone that put Mike on edge, "I need to update you about Tina

Persad. I understand from your director that you're helping to locate her. I'm sorry to say that I think she's probably dead."

Mike would later recall some details he had furnished her with, but for the time being, all she heard was a bunch of words that weren't making any sense. She eventually zoned in again to hear him say, "I understand you worked with her closely on Five Eyes projects in the past and she was a friend. I'm sorry to be the bearer of bad news."

"I ... yes, I did. We did."

"Would it be possible for you to come here to my office and tell me about your last meeting with Tina? I believe from Oscar Marsh that you were probably the last person to see her before she disappeared."

"What? Yes, of course." Mike was on automatic pilot. "I'll need to clear it with Leonard – Leonard de Vries, my director."

"May I suggest that you speak to him now? Subject to his agreement, could you come across to Marston House at midday?"

"Yes, yes ... I will."

"Thank you. I'll see you then."

The graphite-grey soundproofing was severely tested as Mike let out howls and screams as she sobbed into her hands.

"Tina, I'm so sorry. I am so sorry."

———

Leonard had recommended that she take a taxi across town.

On arriving fifteen minutes early, Mike ambled through a Georgian arcade that contained shops ranging in size from a postage stamp selling hand-made bow ties to a large gallery with a wide glass window devoted to one heavy-looking oil painting whose frame was worth more than the artwork.

At the end of the elegant corridor, she came out into a court-yard with several doors on each of the other sides. Marston

House was not in fact a house but three storeys of old offices accessed by a dark entrance tunnel. She rang the bell and waited for the door to be opened.

Once inside, it was as she expected. It looked as if the war effort had been coordinated from here and English Heritage had deemed that it shouldn't be touched for the sake of posterity. *What gives such places their distinctive smell? Damp? Furniture polish?* She was pondering this when a young woman in a black suit took her up some stairs to a waiting room with library shelves along one side. Three leather chesterfields and two side tables sat awkwardly on a threadbare, maroon rug, preventing easy access to the tall window. She sat down, trying to peer into the courtyard.

The door opened, and in walked a man in his forties with an irritating quiff of blond hair and wearing a two-piece tweed suit with a yellow-and-ivory-striped silk tie. He didn't need to introduce himself, but he did: "Hello, Miss Kingdom, I'm Gordon Overton."

He extended a hand, which she shook. At this point, she would normally ask people to call her Mike, but for some reason she held back.

What is that reason? she asked herself.

Because I hate this man, was the answer.

In her years in London, Mike had discovered that the secret-squirrel world of the British differed wildly from its US counterpart. The men fell into one of two camps: the friendly majority of casually dressed types and the popinjays. Gordon Overton fell heavily into the second group. Even when conveying bad news about one of his colleagues, he couldn't hide his vanity or the need to display his status. He sat down on the adjoining sofa and stared at her. His eyes were blue with small, black pupils, and he had a wart on his lower-left lid.

He repeated again that he believed Tina to be dead. Unfortunately, he could say no more at this stage. Why put it so starkly?

Why not say she was still missing? There was a sadistic side to him that was beginning to irritate her.

"Do you know why she might have decided to disappear? Did she ever mention this to you?" he enquired.

Mike didn't need to lie. "No, never." What was he talking about? She had flown to Paris. Had she been found floating in the Seine?

"May we go back to the weekend she spent with you in Wiltshire? Please tell me about it. We're trying to piece together her movements." He was leaning towards her with his hands resting on his knees, trying to appear concerned. He looked like a doctor who had another appointment in five minutes.

A thought flashed through her mind. Leonard had said it was the Brits who had suspected Tina of something and had tipped off Brent Comer that she had spent the weekend at Mike's house. Did the Brits still suspect Tina and Mike of anything? And where did Oscar fit into this? Did he work for this asshole? She wouldn't mention anything about Oscar unless it was raised.

"She came down for the weekend and told me she'd been on a trip to the Caribbean. She arrived on Friday evening, as I did, from London."

"Together?"

"No, separately."

"Then what?"

"We went to the pub and talked about everything other than our work. You know how it is."

"I do. So you only discussed girlie stuff?"

Fortunately for him, the heavy brass table lamp was out of reach. At that second, Mike flipped from grieving friend back to her usual ballsy self. "Yeah, periods, tampons, heavy bleeding ... you know how it is."

He sat back upright and there was a moment of complete silence. "I meant non-work issues."

The balance of power, however, had shifted.

"Why did you suspect Tina, track her to my house and tell Brent Comer that I was also suspect?"

Gordon Overton wasn't to know that Leonard had told her this. "I'm sorry, that's ... we cannot discuss any of that."

"You realise that I was suspended as a consequence of your actions?"

"They weren't *my* actions." He had lost the initiative.

Mike had had enough. "Tina and I had a great weekend, and she drove home to London. She left at 8.30am on Sunday, but you already know all this, having tracked her phone. After that, I haven't a clue, and I haven't heard from her since."

The atmosphere in the room was getting frostier.

"I'm sorry, truly sorry." He sounded sincere for the first time, or perhaps he was trying to sound sincere for the first time.

She shrugged but didn't respond.

"Do you have any idea at all where she might have gone?" He was now genuinely trying to sound reasonable.

"If *you* don't know where, why do you think I would? Where do *you* think that she might have gone?" Mike was trying to find out how much he knew.

He was evidently not used to staff of lower rank asking him questions. "We're investigating, but there's a lot we don't know yet."

They carried on not telling each other anything for another few minutes before he brought the meeting, if that's what it was, to a close.

He walked to the door, opened it and called a woman's name into the musty corridor.

"Goodbye, Miss Kingdom, and thank you for coming." He shook her hand, staring rather pointedly at her khaki forage cap.

She took it off and smiled at him. "No problem ... and thank you."

His face was frozen in a strange expression as he avoided staring at her bald head.

The same woman who had brought her up from reception appeared and escorted her back down.

Once out in the courtyard, Mike decided not to go straight back to the office but to take advantage of being in a different part of London to her usual haunts. She fancied lunch alone. She was only two streets away when she saw a Lebanese restaurant and found a table at the back near the kitchen door.

With a lamb, feta and lentil *fattoush* ordered, she reflected on what had just happened.

CHAPTER TWELVE

In Tobago, Darren was about to meet his friend Eric. They had agreed to go fishing together off Buccoo Reef for tarpon, using flies made of orange and green feathers attached to heavy line. It was also an opportunity to have a private conversation – with just the two of them. Despite the unequivocal instructions and ultimatum that had been delivered in Brightlingsea, Darren had to wait for Eric to return from a visit to his farm near Luberon in Provence to be able to action it. The journey back had apparently been awful, with delays in London while waiting for the connecting flight. There were no direct flights from Paris.

As they were heading out to the deeper water, the horizon narrowed, and the individual palm trees on the shore merged into a green line. There were towering, white clouds in a periwinkle-blue sky, and the sea was choppy but not rough.

Darren waited until they had finished their fishing and were sitting on the white leather seats enjoying a rum punch and snacking on roast jerk plantains and aloo pies. They had caught fish, but no tarpon. This didn't bother him as this wasn't the main reason he was bobbing around on the motor cruiser.

They had finished speaking about the weather in France and the strikes in Paris.

"How was your trip to England?"

"Well, Eric, unfortunately, I have some bad news. My bosses gave me a bollocking. They told me they'd heard through the grapevine about the meth production and wanted it to stop immediately. Every ounce of anhydrous ammonia must be used for legitimate purposes and end up in the USA or Europe."

"What had they heard?"

"They didn't specify, but they said the European Union Drug Agency is now looking into the route and the source. It's getting too risky."

"It's not that easy. You have your bosses, I have mine, and they won't take kindly to any interruption of supply."

"I'm sorry, really sorry, but the load last week will be the last. If not, I'll be crucified – literally."

"If my bosses are un'appy, you'll also be crucified ... next to me ... with most of your teeth already extracted. Anaesthetic will not feature 'ighly, *si tu compris*? Stopping is not an option. We're in too deep." Eric's voice had hardened, and his underlying French accent had become more evident. He was stressed.

Darren swallowed his drink and poured another for them both from the vacuum flask that kept the punch cold; his hand was shaking. His voice wavered as he said, "Damned if we do, damned if we don't?" with a nervous laugh.

"We're both in this far too deep, *mon cher*."

"What can we do?" His voice was almost unrecognisable.

It was Eric's turn to take a drink as a large fish broke the surface away to starboard, jumping into the air and creating a splash; neither man paid it the slightest bit of attention.

"I went to France for several reasons. One was to change the route that our product arrives in Europe. Trust me, we've also dealt with some other" – he searched for the most apposite word – "inconveniences."

"Eric, I have a great life out here. I don't need hassle. I don't even need the money that much. I need to draw a line under this ... it was a mistake; I'm sorry, really sorry."

"You really aren't getting it. There's no going back. You haven't grasped who you're dealing with. You swam into a shark's mouth, and as you know, the rows of teeth point backwards – there's no way back out."

Darren looked crestfallen and slumped into the soft leather. "What have you got me into?"

"I've got you $120,000 a year tax-free for doing nothing and, very importantly, nothing illegal. Your only commitment is to provide the anhydrous ammonia to yet another customer. What they do with it is none of your concern, and no one in law enforcement anywhere in the world will come after you. Why are you bothered?"

Darren wanted to explain that the clear instructions from the 'family' back home had been presented in equally non-negotiable terms, but he said, "My bosses are very successful and worried about their reputation."

"In France, I dealt with the ... let me call it a 'leak'. It won't 'appen again. So I'd recommend you tell them you've stopped supplying me, but, actually, leave everything as it is. They'll be 'appy, you'll get your money, and my bosses will get the raw material. Everyone is 'appy" – he put a piece of spicy plantain in his mouth – "and you aren't down there swimming with the tarpon."

Darren looked from Eric's reassuring face across the beautiful Caribbean, all the way to the horizon. He thought about his alternatives.

He was between the devil and the deep, blue sea.

———

The smell of Middle Eastern spices and the sound of Arabic music filled the room.

It had been years since Mike had eaten a Lebanese meal, and she had picked the perfect day to correct that. She desperately needed a distraction, and it had done this – for five minutes. Sitting alone in a restaurant merely speeds up time; it's like drinking seawater when you're dying of thirst – it makes it worse. In the restaurant, after her second sip of bottled water, she went back to what had just turned her world upside down.

There were no tears. It wasn't grief or even guilt that washed over her; it was anger.

She now had only one purpose, which was to find out who killed Tina and why. Leonard could either give her *carte blanche* or she would resign – again. She still had the resignation letter on her laptop that she had written ten days earlier.

What had just happened in Marston House? Why did Overton think Tina was dead? Mike was completely disorientated, having thought she had made brilliant progress.

She picked up the laminated menu that was propped up between the salt and pepper mills and began rotating it like a steering wheel. Her hands needed to be doing something.

In fact, it was Marston House that preoccupied her. She'd been to the Brits' big, new offices in London several times; they were slick and cutting edge. It's where she believed, perhaps wrongly, that Tina was based and people like Oscar worked. Was she wrong? Marston House was like something out of the 1940s.

And speaking of the war years, who or what was Gordon Overton?

He was a relic of that time, coming from privilege. She imagined him having been born, preformed, at about age fourteen. Yet despite this head start, he'd been destined to remain frozen at this mental age, with an arrogance and an ignorance – reinforced at school – that merely had become more engrained in his ageing body. And he was only in his forties! How did the Tinas and Oscars of this modern world deal with having a Gordon as their boss?

Her thoughts went to Leonard and the fact that everyone has their crosses to bear.

She was proud of herself that she hadn't lost it and laid into Overton – it had been tempting. The fact that she had managed to control herself was slightly unexpected, but it may have been because she recognised deep down that he was central to finding who killed Tina.

He was stupid enough not to realise he had blown his one chance. She had gone across to Marston House fully intending to tell him all about her discoveries: her visit to Janet in Featherstone and Tina's flight itinerary to Paris. But from the second he had walked through the waiting-room door, that wasn't going to happen. And what was with the waiting room? Did she not warrant an office or a meeting room?

The food arrived, and she told herself to eat slowly as a combination of nervous tension and sitting alone might mean that the meal would be finished before the waiter had made it back to the kitchen.

After the first few tasty mouthfuls, she calmed enough that she began to think straight. If Tina were dead, Mike needed to wise up quickly. Her death appeared to have thrown Overton, and it might be that he was taking some heat for having lost track of an operative. Tina had – for some reason, good or bad – chosen not to tell him or Oscar what she was up to. This was odd, but whatever the reason, she had ended up dead. This was always a risk, given the job she was doing; however, operatives normally rely on their office support and the wider network, but in this instance, she had chosen to fly absolutely solo.

Thinking of Oscar, she wondered if Overton had been monitoring his phones. It was strange that Oscar had sent her a message to phone his boss.

The questions were stacking up like planes over Heathrow, but, oddly, this didn't faze her. It gave her purpose. As she used the last of her pitta bread to wipe her plate clean, she tried to devise a plan of action. What first? After clearing it with Leonard, she would check out any news reports of bodies having been found. This might be in the public domain or might have been suppressed. After that, it was a toss-up between going to see Janet again or to make surreptitious contact with Oscar. She settled on the latter, as Janet may have been contacted by someone from Overton's office by now and may be distraught.

Oscar's office and any official lines of communication were out of bounds. The type of conversation she wanted to have with him couldn't be done on his private mobile. She needed to find out where he lived. Until she knew about his relationship with Overton, it was probably best to avoid any traceable calls or messages. So she said out loud, "Oscar Marsh, where do you live?"

A waiter brought her a small, strong coffee, even though she hadn't ordered it. She explained this and declined, but he asked her if she wanted it anyway, free of charge. She accepted it after all.

While sipping it, her mind went back to Zara. Her accident now felt more sinister. One death is suspicious, but the potential deaths of two people working on the same project must surely be linked, and is even more worrying.

She couldn't handle thinking about what Tina had suffered in her final moments; it was all too disturbing. Instead, she mused on why no one would tell her what Tina had been suspected of doing. Mike had asked both Cromer and Overton, but with no response. She would find out or pressure Leonard into telling her in detail. It must be a good starting point. It was obviously serious enough to lead to her own suspension, whether this was so-called 'automatically triggered' or not.

Something in Tina's life or work was so serious that she couldn't tell Mike or even hint at it. Now it was too late to ask.

Tina, help me. Give me a clue, Mike was begging inside her head – but Tina had already sent her a clue.

———

Leonard appeared to have his head in the wastepaper basket as she entered his office.

He sat back in his chair, breathing heavily from the exhaustion of bending over. He was clutching the white cardboard base of a pack of sandwiches he had eaten earlier.

"What are you doing? Are you reduced to sniffing food wrappers?" Mike asked.

"Nah, I wrote down a code and threw it away."

"Not the nuclear codes, I hope."

"Nah, they're written on the executive washroom wall."

"I can believe it."

"How are you? How was Overton?" He was smiling, but that might have been him trying to regain his breath.

"Well, I'm not likely to put him on my Christmas card list."

"He's old school. I deal with him all the time. One of his agents has gone missing, so cut him some slack."

"You've lost one too: Zara."

"It was an accident."

"I don't believe it, and neither do you."

He didn't answer.

"And what's with Marston House?"

"Aw, Brits like him feel comfortable in places like that; it reminds them of when they ruled the world."

"He told me nothing about Tina except that he thought she was dead. He wouldn't tell me anything else or why she'd been under suspicion while you were away."

"I didn't know she was dead. As far as I heard, she broke the rules and contacted someone on the Red List. She had already been warned."

"I'm guessing you're not going to tell me his name?"

He laughed. "That'll be a no."

She changed tack. "I want to take next week as leave."

"Really? Mike, I don't think that's a great idea."

"Leonard, I either go on leave next week or I resign – again."

"I don't want you interfering. Let the Brits deal with Tina and any aftermath." Here, Leonard was in severe difficulty, needing to keep Mike close to him while matters were resolved.

"I can't."

"OK, I'm not going to fire you, but I'm telling you not to get involved. Don't send me a postcard, but ring me if you find her," he said, smiling sardonically.

———

Wazz was in the flat and had finished a call advising a prisoner how to approach their parole application. He had cocked up his own possibility of early release by getting into a fist fight with another inmate; his timing had been awful, and although it had been self-defence, this hadn't been accepted by the parole board. He now belonged to a volunteer group of ex-cons who tried to help prisoners not to make the same mistakes. His own had meant that, instead of being released part of the way through his sentence and put on licence, he had served his full tariff of two and a half years.

The jury at the Crown Court in Kingston-upon-Thames had found him guilty of possessing a Class B drug, namely cannabis, with intent to supply and the judge hadn't allowed any mitigating factors despite the defence barrister making several valid submissions. Wazz had shared digs with three other friends, and all of them smoked weed, but, unfortunately, the shoebox containing their supplies was in the bottom of his wardrobe with his fingerprints all over the packets. His fickle friends had dropped him in it and avoided prison.

Oddly, it was prison that had saved Wazz. After the anger and desire for revenge had receded, he knuckled under and used the order of prison life to sort himself out. He started reading extensively and took a series of exams that he had flunked while at school. He had started a degree but never finished it, and this was his main aim once he was out.

His other aim was to be a more positive part of his son's life; this had meant he had moved to Spain where his ex-wife had relocated and remarried. The degree was put on hold until he met Mike and returned to London. He had a handful of days to go before his final exam.

After his phone call, he needed to change for work. He was halfway to the bedroom when the front door to the flat opened. Something about Mike's facial expression stopped him from making a flippant remark about Sandra from Accounts.

She collapsed into his very big arms.

CHAPTER THIRTEEN

It was after 9.00pm, and Wazz had long since left for his night shift. Mike craved two things: alcohol and to shave her head.

The few tufts of hair that continued to grow after her accident were annoying in several ways: firstly, they reminded her of the blackest day in her life; and, secondly, why had her hair not completely fallen out? Hats, wigs and completely bald were all very acceptable; a few sparse clumps were not. Mike did black and white, not grey, and she definitely didn't do fifty shades of anything – there was yes and no, right and wrong.

With a shiny scalp, she emerged from the bathroom, went straight to the fridge and took out a can of tonic water that she added parsimoniously to a large glass of Gordons gin. There was no ice or lemon in the fridge, which was a relief.

The drink was part of an acceptance ritual.

———

It happened rarely in her professional life, but a search at work had gone well. It turned out that Oscar Marsh lived in Yiewsley, a so-called 'village' in west London. She had no idea where this was, but she had found out it was five miles south of Ickenham, near the M4. She had decided to wait in the office until 6.30pm and ride out there.

A short bike ride later, in a block of flats called Beck House, overlooking the Grand Union Canal and near the flight path to Heathrow, she had found number fifteen on the third floor. She had pressed a bell under a thin piece of handwritten card proclaiming "O. Marsh".

He had answered the door wearing his work clothes minus his jacket and tie. There had been a smell of cooking, but one that was hard to define. "Oh, h-hi, Mike," he had stuttered, looking beyond her as if she had turned up with a SWAT team.

"You were easy to find."

"I wasn't trying to hide."

"Can I come in?"

"What? We were about to eat."

"I don't need food. I want a five-minute chat."

He had stepped back with some reluctance and peered through a door into what was probably a small sitting room. "Kerry, it's a work colleague. I'll be a couple of minutes."

Oscar had directed Mike into the kitchen, where something was bubbling in a gas oven; the cheese topping to a pasta dish had been beginning to colour.

"Relax, let's make this quick," she had said, but he had used his hands to indicate that she should whisper. "What's happening?"

"Mike, I really shouldn't be talking to you; I'm sorry."

"What has Gordon O, or M or Q or whatever you call him, said?"

"Mr Overton found out we'd been in contact. He was OK, but he told me never to do it again without his authority."

"Really?"

"Yes, really."

"Have you made any progress finding Tina? He says he thinks she's dead."

"No, nothing."

"Why does he think she's dead?"

"I didn't know he did."

"That's what he said when I met him in your offices ... Marston House."

"I've no idea, and I don't work there."

"Have you continued to look for her?"

"No, I'm on other projects, but I thought we hadn't heard from her or found her car."

"Has anyone spoken to her family?"

"I expect so, but I don't know if that helped anyone."

"Oscar, I don't know what's happening either, but I'm worried sick about what happened to her. Overton knows more than he's telling you or me."

"Mike, I'm sorry."

"Why was Tina suspected of contacting someone on the Red List? Do you know who that was?"

"No" – he had looked genuinely surprised she was asking him – "and, anyway, it's not just us who devises that list. It will have automatically been triggered and communicated to the bosses."

"You have no idea?"

"No, but you have as much a chance of finding out as me."

Mike had hit a brick wall. "If I need to contact you, I'll leave a note in your mailbox downstairs. I won't phone or contact you at work. Let your wife or girlfriend know, OK?"

"Kerry's my aunty."

"This is my address, in case you need it." She had handed him a note she had written in advance.

"If I want to know your address, I can find it; I'm an analyst."

"Oh, yes, sorry."

"Thanks, Oscar, and relax. I won't get you into trouble."

His face had suggested that, whatever she said, landing him in trouble was a near certainty.

————

She had ridden back to Ickenham, where she was now sitting at the kitchen table, taking long sips of the gin and tonic following her shower. On the fifteen-minute bike ride, she had reflected on what Oscar had said and not said.

Mike had thought she was probably further ahead than the Brits, but Overton had taken the wind out of her sails. She wondered whether he knew what Tina had been up to or whether he'd merely been informed once her body had been found – if it had been found. Secondly, Oscar was now on his boss's radar and was scared to get involved any more.

She wanted access to the Red List, but this was way above her pay grade – which was odd because she was unlikely to have a pay grade for much longer. How could she find out who Tina had tried to contact?

————

In Arnos Vale, on the west coast of Tobago, Darren Boswell was on his way to a meeting.

He had reflected on what Eric had said and concluded that he had no choice but to let the relatively small amounts of anhydrous ammonia continue to be supplied for the meth production. Eric had explained that people had been killed in Europe for messing things up and everything was back on track; the cartel had too much to lose. It wouldn't happen again.

Darren instead turned his attention to reassuring his cousin that he was a reformed character and devoted to driving forwards the half a dozen projects he'd been given.

One of the two most pressing of these concerned the

construction of a new natural gas treatment plant in a location not restricted by governments that were becoming more environmentally conscious. This meant finding a place that could be easily supplied with natural gas from the Venezuelan field that lay under the sea, spreading almost from Panama, across the top of South America, around Trinidad, and on eastwards to Guyana and probably beyond.

He had arranged to have a second meeting with a contact he'd been given – a real estate agent selling small Caribbean islands, whose name was Hector Candelo.

Darren walked up the hill, avoiding the concrete rain channel alongside the road while also dodging the traffic. A small, bright-pink-painted hotel appeared. He made his way through the building to a covered terrace; it was open on one side, with tables laid for lunch. He selected one that gave views down a wooded valley to the sea below and was immediately next to a gutter full of seeds and nuts at table height that ran the length of the restaurant. The feasting birds flew off in an explosion of colour as he pulled out his chair, only to return immediately for their free food. There were blue-grey tanagers; motmots with their piercing, red eyes; yellow kiskadees; and a single chachalaka, the size of a pheasant, which walked languidly along the gutter inches from the lunchtime guests.

Darren ordered a red wine and waited, never failing to be blown away by the local birdlife. Back at his villa, he had a feeder that dispensed sugar syrup, which attracted a host of hummingbirds.

Hector walked onto the terrace and wove his way through the tables. He was wearing a black jacket and a white, open-necked shirt, and he carried a blue folder under his arm. They shook hands, and the chachalaka that had slowly been approaching along the food trough looked at Hector and flew down into the trees, screaming its name out to anyone interested. Hector tended to have this effect on anything coming into contact with him.

After the obligatory small talk, Darren asked, "Have you made contact with the owners?"

"I have. They're interested in your proposition." His black skin had an oily sheen from sweating in the midday heat and humidity.

"You've brought some more details?"

"I have." Hector opened the file and took out some folded A3 plans and maps of Espanto, a rocky island about a mile long by half a mile wide. It was 150 miles away from Tobago at the southern extent of the Lesser Antilles near Grenada.

"And the approach?"

Here, Hector handed over an official-looking British Admiralty chart in blue and yellow that was covered in numbers, which showed the depths of the sea off the island. Darren had been given a checklist, and the approach for tankers carrying natural gas was at the top of this. Without a deep-water channel, the island was of zero interest. He took his time perusing it.

"There are some buildings?" Darren was flicking through aerial photographs, including some that looked many years old.

"They're abandoned. No one lives on the island."

"But they did?"

"Probably fishermen, but nobody permanent. The island had a reputation from when the Spanish were sailing around the Caribbean. It's why it's called Espanto ... it means 'menace'. They were trying to frighten people away."

They went on chatting and eating while staring out to sea.

"Where are you from, Hector?"

"West of Georgetown, Guyana, but I've lived all over the Caribbean."

"Now if there was an island off Guyana, that'd really interest my family."

"There are. There are islands. You didn't say you were interested in something that far south."

Darren was thinking that a certain family member in Monaco would be very, very interested to know that there were islands in the new oil and gas fields being explored and now developed off Guyana, the old British Guiana.

"Are they like Espanto?"

"No, absolutely not. They're in the estuary of the Essequibo River as it flows into the Atlantic."

"They're smaller?"

"Some are small, some are large. Hog Island is twenty-three square miles. It's bigger than Tortola in the British Virgin Islands."

"Really?"

Darren could see a way to regain the favour of his cousin if he could acquire a site or an island off or in Guyana, an area of real interest to Johnny.

———

It was Saturday afternoon, and Mike was roaring down the A303 having passed Stonehenge on her way to Rodbourne.

Saturday was Wazz's busiest night, and she wanted to leave him in peace and not have to work in silence while he slept. Equally, he wouldn't disturb her when he came in at 3am or 4am, and he could slum it around the flat unshaven and in his underpants if he wished. His university course should end very soon, at which time she hoped he could be convinced to sell the flat and move to Wiltshire. Their relationship was strained by the current arrangements, and they were becoming irritable with each other. Wazz described the pair of them as "two shits who passed in the night".

Mike was feeling mentally unstable and needed a few days to put the last week in some sort of order.

She had searched, but there was no mention of a body having been found anywhere. This was incredibly frustrating but perhaps not surprising. She would check two or three times a day until it was announced, and if it wasn't announced, she would start hacking into places to find out.

It had been on a whim that Mike had decided to take herself away to Wiltshire; peace, detachment and objectivity were what the doctor would have ordered – that was if she had found a medical professional who wouldn't have immediately sectioned her and thrown away the key.

As she rode into the village, it looked as if it hadn't changed for a hundred years, and for the most part, it had not.

She disturbed the Muscovy ducks by wheeling the bike across the footbridge to the tunnel and through to her back gate. No one had opened it while she was away, and the small piece of white paper was still where it had been placed ten days earlier. There was even a large cobweb strung across the gate. Everything in the back garden looked as it had been left, if a little unkempt. With the bike under its cover and the house key in her hand, she opened the back door.

She unpacked her rucksack and changed into lighter clothes. The house smelt musty from being shut up.

There were no signs of microphones or cameras. Two other pieces of white paper were also still in place: one in the lounge doorframe and another wedged in the front door. Most importantly, the hidden camera in the lounge on the bookcase was still there and working; she was confident no one had broken in while she'd been in London. Despite Leonard's assurances that no further action had been ordered by Brent Comer, Mike remained untrusting of the Agency.

She picked up the post from the front doormat and took it to the kitchen. A microwavable ready meal from the small freezer compartment removed the need to even consider a ploughman's at The Green Feathers, but perhaps tomorrow?

After opening the letters and discarding the circulars, she found a badly handwritten note. It simply said "I have something for you, Jess". Mike was intrigued, and at 7.30pm, she walked the few yards along the High Street, opened the old door and was strangely reassured by the tinkling of the bell. She could have saved Pavlov a lot of time with his research.

At that time of a Saturday evening, The Green Feathers was half-empty, but the London set were beginning to come in for their ritual three hours of immersion in Wiltshire culture in front of a log fire. The curtain was pulled back, and Jess appeared. She said hello and promptly disappeared. When she pushed her way through again, she was carrying a pint of beer and a small bowl of gherkins. Mike hadn't intended to drink as her trip was meant to be avoiding the rest of humanity for two days, but she smiled and sat down at a table.

"You've been a long time." There were no pleasantries, and Jess thrust the machine forwards waiting for Mike to tap her card.

"I've been in London."

Jess reached down into the deep, sagging pockets of the brown cardigan and pulled out an envelope, which she handed across. "This came for you. It said not to push it through your door. Dunno why."

Mike took it. "Thank you, Jess."

The brass bell tinkled, and two couples dressed entirely from an early Boden catalogue came down the steps, squinting to see if any of their friends had already arrived.

The first mouthful of beer tasted good and removed any trace of the lasagne that had been slightly dried by the microwaving. She picked up the white envelope on which was handwritten "Jess, please give this to Mike Kingdom when she next comes in. Please do not post it through her door. It's a surprise. Thanks." In the centre of the envelope in bold lettering was typed "MIKE KINGDOM". This wasn't the outer envelope in which it had been posted, and there were no other marks on the outside. She eagerly opened it.

Mike,

Either I have made contact with you by now, and we can laugh at this over a drink in The Green Feathers, or you haven't heard from me, in which case things might have gone wrong.

I don't know who will see this note so I'll restrict what I write. I'm currently trusting nobody – that's nobody.
I'm not using phones or the internet, which is why there has been radio silence, and I didn't post this to your cottage but to Jess. I hope it gets to you.

Don't trust anyone in my company or yours. You need a thick skin in this business, or you'll sink.
Look under your lifesaver.

Here are pictures of three people who might be relevant. No idea who they are.

I'm off abroad.

T

CHAPTER FOURTEEN

On the Friday evening, Darren and Hector had taken a taxi and were being driven the twenty-five miles northwards from Cheddi Jagan airport to Georgetown; it had only been a ninety-minute flight from Port of Spain.

They were on the East Bank of the Demerara Public Road, passing the inappropriately named Garden of Eden Power Station, which was a nightmare vision of pylons and wires with no sign of an apple tree. At the entrance, a sign proclaimed "This facility is operating under level 1". It looked as if it would struggle to operate at any level. Another sign by the road read "Safety begins here", although it was possibly facing the wrong way.

For the whole journey the road followed the red-brown Demerara River, flowing on its way to the Atlantic Ocean. It was either right next to the road or hidden by houses and fields to the left. The landscape was green and flat, punctuated only by the occasional tall, thin palm trees.

They had passed through several villages named after the historic sugar cane plantations; ironically, almost all had biblical names. As well as the Garden of Eden, the taxi had already passed through the Land of Canaan, which was surely a promising sign.

Darren was trying to imagine the sickly smell of molasses when there had been 200 operational rum distilleries.

The new bridge the Chinese were building across the Demerara River came into view. Gradually, Georgetown's suburbs began to engulf them, and, in what seemed like minutes, they were getting out of the taxi in front of the Devonshire Hotel. From the outside, it resembled a three-storey colonial house painted in pastel colours.

Darren and Hector walked into an inner courtyard that was open to the sky and built in a Spanish style with ornate, white metalwork on the balcony supports. They were asked to take a seat in one of the brown faux-leather chairs and given a strong coffee each while they were checked in.

The only other guests or visitors were two men smoking thin cigars and conversing in guttural Russian.

Darren couldn't quite put his finger on why he had felt uncomfortable, even unsafe, since he had landed at the airport. After all, he lived in Trinidad and Tobago most of the time, where despite the daily killings, he felt reasonably secure. Hector also was on edge, appearing to repress his desire to look around constantly; this went beyond his normal suppressed aggression.

After the formalities, they both climbed the stairs to freshen up in their rooms; there were no lifts. Darren opened the door while hearing the belly laughs from the Russians below him. He was confronted by darkness, which was only partially relieved by turning on the double wall light. The bed was covered with a crocheted counterpane in the colours of the rainbow, and the curtains were a depressing brown. The room smelled of insect repellent, which wasn't surprising as the aerosol can was occupying pride of place on the dressing table, though its purpose was unclear as a large cockroach wouldn't need to lower its antennae to get under the door from the corridor with its one-inch gap.

This likelihood was proven to be reality when he stepped up into the bathroom, which ran the length of the room but was barely the width of a human being. A pair of cockroaches were mating on the floor or possibly one was eating the other; it was hard to tell. He checked himself in the rusting mirror, washed his hands and dried them using a damp, folded towel that begged so many questions, all of which were best left unanswered.

There was no safe for his passport and wallet, not that if he would have trusted putting anything one it. Instead, he shoved all his valuables into his pockets, not bothering to unpack his small item of hand luggage, which contained a change of clothes and his washbag. He was only staying one night before returning to Trinidad.

As agreed, they met downstairs after breakfast the next day before visiting two large, derelict industrial sites on the banks of the River Demerara. Some sites – including an island further north on the Essequibo River, about fifteen miles away – might be visited on a subsequent trip. Firstly, however, Darren had a courtesy appointment.

After leaving Hector back at the hotel, he took a short cab ride to the British High Commission.

The taxi had been booked for the whole day, and Darren asked the driver to wait for one hour somewhere close to Main Street, as he wouldn't be long. On getting out of the car, his sense of unease grew even stronger. The low, white building at the roadside was topped with two rows of coiled razor wire and a forest of security cameras on poles. The entrance gate was behind a raised black barrier that would stop a tank, and there was a row of very heavy planters to dissuade anyone from driving too close. The cheery posters promoting education at British universities couldn't lighten the effect.

His courtesy call complete, he returned in the taxi to the

hotel to pick up Hector, ready to visit the potential sites for a new anhydrous ammonia plant with river frontage. He was keen to deliver what his cousin was looking for, so he could demonstrate that he was making reparations and applying himself.

The first site was a completely demolished rum distillery with its own wharf. He would need to check the water depths throughout the year, but it had been used for almost a hundred years, so initial indications were good. At first sight, it was also near perfect in terms of dimensions, neighbours, road access and so many other factors. He walked out to the middle of the plot and stood on a concrete foundation. In some respects, this was a waste of time as everything had been reduced to ground level and removed from the site.

Hector walked in a tight circle around Darren to avoid being in the 360-degree video Darren was taking on his phone to send across to Monaco via Essex. If he had paid more attention, he may have seen the two men on the fire escape of the disused factory next door who were watching their every move.

———

"Do you want another beer?"

"What? Oh, yes ... sure, thank you." Mike had drunk the first cold pint without noticing; her mind was racing all over the place. She had even eaten the gherkins.

Tina's note and the photographs hadn't left her hand. When had it been written and posted to Jess? It couldn't have been written before Monday, and therefore it couldn't have been delivered before Tuesday. She would ask Jess when it had arrived.

Oddly, it felt like her friend – her one girlfriend – was in the pub with her. She had examined the single sheet of white, unlined paper as if it had a secret watermark or hidden code in or on it. Every word had been read and reread until she could recite it. What did it mean? What was written between the lines?

The fact that she hadn't made contact with Mike meant things had gone wrong and she was dead. Her reluctance to even commit anything detailed or specific within a private note, hand delivered by Jess, told Mike that Tina really, really didn't trust anybody, but why? It was so serious that she had decided to not use phones or any electronic means of communication. She'd been so worried that her company or Mike's was checking up on her or perhaps chasing her. What had she done?

Jess brought out Mike's beer.

"When did the letter arrive, Jess?"

"Yesterday."

"I don't suppose you saw where it was posted?" Mike was unaware that letters no longer displayed the sorting office where they were first franked.

"No ... and I don't get many letters." This was less than helpful.

"Thanks, Jess."

This meant it wasn't sent immediately, although she could have asked anyone else to post it, which was likely if she were now in France.

If Tina was this concerned and careful, then Mike must be as well. She, too, couldn't leave a history or trail anywhere – on phones or computers. Patently, she would have to use her most untraceable methods while using search engines so as not to leave any footprint. And she would have to do all this alone – with no discussion with Leonard or Oscar or, if she were honest with herself, any other person.

As Mike had sensed, it had been in The Green Feathers, when she had mentioned Zara having been knocked down, that Tina's demeanour had changed. Perhaps she had felt her project or projects had been compromised and her cover blown.

Then there was the sentence "Look under your lifesaver".

Mike was keen to get back to the cottage to see what was under her coffee machine. Had Tina written something? And who were the men in the photographs?

There was a lot to take in.

While drinking the next beer, which Jess had served unasked, she stared at the men who had been photographed in what resembled Central London. The first looked furtive with small, dark eyes set close together. His blond hair was slicked back, making him appear older than he actually was. Mike thought he was in his mid-thirties. The second was taller with curly, brown hair and was wearing a shearling coat over a suit and striped tie. He was in his mid-forties. The final one was tall and well-dressed, yet his black hair was down to his chin with a central parting. Was he an ageing hippie? His skin was swarthy or tanned, and he had a long face. He was about to get into the passenger door of a very expensive Aston Martin. Mike would use the registration number later to find his name and address; she had ways to do this via both the DVLA and his insurance company.

Tina wasn't sure if any of these men were important or not, and for whatever reason, she was unable to tell Mike exactly what she was up to; she could only leave the subtlest of hints. There was so much more in this note written between the lines, Mike could feel it deep down. Actually, she couldn't feel anything deep down, having already drunk two pints of beer so quickly; walking home in a straight line might be a challenge.

Someone called Tommo, judging by the shouts of encouragement from his friends, had stood up, was waving a handful of notes in the air and was calling for drinks all round. Whatever his position in a hedge fund in the city, he was about to be cut down to size. Jess came out from behind the curtain and told him to fuck off, much to the amusement of the young farmers, but to the disappointment of Vic, the overweight pub regular who was sitting in his favourite seat in the corner and who was enthusiastic about any and all free drinks on offer.

Vic lived in the High Street, where he spent many a day in summer spraying children – and indeed their parents – with a hose from his garden. He never missed an opportunity for an unexpected free pint of beer. He leapt up – well, more accurately, set his bulk in motion – before waddling over to Tommo and suggesting that he might be able to rectify the situation. Having taken the order for everyone on the table, Vic pulled back the curtain and passed this on to Jess in the kitchen behind.

"Fuck off, you'll have to wait," was a huge improvement on the first response.

Vic nodded knowingly over to Tommo before sitting back down in his favoured chair, its wafer-thin cushion incapable of puffing out any more dust, having been compressed from years of fine service. He winked at Mike who was sitting at the next table. "Did you see they men in the end?" he asked conspiratorially in his broad accent while leaning towards her.

"What men?" She was frowning.

"I think it were they two blokes who were 'ere before. The ones who look like they're flogging dictionaries."

Mike had no idea what he was talking about.

Vic lived alone and spent a disproportionate amount of time in his front garden, craving human contact. Rodbourne had no need for a Neighbourhood Watch scheme.

"No ... when were they back?"

"An hour ago."

Mike made an assumption about who they were and was wondering why Brent Cromer's men had returned. He was no longer director. Whoever they were, she now had a problem: she needed to get into her cottage to retrieve her stuff and see what Tina had put under the coffee machine.

"Did you see them leave?"

"They buggered off towards Salisbury in a black Jeep Cherokee, I think it were."

"Thanks, Vic." On standing up, she became aware of her unsteadiness and, with the note in her hand, made for the fireplace.

"I ordered thee a pint," he said as she passed him.

"You drink it; I'm going."

Keeping the photographs, she threw the note into the flames and waited, watching it curl and burn. Although mostly symbolic, a gentle prod with a poker destroyed all traces of it. There was a sign warning customers not to touch the fire, but nobody took any notice, not even the green woodpecker whose glassy eyes came to life as the flames flickered.

As she walked between the tables and up the steps, there were various friendly shouts of "Goodbye," "Part timer," and "Shut the door behind you."

The cool air was striking as she stepped out into the wide street. There was silence, which only served to heighten her nervousness. Not a leaf was moving, and there was no sign of activity, despite her looking behind herself after every few steps to check. How could such a short walk take so long?

On entering Church Lane, the illusion of security provided by the lonely streetlamp on the corner gradually faded as she walked into the darkness using the torch on her phone.

———

It was early on that Saturday evening, and a Serbian lorry driver was heading south from the port of Le Havre in northern France. It would be a clear night and, with his stomach full and the cab already warm, it should be an easy run down to Clermont Ferrand after picking up a container forty minutes earlier.

The journey southwards around Paris was uneventful, and he was thankful he could listen to the commentary on the Russia versus Serbia football match. Unfortunately, the game began to go downhill as Anton Miranchuk scored from the penalty spot after twenty-one minutes and, by the end, Russia had won by four goals to nil. However, it had passed a couple of hours, and there was always the match against Cyprus in four days' time. Unfortunately, he wouldn't be alive to listen to it.

Four and a half hours later, while passing a village on the A71 near Bourges, he was pulled over by an unmarked police car with flashing, blue lights and approached by two heavily armed officers. One opened the door, climbed up into the passenger's seat and ordered him to drive; the other jumped back into the car, which followed them off the main road and along a country lane. Forced to pull up in a layby, the driver was manhandled down a bank, through dense trees and unceremoniously shot. His phone, wallet and any identifying paperwork were removed from his clothing.

While this was happening, a passenger from a Citroen, already parked nearby and waiting, jumped up into the cab and settled in the driver's seat, preparing to drive off. The 'policemen' removed the flashing-light unit from the roof of their car and put it in the boot; they, too, prepared to leave.

Thirty minutes later, the lorry was driven into an industrial estate on the outskirts of Bourges and round to a nondescript unit located at the back. It was reversed through a pair of high-security doors into a large, empty space where three men were waiting to unload the container.

It would take four hours to remove the transparent packets of meth from their hiding place, within the bright-red fire extinguishers. The process was slow and produced so much bulky waste that it needed to be loaded into another lorry, ready for disposal in a landfill site.

Inside the warehouse, there were also three Peugeot Boxer vans with their rear doors open ready to receive the drugs. The transfer was overseen by Jochem, a thickset Dutchman with pale lashes and eyebrows contrasting with his tanned face. His side-kick walked around constantly, saying nothing but not missing anything. It was a well-oiled machine run by a gang boss in Rotterdam.

Staying under the radar was paramount. There was no need to rush or to take risks and blow what was a dangerous intervention. All in all, it would take a week to distribute the drugs all over France, where it would have a street value of over €10 million. This would all need to be done without drawing the attention of the Morcodo network – the biggest drug cartel in Europe, which was run from a French prison by its Moroccan head, Ayoub.

That the Dutch thought they could take on the Moroccans and win was, in itself, hard to believe. That they might hijack and steal €10 million worth of meth without reprisals was naïve or, as a minimum, ill-considered. As it happened, it took three hours before the Morcodo cartel members in Clermont Ferrand got wind of what was happening.

In France, a gangland war of epic proportions had begun.

CHAPTER FIFTEEN

A muntjac deer shrieking in the dark had done nothing to calm her nerves while she walked back to the cottage. She opened the front door slowly, went inside, immediately bolted it behind her and turned on every light.

There was only one thing dominating her thoughts: what had Tina written or hidden under the coffee machine before she had set off back to London thirteen days ago?

Once in the kitchen, she pulled down the blind before unplugging the small, black Bosch coffee maker that she referred to as her lifesaver. There was nothing underneath, not even a note. She held it over the sink and tipped out the water from the reservoir.

While tilting it, she saw a piece of masking tape stuck on the bottom of the machine. In scratchy writing using a blue ballpoint pen was the name "Gordon Overton". Mike rotated it and searched every corner, but that was it: one name and probably not the one that had triggered all the alarm. After all, he was unlikely to be on the Red List. Tina must have written the name and stuck it on the machine while Mike had been upstairs, showering before she left for London. This was right after she had used Mike's laptop to search for something.

The frustration that coursed through her veins was almost unbearable. Fortunately, there was no one nearby to try to offer advice or receive the full force of her anger. She was so excited that Tina had given her Overton's name, but she couldn't handle not being able to do anything with it or she would trigger every alarm in the CIA's system and probably at the British security service as well. She burnt the piece of masking tape.

Mike put the coffee machine back in its place on the kitchen worktop and looked around. There was no sign that anyone had been in her house. If Brent Comer's men were to reappear, she could handle it – although she couldn't get her head around why they would turn up at her door. They must know she would phone Leonard instantly. Perhaps Vic had been confused.

Tiredness kicked in. Would it be better to leave on all the lights in the cottage or would that be an utter waste of time? Her last thought as she sat in the lounge was that Tina's note had been burnt as had the piece of tape attached to her coffee machine. No one would ever know.

She never got around to pondering what Overton was up to or whether he was connected to one of the men in the photographs, because she fell into a deep, deep sleep.

———

Mike woke up in an armchair a few hours later, disorientated and with a dry mouth. The first thing she did was check the news reports around France and elsewhere, but she found nothing.

She drank a glass of water and sat in front of her laptop at the kitchen table. It would take her a few minutes to set up her system such that it concealed her internet activity. In fact, she configured it to disguise where her calls and searches originated. To all intents and purposes, she was now someone working for

UNICEF, the United Nations Children's Fund, based in New York.

It took all her self-discipline not to check out Overton some more. What she heard in her ear was Dylan, Wazz and Tina screaming at her to take a breath and think before she dived in.

Instead, she searched for the men in the photographs. There were no good matches for the first, and there was no other way to find out who he was. The second turned out to be an apparently well-known football commentator on TV called Edward Bunting. He lived in West London with a glamorous wife and family.

The third was the easiest to identify, with her having the car registration number in addition to an image of his face. He was Peter Swift, a billionaire Brit living in Monaco and Cannes, but originally born in Brightlingsea, Essex. How was he relevant, or was he relevant at all? She'd been hoping the photograph would provide some obvious link to Overton, but that was very wishful thinking. The man looked a bit like Rasputin.

Peter Swift was yet another connection to France. Tina obviously had no idea who he was or if he were relevant. A quick look showed that he had made his money through mineral and chemical companies around the world. Mike couldn't really see how he might be connected to CHOGM. She would return to this later. There were other routes to pursue first.

Tina had given her enough hints in her letter about where to start. "You need a thick skin in this business, or you'll sink" was almost verbatim what she had said about the surface of the tar pit in Trinidad where she had met Sheldon Douglas. It was early evening in Port of Spain, and Mike was tempted to call him – but to say what? They had never made direct contact, and he wouldn't know her name. Washing and drying her plate gave her time to think it through.

Anyone and everyone she now contacted might be a name on

the Red List. She was playing Russian roulette, but with no alternative.

Mike had made a note of two of Sheldon's numbers while she had access to the system at her office. She dialled the first, and he answered after a half a dozen rings.

"Sheldon." He emphasised the second syllable.

Thereafter, the conversation involved Mike pretending to be Jana, who worked for the Brits and, in particular, for the person he had met at the tar pits on Saturday, 1st March. Mike had randomly picked her aunt's name out of nowhere.

Sheldon sounded cautious and was probably trying to make sense of the US dialling code.

Mike needed to explain this: "I'm in New York, in case you're wondering about the number. The reason I'm phoning is that she has gone missing." Mike was at a disadvantage here from not knowing the alias Tina had used.

Sheldon was still not convinced.

Mike persevered, "I'm trying to find her. I'd like you to help me. Two weeks ago, she was at my house and told me about the tar pits and all about the man with the interesting way to dispose of his Carib bottle tops."

He relaxed slightly, but he said he had no idea where she was.

"She said she met Hector Candelo outside the TEMA building in Tobago on your recommendation. I'm going to phone him next. Should I trust him?"

"No way," he responded, and then he went on to make it clear from his answer that he didn't know Hector and had only met him twice.

"I'm worried about her. What did he want to talk to her about?" Mike was groping in the dark.

He explained he had put them in touch, but he had no idea what it was all about. His heavy accent and use of patois meant Mike had to concentrate.

"She didn't fly to Tobago without some idea of what Hector had to offer. What did he ask you?"

"I can't say, man."

Mike then played her ace card and dropped into the conversation how it had been her who had found Sheldon in the first place, and how it was to her that he should be grateful. She ended with, "You want to go on working with the Brits, don't you? If so, tell me enough that I can find her, please."

With Sheldon, money always talked. Loyalty was for losers. He denied all knowledge, but he said Hector had said something about meth, and he wanted money for the information.

"Meth being made in Trinidad or being imported into Trinidad?" she asked.

"You crazy?" Sheldon had clammed up, saying that such conversations were very dangerous.

"If I don't find her, your income from the Brits stops, so why don't you think about that and where she might be. Any ideas?"

He explained that Hector had met somebody in Tobago, but he didn't know who.

"Made here or imported here?"

Sheldon hesitated, but he finally said it was likely to be made locally.

"Where?"

He had begun to lose patience and explained that, if he knew that, he wouldn't need Hector and would want the money himself.

"What if I call Hector and ask?"

He had exploded: "Yuh dotish awah?" (meaning "Are you mad or what?") Sheldon warned Mike not to mention his name and stated that this was all suicidal.

"Why's that?"

Apparently, Hector was a snake and a hustler.

"Where is she, Sheldon? Think hard."

His reply was graphic, explaining that if anyone asked about meth production, they were likely to get hacked to pieces with a machete – and that's if they were lucky.

"When I see her, I'll tell her you were helpful, OK?"

He had said nothing in reply.

"One last thing. What name was she using with you?"

"Alice Dee."

After the call, Mike flopped back and tried to make sense of any of it.

Before she tried to phone Hector, she would do a bit more research on him. At least when she called him, she would know to use the name Alice Dee.

————

At that precise time, Hector was in the hotel courtyard having a rum punch with someone he knew as Johnny Boswell. The visits to the two adjacent sites had gone well, and his client was very happy. They were sitting among the pot plants, enjoying the moving air from a fan swinging back and forth from the wall next to them. They were chatting about the history of demerara sugar and its many uses.

Hector's family had been slaves on the Peter's Hall plantation; not cutting sugar cane but digging three canals that provided irrigation water. There had been over 200 plantations at the time, and, together, they produced enough sugar to make British Guiana the largest rum producer in the British Empire. The high humidity and constant temperature were perfect for the distilleries. By 1881, Hector's family were free, un-indentured and working on the now 1,000 acres of cane fields.

Hector had left Georgetown in 2020 after the elections, when the tensions between the Indo-Guyanese and the Afro-Guyanese had made his family's life intolerable. He told Darren that he went straight into real estate in Scarborough, but in fact this was rubbish as he had become a taxi driver on Tobago.

It was while he was explaining a well-rehearsed lie about why he had so many wonderful islands for sale – conveniently omitting any mention of taxi driving – that a cab turned up. The driver came into the courtyard and asked for Johnny Boswell.

"We'll continue this conversation in Scarborough. I need to settle up." Darren finished his drink and walked to the man at the reception desk, who had a piece of paper ready. Paying the bill for both of them took no time at all.

The driver stepped in to take the carry-on bag that Darren had at his feet and then turned towards the exit.

"Thank you, Hector. Enjoy your few days here. I'll get home late tonight, but I'm looking forward to a day fishing with my son tomorrow."

They shook hands, and Hector was left on his own. The receptionist, Chico, walked across the tiles to the small bar and began making another punch – a bottle of rum had already been secretly added to Johnny Boswell's bill. He brought it over and placed it in front of his friend Hector, and they exchanged a few words on the gullibility of the British.

Left on his own, Hector was feeling the best he had for months. It looked like he might finally have organised an introduction to a deal on a big piece of land. He toasted himself – it had taken a long time. For the next three days, he would see his family near the Essequibo River, all courtesy of Johnny paying for the visit. Why not take advantage of this free trip home?

He took a big sip and laughed to himself. Back in Scarborough, he had $4,000 in cash hidden away in his roof space. Some of it came from a Dutchman or German, he didn't care which, who had paid him for information on the meth lab in Point Lisas. It was easy money. That British woman had also come up with $1,000, but no passport – yet. He had quite fancied one, but too bad.

He must look at the positives. His life had turned a corner.

With his shirt sticking to his back from sweat, he climbed up the stairs and moved along the internal balcony to his room, looking down at the armchairs where he had so successfully convinced Johnny Boswell of the merits of the first site with its easier connection to the Demerara River. The irony that it was probably his ancestors who had dug the canal in the first place wasn't lost on him.

A little later, Chico was looking up at the balcony when the two Russians came downstairs carrying their bags, as they were also checking out. It was a busy time in Georgetown.

———

She was kneeling on the work surface changing a light bulb that had plunged half the kitchen into darkness; this had been the only excitement in Mike's evening, apart from the scratching of a mouse somewhere in the ceiling above her. Her research on Hector had been interesting, not least the fact that he was Guyanese.

Once back at the table, she pondered the last line of Tina's note: "I'm off abroad".

It came to Mike in a flash not dissimilar to that she had experienced ten minutes earlier when the bulb failed. Tina was telling her that she was going abroad so Mike didn't waste time looking for her in the UK. She would also know that Mike would search for flights eventually, using the name Christina Persad, and this would lead to her discovering the date on which she had left the UK and that she had gone to France.

The note was also trying to indicate in a cryptic way that Mike should start with Sheldon. This would probably lead, via Hector, to some connection – whatever this was – that would explain why Tina was doing something in France. She was trying to tell Mike all this without another human being aware of any of it, even her work colleagues.

Before Mike tried Hector's phones, she wanted to do some

more research into meth production in Trinidad and Tobago. After all, this was the information that Hector was trying to sell to Tina for $10,000 and a new life. She grabbed a coffee and settled into her research.

When she next came up for air, she realised that perhaps speaking to Hector might give her a new direction or a hint; she didn't expect him to mention any other names or addresses as that information was too valuable to him. She pulled up the numbers on her screen and dialled.

His first phone was turned off.

She tried the second, which at least rang but, sadly, remained unanswered. It didn't go to voicemail, although she wouldn't have used that facility anyway. That he hadn't answered had surprised her, as hustlers like Hector lived and died by their phones.

———

This was true as Hector was lying dead on his hotel bed with his hand awkwardly reaching for his mobile.

PART TWO

CHAPTER SIXTEEN

As Wazz had said many times, patience wasn't Mike's middle name. She tried the numbers again an hour later, and when there was still no reply, she turned her attention to the laptop on the kitchen table.

With everything plugged in, she began with Sheldon's phone messages, looking for when Hector made contact at the beginning of March or just before. The name Alice Dee popped up in one text from Sheldon at 6.33pm on 1st March, in which he said he would set up a meeting. Mike had seen this before in her earlier searches, but, of course, the name Alice Dee meant nothing to her then.

Trying to follow what happened was a hit-and-miss affair. There could have been face-to-face meetings or phone calls, or they might have used other phones and devices. If this were the case, Mike wouldn't be able to access these. She swapped over to Hector's phone and checked the twenty-four hours before he contacted Sheldon. Who had he spoken to, messaged or met?

There were dozens of messages and texts, which wasn't surprising, given his life as a hustler. She ordered them on her screen into three columns headed "Irrelevant", "Not enough information" and "Possible".

The ticking of the clock in the small kitchen became louder, or it could simply have been that it was silent outside in the village at that time of night.

In the column marked "Possible", there were four names. One he had called three times just before calling Sheldon. Hector had messaged and met him on two occasions very recently; he was identified only as 'LoverBoy'.

She stood up, walked into the lounge and flicked on the light. Her eyes needed a rest from the screen for two minutes. After pulling back the curtains, she looked across at the cottages opposite, which were barely illuminated by one of the three street lamps from the High Street. There were no signs of life; the village was asleep. Church Lane was a cul-de-sac, which was perhaps symbolic as this was where Mike spent her life – both in reality and online – following ideas up ever-narrowing lanes only to find dead end after dead end.

Her break over, she went back to her screen and moved from the period around 1st March to the present moment. Who had Hector been in contact with over the last few hours?

Here, she had success. His calls and messages were all to family and friends in Guyana.

A few clicks later, she had located his phone to the Devonshire Hotel in Georgetown. No wonder he wasn't answering her calls; he was back with his family. She would try him one more time – it was 8.00pm in Guyana.

A voice answered, "Who is this?"

Mike was temporarily thrown, she wasn't expecting him to answer, "Hector, I'm a friend of Alice Dee. I wondered if we could have a chat about the proposal you put to her in Tobago."

There was a pause, followed by, "What's your name?"

"Jana Smith ... we've never met. I work for a sister organisation to Alice." Jana now seemed to be the default name that flashed into Mike's mind whenever she needed an alias, but her aunt wouldn't mind.

"Miss Smith, this is Inspector Khan of the Guyana Police Force. May I ask where are you ringing from?"

"New York." She was still hiding her location.

"I'm sorry to tell you that Hector Candelo has been found dead. Do you have any information that might help us?"

"No ... sorry, no. We've never met. I was given his name by a friend."

"Is this a personal or business matter?"

"Real estate enquiry. I believe Hector is an agent for certain properties. It doesn't matter; it isn't that important. So sorry to hear that he's dead. How did he die?"

"He was murdered in his hotel."

"Oh."

"Miss Smith, if I need to contact you, should I use this number?"

"What? Yes ... but I'm not sure that I can be of any help."

"I must get back to our investigation. Goodbye."

Mike slumped back in her chair and looked at the ceiling. What could possibly connect Zara's and Tina's deaths with Hector's?

One word was going around and around in Mike's head: Guyana.

———

The sun was just under the horizon and producing a pale-gold glow in the eastern sky above the village. Mike was completely unaware, playing with a pencil and deep in thought. The night had passed without her noticing.

She was trying to make connections: Tina was looking into threats to CHOGM in Guyana, and so was Zara. Hector was

Guyanese and had asked to meet Tina. Hector was murdered in Guyana. How were they all linked?

Mike went back to her searches of Hector's phone and the identity of LoverBoy.

She almost screamed. There in front of her, she could see a message that asked Hector to pick him up outside the factory where he worked, mentioning a specific road. She checked quickly and found that he was a factory worker in Trinidad employed by a company that produced fire extinguishers and related products. LoverBoy was Hector's source working at the very small facility in Point Lisas and living nearby; he was a Trini and not Guyanese.

It suddenly dawned on her that she had already checked out this company: it was Pyrandox, run by Eric Fournier. There were only seven employees in Trinidad. This felt like real progress.

It was while she was idly zooming in on an aerial photograph of their Point Lisas factory that something clicked.

After a lifetime of pursuing drug cartels and distributors, her eye naturally fell onto the adjoining anhydrous ammonia plants and the port facilities. Although her previous interest had tended to be in cocaine and heroin, she automatically associated the words 'anhydrous ammonia' with crystal meth. It set her mind racing. Unknown to her, she was making the same connection that Tina had made.

In her experience, Trinidad wasn't known as a centre for meth production, but she hadn't realised it was such a huge producer of one of the main ingredients. This was all overwhelming, and she made a note for the future, but it was probably not relevant to today's problem. She moved on from LoverBoy to the next name on her list of Hector's contacts: Johnny Boswell.

Here, she struck gold – or should that be oil or natural gas?

The details of the trip to Georgetown to show Johnny two possible development sites for a new ammonia plant came up in a message on Hector's phone. The dates showed they were together in the Devonshire Hotel yesterday, only hours before Hector was murdered. Mike was now like a missile locked on to a target.

Somehow, she had unconsciously put some frozen bread into the toaster and, afterwards, spread some margarine and jam on it. It was consumed without her noticing what she was eating, as she tapped away at the keyboard.

When she saw that Johnny Boswell was a director of the ammonia plant in Point Lisas, she almost went into overload. Time to take a break.

As she walked around the kitchen and into the lounge, she saw some leaflets that had been delivered the day before: the parish newsletter and a notice that the village hall was closed for two weeks for the filming of a TV series. Her heartbeat had slowed by the time she was back in the kitchen.

When Mike discovered that Johnny was from Essex, even she needed to stop and stare at the ceiling. She had made more progress in five minutes than she had in ten days.

Dylan's voice was screaming in her ear: "*Slow down!*"

Mike listened subconsciously and spent five minutes calmly calling up photographs, biographies and old addresses; in fact, all the boring stuff about Johnny Boswell. It felt like he was the key to some lost kingdom, to some parallel world.

What did LoverBoy, Eric Fournier and Johnny Boswell have to do with any of this? She couldn't see any connection yet, but she convinced herself it was only a matter of time before she found it.

Her success over the last few hours had pumped her up, but there were still messages on Hector's phone to check. The next one was to Alice Dee, and it simply had a name: Alexei Savin. Mike wanted to check him out, but she would need to be extremely careful and put every conceivable cut-out and barrier in place.

She spent time reassuring herself that there was no way anyone could track back any searches to her, and she continued to use the identity of Jana Smith from UNICEF in New York if anyone were interested. Everything on her kitchen table was neatly organised, from her notebook and pens to her packet of cigarettes and lighter. She was ready.

"OK, let's see who you are," Mike muttered to herself.

Savin was Russian, but he very much flew under the radar. He was an oligarch by any other name, but he wasn't the sort who bought Premier League football clubs. He lived in many places, but London and Monaco were his preferred bases when he wasn't on his superyacht, the *Bellis Mare*, which he appeared to keep moored in the Maldives most of the year.

In the handful of photographs she found, he was a very tall man with broad shoulders who stooped as if embarrassed by his height. He mostly dressed casually and seemed to be happiest in old knee-length shorts and flip-flops. There were none of the hand-made suits and bling favoured by so many of his compatriots in Monaco or elsewhere. He had a disarming smile and a few tattoos on his left calf; otherwise, he was nondescript. He could have been any other rich Canadian or Australian who enjoyed deep-sea fishing in the Indian Ocean.

Mike couldn't fail to make the connection that his apartment was in Monaco and Tina had flown to France. Perhaps there was a connection, and she'd been drawn like a moth to the flame and, sadly, been burnt?

It was while searching the Agency's and Five Eyes' files on him that she made a key discovery: he was linked to the Russian President with a remit to destabilise the Caribbean and South America, while ensuring that Russia ended up with the extensive mineral deposits. This wasn't public knowledge. His own companies – which had substantial interests in oil, gas and rare metals – were known by the Western spy agencies to be conduits for billions of dollars of investment from the President's own money.

Not surprisingly, in the files she had gained access to, he was a frequent visitor to the Russian Embassy in Georgetown, which was one of the largest in Guyana and the entire region.

Mike picked up the packet and lighter. It was time for a pause and a reward for making so much progress – real progress – in just a few hours. The rear garden beckoned while she marshalled her thoughts, and she headed outside. This was all very interesting and relevant, but how did it get her closer to finding Tina's killers and, if it was all as she now expected, bringing this Alexei to justice?

While puffing cigarette smoke upwards, as if avoiding nearby dinner guests, she walked over to her bike and began picking aimlessly at the silvery metallic cover. Something was still eluding Mike. Why had Tina not shown the photographs of the first unidentified man, Edward Bunting and Peter Swift to Oscar or Overton? And if she had discovered something about this Alexei, why had Tina not told them? What had made her so suspicious and scared of her own and Mike's employers? As it turned out, Tina may have been right to be suspicious of something – it had led to her death. After stubbing out the cigarette on her waste bin, she popped the butt inside and returned to her desk.

The five-minute break had been good for her. It made her slow down and consider what she had learnt and where she should look next. Time was always short, and she couldn't waste it pursuing too many dead ends.

She decided to park the meth production idea; it was probably her overactive mind making connections where there weren't any. Hector was in Guyana to try to get a percentage from introducing this Johnny Boswell to potential sites for ammonia production plants. Mike could imagine that Hector may have trod on some important toes, including Russian and Chinese interests. Perhaps this was why he'd been killed.

Alexei Savin must be involved in some threat to leaders

attending the conference. Perhaps this was why he was on the Red List – that's if he was.

The church bells began to ring, calling the villagers to the Sunday-morning service. The sudden noise sent a flock of pigeons in every direction, with some landing in the hawthorn tree beginning to come into leaf at the bottom of her garden.

Mike leapt up as there was a tapping at her glazed back door. A face peered in.

She let her heartbeat slow down; it was a peacock looking at itself in the glass. When she stood up, it strutted down the path and scampered away to the compost heap at the bottom of the garden, where it turned to give her a disdainful look.

Before she made herself breakfast, she did one last check to see if there were any reports of a body being found. To her horror, a French newsfeed contained a press release from the police authorities announcing that the body of a woman who had been found in the Siagne River near Cannes had still not been identified, and there was a request for help from the public. A name and phone number were provided.

Mike was stunned and sat staring into the middle distance.

Twenty minutes later, she had eaten a piece of toast and peanut butter while walking around and collecting up her things. A couple of huge mouthfuls emptied her glass of milk, and she raced upstairs to pack her rucksack. If she were quick, it would only take her just over two hours to get to the flat in Ickenham before Wazz headed for work.

She left the house and locked the back door, as the frustrated peacock pushed its way through the hedge at the bottom of the garden. Within the hour, it would be back looking at its reflection in her glass door. She manoeuvred the motorbike through the tunnel and past the parked cars of the Sunday congregation. In her rucksack was her passport. She thought she may end up flying to France.

CHAPTER SEVENTEEN

The white taxi slowed to a stop under the palm trees, despite the car having backfired randomly for the whole journey and having one door tied up with string.

Tina was telling the driver her visit wouldn't take more than an hour, while grabbing the bag and sun hat from the backseat next to her. It was 9.00am, there weren't many people about, and a low sun was shining through the palm fronds. At the entrance, she waited until Sheldon Douglas turned up before buying two tickets that gave them access to the Pitch Lake. They didn't pay for a guide; Sheldon was a local and knew how and where to walk. They weren't here as tourists but to have a private conversation.

As they made their way out across the grey surface, he pointed out the processing plant run by LATT, Lake Asphalt of Trinidad and Tobago, which refined and exported the tar, and he showed Tina the peripheral low cliff wall that demonstrated how little the surface of the lake had sunk despite all the extraction over 400 years. It was replenished naturally from beneath. He mocked Sir Walter Raleigh, who had claimed to have discovered it, despite it having been used for centuries before. It was impossible to estimate the millions of tonnes of pitch, as it was known, that had been transported to the UK over that time to be used for caulking ships in the early days and as tarmacadam on the world's roads.

They were standing out in the middle among the brown, oily pools when a local man wandered over casually. He was naked. Sheldon politely told him to disappear, but not before Tina had been mesmerised by his piercings. The man seemed reluctant to leave, so she gave him $5 and asked him to get her a Carib beer. He neither questioned why she should want one at 9.00am or where he was going to get one; instead, he wandered off back towards the ticket office.

Sheldon smiled when he said, in his heavy accent that he thought she would like to see some local colour. He reassured her the man was from a local family and quite safe.

"Well, I can see he's not carrying concealed," Tina replied.

It was Saturday, 1st March, and she was meeting Sheldon at his request. He wanted to pass on information about several ongoing projects, but in addition, he mentioned a new acquaintance of his called Hector Candelo, who had asked to be introduced to someone from the British High Commission – unofficially. This man had some information he wanted to sell.

Tina was Sheldon's handler, and she had met him occasionally over the last two years. She knew he valued his regular income courtesy of His Majesty's Government and wasn't a time-waster. Sheldon was up front about it, saying he didn't know anything about this information except that some of it was relevant to drugs and some to a Russian operation. She agreed to meet this man in Tobago two days later, hoping to catch a plane to get there and not suffer the unpleasant crossing on the fast ferry around the western tip of Trinidad.

The first time she had caught the ferry, the film *Skin*, which is about two white parents in South Africa who had a black-skinned baby, was being shown on the big screen. The only white couple aboard had looked embarrassed throughout, and she was glad for once that her skin was brown. This wasn't her main memory of that trip, on which the wild dipping and rolling of the boat had induced so much seasickness that the toilets were unusable. Racial politics seemed of secondary importance for an hour or so.

This time, having met Sheldon, she tried to book a flight, but they were all full: it was Carnival week. Instead, it was through a contact at the Ministry of National Security that she hitched a lift on the drug surveillance plane; this was something she'd done once before. The weather was good and the journey smooth.

Oscar Marsh and Zara Penfold back in London had checked out Hector Candelo, but there was nothing much on the systems about him. Tina felt safe meeting him outside the TEMA building and was intrigued whether he had any information on her main project, on which she hadn't made great progress. Gordon Overton, her loathsome controller, had been explicit in his instructions. She was to identify threats to CHOGM and maintain her contacts in the southern Caribbean. When Oscar had told her that Hector was Guyanese, her hopes had risen that he might be a new contact to develop.

Watching him approach for the meeting at the appointed time, her hopes had dissipated. The two things she noticed first were the scuffed cheap shoes and the file under his arm. He was wearing a threadbare black suit and an open-necked white shirt. There was a cockiness in the way he walked.

For the first few minutes of their conversation, it was all silly posturing on his part. She let it all ride.

Case officers like Tina were two-way mirrors, reflecting what the contact wanted to see but allowing them to observe it anonymously somehow. Quite quickly, she had him sussed; her job relied substantially on cultivating the Hectors of this world. While electronic surveillance and AI were taking over so much of the secret-squirrel world, it still relied in no small part on the interface between agents and joes.

His early demands, before he would even give her the vaguest idea of what he knew, would test the patience of any normal human being, but she let it pass. He asked for a ridiculous amount of money, which was also a typical bargaining position. It was when he asked for a British passport that she picked up that this wasn't just a routine interaction. His information, in his eyes, meant he might need to leave the Caribbean.

He seemed to only have one negotiating style, which bordered on aggressive. There was certainly no finesse. Tina had let him have his moment of fame and then gently stopped him. Unless he gave her some indication of what he was selling, there would be no progress, and both their trips would have been wasted.

Somehow, he was aware she had flown in on the drug surveillance plane and this indicated to her how well connected he was. She turned this around and pointed out that she was someone serious, and he had an opportunity to join the big leagues, but he had about two minutes before she called a taxi back to the airport half an hour away, never to contact him again. She left a long, long silence.

He began to talk more quickly, but in a whispered voice, setting out all the parameters before he would pass on his information. She gave him the space and time, having to concentrate as his speech drifted more and more into Trini and Guyanese patois.

"Hector, this is your one chance. Either you tell me enough that I want to meet you again or the opportunity is gone *forever*."

Her calmness had thrown him. Hector had grown up having to fight his corner. He looked around and used the seconds to weigh up the situation. For her part, she knew he was about to give her the end of a thread that might lead to something useful.

The sun was burning down on them, and he had rested the blue file on his head to provide some shade. Was this why he had brought it with him? Or was it to look as if he had reams of information? Tina was wondering why they were standing away out in the open and hadn't met somewhere else. She realised he was nervous and the protection of being outside the TEMA building was perhaps for him not her.

He said that his information was about a Frenchman producing drugs. In fact, she hadn't understood him at first, and he needed to simplify and repeat what he said. Such an interesting line of conversation wasn't what she was expecting, but she had hoped it wasn't about a couple of locals producing ganja up in the hills.

When she pressed further, he clammed up and returned to his need for money and a passport.

"Hector, this isn't how it works. No one will pay you anything until they know you're a reliable source. You have to give me something first. Give me a name."

There was silence.

She continued, "You may be used to lots of haggling, but this is about you gaining my trust. Once you have that, we can work together."

He paused, weighing up the situation. "Eric Fournier."

The name meant nothing to her, but at least she had something to pass on to London. However, before Hector left, there was one chance to see how useful he might be. When pressed, he had shrugged and said that Eric Fournier was involved in drugs – that's what he was telling her. His aggression returned.

Never wanting to kill off a potential source, she let him vent his spleen, encouraging him and suggesting that they should meet again and he should call her if he learnt more. She said she would be happy to pay for such information.

"What about Guyana?" he said.

"What about Guyana?" She pretended to have forgotten that Sheldon had said he had two pieces of information.

"It's about CHOGM. You know CHOGM?" He went on to rant about the government and how it was selling out to the Chinese.

"What have the Chinese got to do with CHOGM?" She couldn't believe her ears.

"Nothing." He explained it was the Russians who were intending to disrupt the meeting. They were after important people. British people.

Tina was stunned. This never happened where a 'walk-in', which is what he effectively was, offered relevant information about the issue of the day, unprompted. She asked for a name or more information, but he shook his head, asking again for the money and passport.

She was pleased with the way things had gone. There was enormous potential for the future, but time was pressing. "What's the best number to call you on?"

He gave it to her, and in return, she gave him a card in the name of Alice Dee, account executive at an office supplies company, explaining that she would pass on his request for money and passport to her superiors.

"I thought you were at the High Commission?"

"Hector, I am. Please keep my identity secret, just between you and me." This was a classic ruse to bind the source to the handler in a shared conspiracy. "I'll check out this Eric, and you call me if you hear anything more about him or meth production ... oh, or the CHOGM threat, OK? That's how this is going to work." She didn't want to reveal that this was her main interest and his information might just save her job.

There wasn't much more to be said. He nodded, and they walked off in opposite directions.

———

The next day, she was at the Hilton hotel, high above the Queen's Park Savannah, which was the beautiful green space in Port of Spain. Having had a disturbed night's sleep, she had chosen a stool at the far end of the outside bar and grill next to the central communal swimming pool. Nobody was nearby, and she had a fresh rum punch in front of her. American football was playing on the small screen above the rows of bottles, and the loud Indian and calypso rhythms of Soca were blasting out from the loudspeakers across the pool.

She called a number in London. "Oscar, you saw my message? Anything on our French friend?"

"No, there's nothing, and I mean absolutely nothing, apart from that he runs a fire-extinguisher business, called Pyrandox SARL, throughout the Caribbean."

"I've only got a couple of days out here, and I want to maximise them. So there's nothing on this Eric?" She'd been convinced that Hector's information would link up with other intelligence.

"Nothing, absolutely nothing."

"Oh well, I'll dig around out here and see what I can find. I'll see you soon."

The call ended, and she took a long sip of the sweet, syrupy drink, having taken out the stick with the skewered strawberry. The pool area was empty apart from three local ladies in their sixties wearing swimming caps, who were doing aerobics in the water. Feeling slightly deflated, Tina searched idly on her phone, following each and every idea wherever it led while using the cocktail stick to poke anything and everything within reach, including a line of ants who had discovered a drop of sugary liquid.

The day-to-day life of a field agent working for MI6 has acquired a glamourised reputation. As a minimum, it's ninety-nine per cent tedium with one per cent excitement – and in this assessment, the excitement may have been exaggerated. Most agents' lives were spent poking everything in sight with a cocktail stick with no real idea of what to do next. Tina had just experienced her bit of excitement at the meeting with Hector. For the next few days or weeks, it was unrealistic to expect fireworks.

She hadn't done well on this trip, she knew. With only a couple of days left, she had hoped to have pulled it out of the bag with the lead provided by Hector. Three steps forwards and two back was a frequent occurrence in her line of business, but this was to be expected in a job where the results were completely unpredictable and hard to quantify.

There was only the bottom half of her drink left in the glass – a pale-red liquid comprising mostly of melted ice. The barman came across, and she nodded with a smile. He beamed at her and turned around, glad to have something to do.

Like him, she needed to be actively occupied in order to pass the time and to justify her existence. She couldn't spend the next two days sitting at the bar drinking rum punches, as attractive a proposition as this was; she wanted to meet people, speak to people or at least pick up some threads.

Tina wasn't on a secure line while she was flicking through ideas on her phone, but then she wasn't doing anything worthy of interest by others. The next rum punch was delivered to her on a fresh, small, white linen square to absorb the condensation that would inevitably run down the glass. It was perfect sitting outside yet under shade. The barman left to follow the game on the screen above him.

If she could make no progress on her own project today, she may as well explore further the leads Hector had given her. She started with Eric Fournier. Who was he really? She began searching again on her phone.

She wasn't expecting surprises, but surely there must be something? Something that would give her an opening in Trinidad or Tobago.

Sadly, as Oscar had said, there was nothing odd about him and nothing stood out, which always made Tina suspicious. Normal people all have one or two feathers that stick up. Serious people trying to hide stuff always smooth down every feather, however small. There was little of interest in the Caribbean, and most of her searches were on his farm in France and his business history leading to his role heading up the fire-extinguisher company in the Caribbean.

The waiter came across with the snack menu and put it in front of her.

"I'll have a burger and fries ... like before." She was a creature of habit and had enjoyed it several times on this trip.

He tapped in the order before disappearing along the bar and into the kitchen behind. The football game had finished on the screen, and the local ladies were drying themselves and laying out fresh towels on the sun beds.

Tina didn't notice any of this.

Hector was a chancer, but he hadn't gone to all that trouble to give her a useless lead. He must be convinced for some reason that Eric Fournier was involved in the drug business. Was the fire-extinguisher business a cover? Here, her background in biochemistry came to the fore with the knowledge of the palette of potential ingredients used in meth production. Fire extinguishers would also be handy containers in which to distribute it around the world.

She was mesmerised by what she was seeing on her phone. There, next to his factory was an enormous natural gas treatment plant producing anhydrous ammonia. This was wonderful, and she knew she had stumbled on to some intelligence gold. A wave of relief swept over her. It would be another team in London who would eventually deliver, but she would regain some of the points she had lost after a couple of recent failures and mistakes. You never know when things will work out. It was definitely win some, lose some.

Her food arrived, and she opened the sachet of mustard before smothering the burger with it.

Was Eric doing this by himself, or did his company know about the drug operations back in France? It was surely the former.

After putting down the bun and wiping her fingers, she checked out the parent company in Europe. Unfortunately, this wasn't straightforward. It was owned through a series of companies leading to one in the British Virgin Islands.

Her phone rang. It was Hector Candelo. This saved her chasing him, which was never a good bargaining position.

"Hi, how are you doing?" she asked.

"I've got something big for you. There's a name being mentioned in Guyana. I need some money."

She negotiated with him for a couple of minutes and agreed to pay him $1,000 if he came to Port of Spain. This was no problem. "What's the name?"

He said he would tell her when they met.

CHAPTER EIGHTEEN

Tina was walking at a speed that was as fast as possible before it would be classed as a run.

She was in a long corridor between the departure lounge and her gate at Piarco airport, and after a mostly frustrating twelve-day trip, the flight back to London was only an hour or so away. This, however, wasn't the reason for her marching stiff-legged, her rucksack bouncing on her back. She needed to get past a slow-moving huddle of people almost blocking her route.

This was all about a claim to fame. It would be a story to repeat for decades to come. She had overtaken Usain Bolt.

It's true that he was generously signing autographs and taking selfies with people as he made slow progress to his gate, but this wouldn't dilute her bragging rights. As a record, she took her own selfie while passing him and couldn't wait to tell Mike when she went down to visit her tomorrow. The taste of a large glass of Italian white wine would be a welcome change from the rum punches and mediocre beer that had featured so heavily in this trip.

With any luck, she would have a couple of glasses of something alcoholic on the plane to help her sleep some of the way back to London. She boarded through the aircraft door with a slight sense of relief.

With her seatbelt fastened, Tina put her head back and closed her eyes. There was nothing more she could do until she was home. Hopefully, the information on the meth production would be useful to one of the teams and perhaps to Mike, although Tina had no idea about her current projects. The latter were, however, likely to be drug-related and linked to the Caribbean and Central America. Occasionally, working in silos could be frustrating, if understandable.

There was also nothing she could realistically have done the previous day, and sitting around the pool didn't appeal. Instead, she had decided to take a taxi down to Point Lisas, an hour away to the south. It would pass the time, and she might spot something else she could feed back on the connection between the ammonia plant and the fire-extinguisher factory.

Before ordering the taxi from reception at the hotel, she had sat in her room checking further on Eric Fournier's company, Pyrandox SARL. Surprisingly, nothing had been fed back to her about him from Oscar or Zara. Tina knew he was involved in something shady. She could feel it inside.

It had taken her a long time to make very little progress. There were few photographs, and any addresses were from company reports and listings in many economic jurisdictions where confidentiality and minimal tax liability were the main attractions. The fire-equipment business appeared, to her eyes, to be legitimate; it was international, successful and becoming a market leader. Was it really a front for drug production and distribution?

She couldn't help being intrigued and was disappointed that there were no links already with Eric Fournier. Her experience had mostly been with Mexican, Colombian, Moroccan, Dutch and Balkan cartels and organisations; therefore, the French connection was new to her, as was Trinidad as a production centre. Tina was frustrated. She was a case officer and an operative in the field, not an analyst. Others were meant to supply her with intelligence from all the usual sources. She lacked the skills, the equipment and the access.

In the taxi, she'd been wondering whether Mike would have taken so long to give her useful leads. For the whole journey, the landscape out of the car window had been flat, dominated by the old sugar cane fields and drainage ditches. The Caroni Bird Sanctuary was to the west, extending to the sea under a big, blue sky with backlit clouds. It hadn't been until they approached Point Lisas that the industrial buildings had begun to dominate.

She had asked the taxi driver to park up for half an hour while she walked first to the fire-extinguisher factory and then past the ammonia plant. A woman in red lipstick and court shoes had been coming out of what looked like a small office at the corner of the long, grey factory building.

Tina had walked through the gate and approached her. "Hi, my name's Alice Dee. I'm an agent for office furniture throughout the Caribbean. Is there any chance I could speak to someone about buying office fire equipment?"

The woman had given her a toothy smile and nodded to a door. "Go see Jeremy." She had then wandered across the car park.

With nothing prepared, Tina had tapped on the door and had stepped inside.

———

The office was small, perhaps thirty feet square and divided by a glass wall, and there was no reception desk as such. It didn't look like they were geared up for receiving visitors. A Swiss Cheese plant with its huge, glossy, lobed leaves was climbing up in one corner, where it had reached the ceiling. In the back half, behind the glass dividing wall, two men were talking, one of which was in a white lab coat and holding what looked like a computer printout. Nobody else was around. They both looked up as Tina entered.

Presumably, one of these men was Jeremy, but she never got to meet them. At that moment, a man entered from outside; he could only have been twenty paces behind her.

"May I help?" he asked in English with the merest hint of a French accent.

"Oh, hello. I'm Alice Dee. I was just passing and saw the sign on your factory. I buy and sell office equipment."

"Hello, Alice. Are you English?" He had picked up on her lack of Trinidadian inflections and rhythm.

"I am. Are you French?"

"I'm half French, half English. My name is Eric. I'm the manager here in the Caribbean." He had olive skin, black hair and was wearing red-framed glasses.

"Pleased to meet you." She put out her hand, which he shook gently.

"*Enchantée*. How may I help? You understand that we're wholesale, not retail, here. In fact, we export most of our products around the Caribbean and beyond."

"I guessed that, but I wondered if my company could bulk buy from you. We buy all sorts of office furniture and equipment. We stockpile it and sell it on to new builds and refurbs."

"It's possible, but you understand that fire equipment isn't like desks and chairs? There are regulations and maintenance schedules, you know?"

"Sure, I understand that. It was just a thought as I was passing by."

Eric didn't look entirely convinced that a British woman, even if she were a rep for an office furniture/equipment company would be passing by, as she put it, in this part of Point Lisas industrial area. With the illegal activities in the back corner of the factory, he was always suspicious of anyone whom he didn't know. "Do you have a card?"

"I do." She handed it over.

He reached into his wallet to offer her his.

She had guessed he was Eric Fournier and was revelling in her good fortune. What were the chances of bumping into him? You always needed to ride your luck, and that luck was often made by doing things almost randomly. She wouldn't have met him if she were still at the bar at the Hilton, drinking rum punches.

"Let me get you a brochure, but you can see everything online, I'm sure. Where are you travelling to?" he asked as he reached into a drawer.

"The University of the West Indies' campus, and then back to the hotel. I fly back to London tomorrow."

"When are you back?" He seemed to have accepted her and was beginning to flirt with his eyes.

"Not for a month or so."

"Well, please email me if I can be of any help." He stepped aside and opened the door, reaching over her to form an arch like a guest at a wedding creating a tunnel for the bride and groom.

"I will." She looked at the back of the brochure where the contact details of various factories and offices were listed. "Are you often at the head office in Nice or are you permanently out here?"

"I'm back in France for a week, as it happens."

"Goodbye."

They smiled at each other as a large, white road tanker drove down the side of the factory to the rear doors.

Sitting in her plane seat with the seatbelt undone and her tray table down, she was eating the meal of jerk chicken, rice and peas. At least, that's how it was described on the menu card, but it was a sanitised version of what she'd been eating for what seemed like a two-month trip. She would be glad to get home and spend a weekend with Mike.

As the Caribbean disappeared off the bottom of the screen in front of her, she used two fingers to move the map and enlarge it. Much of France materialised and, in particular, the southern area around Nice and Monaco. With the remains of her meal piled up, she had placed the napkin on top and pushed the tray as far from her as possible; this was about one inch. Tina clutched her glass of Sauvignon Blanc with both hands and stared at the map, seeking inspiration.

It was the response from Oscar, presumably after contact with Zara, that was so galling. Surely the information she had passed back was important? She would be back in the office on Monday when she would ask a lot more questions.

A member of the cabin crew was topping up glasses. Perfect timing. She asked for two ice cubes as the glass had warmed in her hands.

Mike wouldn't have responded like that. When they had worked together at Five Eyes, they'd been in perfect harmony. Tina realised it would take all her self-control not to discuss it with Mike at the weekend. Hell, it might be relevant to what Mike was working on herself. This need-to-know diktat and compartmentalisation were critical to the job, but it sure relied on those at the top collating everything. Personally, she had no great faith in Gordon Overton, effectively her boss, and was grateful their paths rarely crossed – one of the benefits of mostly being in the field. She disliked him intensely. He had similarly never rated her, even before she had made a couple of mistakes and jeopardised a major project.

The 'fasten seatbelt' sign was illuminated as the plane

approached the east coast of the USA, as some mild turbulence had begun. Mindlessly, she moved the map so it was centred on Guyana.

Her thoughts on Hector Candelo tended to swing between two extremes every time he came into her mind. One moment, she thought he was an unpleasant character with nothing to lose, who had learnt some gossip from a friend and saw a way to turn it into money. At other times, she saw him in a different light. While talking to her in Tobago, he had been nervous. She felt he'd been personally surprised to learn about the drug production in Point Lisas, and he was reluctant to give her Eric's name.

However, after the conversation while she was at the Hilton, they had arranged to meet at the airport, immediately before she checked in for her flight to London.

She had eventually handed over $1,000 in an envelope, but only after Hector explained it was his brother, Joseph, who had provided a name in relation to the CHOGM threat.

Joseph worked as crew on a superyacht, the *Bellis Mare*, which sailed the world but mostly the Caribbean and the Indian Ocean. At the moment, it was moored off Georgetown, which gave the two brothers a chance to meet up with the rest of the family. The owner, a Russian, used it as a floating hotel and was only ever on board for a few days at a time. It had recently arrived, and Joseph had been asked to help carry some strange, heavy cargo ashore; it had found a route onto land that avoided Customs, which had obviously been well-prepared. Nothing had been explained to him; he was just part of the unloading team. Separately, he'd been told that the boat must definitely sail on the day CHOGM started. He hadn't really put the two things together before – he was more interested in the fact that he was being paid to have two weeks at home; this had never happened before.

The owner had spent a day in Georgetown, mostly at the Russian Embassy, before flying off in a private jet to Miami. He was called Alexei Savin. Before Tina's plane had left the tarmac, Hector had confirmed the name in a message with a load of emojis. He was probably ecstatic at being given $1,000.

She had agreed that, on her next trip, she would meet up with Hector again and his brother, Joseph, if he were on shore leave. Despite the rocky start, she could see possibilities with her new contact.

If Hector was raw with rough edges, Sheldon had matured into his role. He was now her ideal eyes and ears in Trinidad. Unfortunately, he had heard absolutely nothing about CHOGM. Trinidad and Guyana had good relations, and he couldn't understand who would want to disrupt the status quo. He guessed it was someone off the islands.

Staring at the map of Guyana on the screen before her, she was struck by how unusual it was. Together with Belize, it was the only member of CARICOM – the Caribbean Community grouping of countries – that wasn't an island and, in Guyana's case, not strictly speaking on the Caribbean Sea. She hadn't realised how poor a country it was, but so rich in mineral resources and yet with such a small population. It could become the jewel of South and Central America. Would it have a skyline of glass and metal in twenty years?

Her last thought before she fell asleep was about her own heritage. She was that unusual mix of black African and brown Asian, just like Guyana. The tensions between the two communities so rarely worked around the world in countries such as Uganda or Trinidad. Would it impact the fight to control the riches of Guyana? It wasn't her current problem, though; she needed to get back home and update her controller.

CHAPTER NINETEEN

The crew member was shaking her gently and asking if she would like breakfast. The cabin lights were still half-dimmed.

Tina, in a half-drunken stupor, had agreed to be woken, which was perhaps a mistake. She had only achieved a couple of hours' sleep, mostly thanks to a screaming baby two rows in front. The map, when refreshed, showed an arrival time at London Gatwick of 9.03am. It was Friday, 7th March, and she was almost home.

The plane soon landed, and she disembarked. If Usain Bolt had been on the same plane, he'd been sitting up front, and she hadn't seen him get off or at the baggage carousel.

Later, having hauled her suitcase onto the train, she was taken by the white flowers of the blackthorn, which were now visible, as were the first green flushes of the horse chestnuts – all this had happened in the previous few weeks while she was in the Caribbean. Half an hour later, she was in a taxi on the way to her flat in West London.

When she walked through the front door, there were half a dozen letters on the floor and four phone messages on the land-line from her mother. They weren't important, but when you spend so long abroad, often leaving at short notice, it's useful to provide friends and relatives with a place to leave a message. After all, she couldn't tell them where she was or what she was doing. If her mother had known, she would have had kittens.

Feeling weary, Tina didn't unpack fully but only enough to pull out the dirty clothes, which went straight into the washing machine.

Finally, with a cup of tea in hand, it was time to phone Oscar, so she dialled his number.

"How are things?" she asked when he answered, very keen to hear anything that had happened. It was as if she were an actress who had just come off stage having played a difficult scene. This was perhaps not that far from the truth.

"Gordon wants us to meet at 10.00am on Monday. He's away at the moment," he updated her.

"Right. I can wait until then except for a couple of things. Oscar, was there really nothing on this Eric? Only, having now met him, I'm deeply suspicious. I'll fill you in on Monday about what happened when I bumped into him."

"No, there was nothing. Nothing ... anywhere," he added, and then he referred to the range of sources available to him that he had searched.

"Get back to me if anything comes up, or if not, we'll chat on Monday."

"OK, will do. Anything else?"

"Yes, let me pass on to you half a dozen names I've been given by various people. Will you check them out?"

"Sure."

She sent him a prepared list rather than reading them out. "Received?"

"Yes."

"Great, I'm tired and looking forward to a quiet weekend. See you Monday."

After the call, the afternoon went by in a blur as she fell

asleep for an hour and, afterwards, forced herself to finish a few chores.

———

The three-hour drive to Wiltshire was tedious, as she was caught up in the mass exodus for the south coast and Devon that happened every Friday.

She had ground to a halt on the M25, even before the M3 turning. There was no point getting upset, and she told herself to smile and enjoy the view, which turned out to be mostly supermarket delivery lorries, it seemed.

The loud ringing of the phone through the car's speakers frightened her; the volume had been on full.

"Hi, Oscar, I'm in the car."

"Can you speak?"

"Yes, I'm on my own."

"That list of names you gave me? Only one was interesting. I can see all the public references and loads of general stuff, but it's blocked on our main system, if you know what I mean? It's marked as 'refer to O only'."

"Really?"

"Yes. I thought you'd like to know."

"If he knows about him, I can relax. It can wait 'til Monday. Perhaps, he'll tell me why."

"I'd forgotten that Zara had submitted a list of names in a request to me a few days ago. I'd passed it on through the usual channels, but it looks like it got nowhere. That name was on her list."

"Stranger and stranger. Thanks for letting me know. Have a great weekend."

Despite the heavy traffic, which thinned out eventually, the next couple of hours passed in a flash. There were too many thoughts in her head. Her mother, a doctor, had always told her that you can check everything a thousand times, but there's no substitute for gut instinct. It's a very distinctive feeling that something – something without definition – is wrong. Tina had that gnawing in her stomach now.

As she crossed into Wiltshire, another gut instinct came to the fore. This was why she felt she was so suited to her job: she could smell when a contact might be useful or might be a waste of time, effort and resources. Something about Hector, despite the obvious negatives, gave her the feeling that he had grasped having only one chance to impress her. Most people would focus on his aggression or his scuffed shoes as if this were a blind date. She hadn't met him as marriage material, and she didn't even need to like him. In fact, she rarely did like her contacts, but in Hector's case, there was something about him.

Words are cheap. It's actions that matter.

How he had found out about Fournier was for another day, another visit, another meeting. It was when he had also told her about CHOGM that he had proved he would be extremely valuable across the board, as might his brother. She hoped he'd been discreet when asking around.

Now, remarkably, Zara had discovered this same name somehow, and Gordon Overton was aware enough that he had blocked general access – yet Tina wondered why she hadn't been told. It was very likely to be relevant to her project, but she'd been excluded from the intel. How was she meant to operate out in the field? Couldn't she be trusted?

She parked her thoughts. The village sign for Rodbourne appeared ahead, partially hidden by some brambles. It felt as if a weight was lifting from her shoulders as she turned into Church Lane. A weekend with a friend was what she needed, and especially a friend in the business, which would remove some of the pressure of watching her words and having to lie – a barrier that severely limited the pleasure of any social visit. Even though she spent her life lying, she was conscious that, every time she did it, a small piece of her own character was corrupted and the membrane protecting her soul punctured.

Having parked the car, she walked towards the cottage. When Mike opened the door, they shared an emotional hug. Tina picked up her bag and stepped inside the warm cottage, where they began by talking about everything other than work.

The pub beckoned. It was a chance to bitch about other people and complain that the beer and wine were too warm. The evening had turned cooler, so they dressed accordingly. Mike put on a tight, red, knitted skull cap and her usual sweatshirt and jeans, and Tina tied back her thick, glossy, black hair, having changed into a lumberjack shirt and dark trousers.

It was in The Green Feathers that they relaxed and started talking shop, albeit in their usual guarded way.

"Right, tell me about the trip." Mike wasted no time when they were sitting down, cocooned in a buzz of conversations.

Tina mentioned her strange meeting at La Brea Pitch Lake and why Sheldon had asked to see her. After most of a glass of white wine, she described Hector and said she hadn't liked him much, but this was par for the course.

Tina asked Mike about her week, and this was when it all began to go wrong. Mike mentioned that a memorial service had been held for a member of staff. Mike had clearly been affected and hated her new boss.

Tina asked who had died, and it was when Mike had said, "An analyst called Zara ... I don't think you've met her," that Tina had felt a shiver pass over her body.

She put down her wine glass and stared at Mike.

"She was knocked down while she was out running three days ago. Never regained consciousness."

"What? They sent me some of her intel last week while I was in Port of Spain. Did they get the driver?"

"No, not that I've heard. She was a great kid ... came from Philly."

Tina reflected for a minute. "She was really sharp. The stuff she sent was spot on. That's sad news." It was the intel from Zara that had been the most relevant, and she had patently made further progress leading to her asking through official channels about a further list of names. Who had decided that this was a problem?

They finished their drinks and stepped out into the cool night air. Tina had become nervous, and she looked up and down the empty village High Street, illuminated by its three lonely street lamps.

"What's up?" Mike asked.

"Nothing," Tina replied, "I'm still on edge from the trip. It takes me a few days to calm down." But this was miles from the truth.

"You can relax; we're a hundred miles from London in the middle of nowhere. It's one of the reasons I chose here. Let's get a good night's sleep."

Chatting about what she thought was a bright star high on the horizon, they had walked along and into the dark of Church Lane. Sleep wouldn't come easy that night, Tina was sure.

———

She was right. The clicks and creaks of an old thatched, terraced cottage weren't conducive to an undisturbed night. Light crept in through the curtains as the moon revealed itself from behind clouds. Her breathing grew louder, but this might have been because the sound was reflecting off the white-washed walls of the very small bedroom.

There had been a series of storms forecast overnight, but these hadn't materialised.

With absolutely no reason to do so, given how tired and jet-lagged she was, Tina rose early the following morning, needing a strong cup of tea among other things. It gave her a quiet few minutes to think on her own. She heard Mike coming down the stairs.

"I know this is a bit odd, but can I use your laptop for a few minutes to check something out? It's been bothering me all night. I don't want to use my phone,"

Mike stared at her through sleepy eyes, not quite grasping everything.

Tina reassured her, "Not if it's complicated, and I don't want to see anything you're doing."

"I know. OK. No problem, let me set it up for you. There's not much interesting on there anyway. Clear the search history when you've finished."

Mike gave Tina access and went upstairs to shower and finish dressing. This took fifteen minutes.

"Success?" Mike asked when she came back into the kitchen.

"Sort of ... thanks." Tina was now fully in work mode, and she kept her face from betraying anything about what she had just discovered. It was inconclusive but odd enough to give her plenty to think about on the journey home.

"What's up?" Mike was now fully awake.

Tina merely smiled.

"Are you in danger?"

"I don't know." She paused, but the decision had been made and the line was about to be crossed. "Something's not right. When I met my new contact in Tobago, he gave me a name that could be relevant to your project, I'm guessing. I passed it back to my boss, and he appears to have kicked it into the long grass. Why? Why not pass it on to you and everyone via Five Eyes?"

"What name?"

"Eric Fournier. He runs a fire-extinguisher company in Trinidad. There was nothing more I could do on my project, so I paid a visit to his factory and bumped into him. He's shady; real shady."

"Why not share it? That sounds crazy."

"Well, I've told you now. I won't say anything else. Perhaps you could accidentally discover him yourself and check him out. Don't mention me. I'd better get going. I want to get back to London ready for the debrief meeting tomorrow. I'll perhaps learn more."

———

Tina was distracted for the entire drive back up the A303, M3 and M25.

However, she was partially relieved to have unburdened herself by telling Mike about Eric Fournier. This information should have been shared among the community. Unfortunately, what she had found using Mike's laptop was even more worrying. She no longer trusted anyone at her head office and wanted to see for herself, as for all she knew, Oscar could have been lying about the restrictions. Nonetheless, he was most likely to be telling the truth, and from a few enquiries, her suspicions began to fall on Gordon Overton. There was something about the man.

Unless she was missing something.

This was always a possibility in a profession where one had the advantage of being told secrets, but not *all* secrets, and of course, one was lied to constantly. Most of this wouldn't have mattered apart from one thing Mike had said to her in The Green Feathers: Zara had been killed.

Tina couldn't accept that she had died as the result of a hit-and-run. Things were getting serious. She needed to be very cautious herself, being aware more than most of the shifts in tectonic plates and how easy it was to be crushed or buried where they intersect.

It had been a spur-of-the-moment action. While Mike was upstairs showering, she had opened a kitchen drawer and found a roll of masking tape and a pen. She had written the name "Gordon Overton" on a short piece of tape and stuck it to the base of Mike's beloved coffee machine – her 'lifesaver', as she called it. Tina had no idea how and when this might be useful. She simply felt it might be in the future and that, if Tina directed her to it, it might give Mike a lead.

It was somewhere near Andover as she passed two traffic officers travelling at sixty-five miles an hour that she finally made a momentous decision. Having pulled off the A303, she turned off her phone and took out the battery.

She had decided to disappear for her own safety.

CHAPTER TWENTY

In a layby, she opened her bag and took out her purse, in which she found £130 and $225 in notes. This was important, as she no longer wanted to use credit cards or anything traceable.

The traffic on the A303 and the motorways was light on that Sunday morning, which helped her to monitor the vehicles around her. Near Heathrow, she made the final decision to not even return to her flat, but to drive around the M25 to Essex and her sister. The fuel level in her small car was showing below a quarter full. She pulled into South Mimms service station and filled up, paying with cash.

She continued her journey, and at Brentwood, she turned off for the village of Featherstone, having rehearsed her story a hundred times.

She hadn't been able to give Janet any warning, so it was a complete surprise when she rang the doorbell just before midday. After the initial shock and hugs, Tina explained that her recent trip had been cut short, and she was at a loose end for a couple of days. Sitting on the sofa in the lounge, she filled in a few of the blanks. Janet was the only family member who knew she worked for what had been vaguely referred to as the FCDO.

Details of what she actually did had been left out, but some of these needed to be filled in as Tina wanted to stay for a while, use her sister's credit cards and borrow her car.

Janet was frightened for Tina. For years, she had put two and two together and, well, imagined awful scenarios that involved her younger sister in scary places around the world. The truth was in fact worse, and what she had just been told did nothing to reassure her, but at least there were some things she could do to help.

For three years, and with Janet's knowledge, Tina had left a bag in the back of the airing cupboard purposefully for an emergency like this. In it were a passport, $2,000, some other bits and pieces, and a phone that needed to be charged before her trip into London tomorrow. It was an unplanned bonus that she had her suitcase from her trip to Wiltshire in the boot of her car. That evening was spent doing another load of washing and reassuring her sister over glasses of Baileys on ice.

On Monday morning, after a long breakfast, Tina moved her car down the road and parked it under some trees and behind a camper van. It was out of sight and could stay there for weeks if necessary.

Once back in the lounge, she began some searches, regretting that she didn't have most of the requisite skills like Oscar or Mike. Tomorrow, London beckoned, but for the time being, she felt a little calmer.

This didn't last long.

While driving Janet's car to a supermarket in Brentwood, she had turned on her phone to check for messages. By doing this in a carpark a few miles away, no one would be able to track her to Janet's. Under a sky full of fast-moving grey clouds, she heard Mike's message about Brent Cromer's men taking her equipment. Several women pushing their empty trollies back would have been surprised to see her leaning back in the driver's seat, staring at the padded roof of the Vauxhall with her hands on either temple.

What? What's happening?

It was so tempting to call Mike back, but this would have been crazy.

As she watched the shoppers going about their daily lives, things gradually began to fall into place and her decision to disappear seemed to be justified – and perhaps even essential. Tina knew she had brought this upon Mike, and if she could, she would put this right, but it might mean an enormous cost to herself and possibly put her life at risk.

————

Gordon Overton lived in the upper half of a Georgian townhouse at the back of a museum. On the façade, as he had mentioned to his staff several times, was a blue plaque celebrating the life of a poet no one had heard of. He was part of a fast-disappearing breed of old-school-tie types – except that, even in this, he was an impostor. He neither came from money nor had gone to anywhere like Eton or Harrow. He had been to a private school called Cheddings, which no one had heard of either. It specialised in sport – a sure sign that, from the calibre of the intake and the ability of the teaching staff, academic achievement wasn't the first priority. As he was always looking to improve his chances, his accent became ever-more clipped and his hair more foppish.

In MI6, he revelled in the power that his rank gave him and the perks that came with the job. In particular, it gave him membership of a club to which he would never have had access. He ate there two or three times a week, accompanied by any guest whom he could use as a reason to put the tab through as a business expense. He had become a creature of habit, which was another indication of his unsuitability for the job. Tradecraft was something his case workers and agents in the field did. It didn't apply to him while walking half a dozen streets in London to his house or club, which he did most lunchtimes.

He had gradually become what he wanted to be. This had happened because he'd been given the opportunity through a family friend who happened to be high up in the service. Whether he was good at his job or looked like he was good at his job didn't matter.

Tina had decided to do what she did best: trail him for a couple of days. There were some questions that needed answering. Normally in the secret-squirrel world, there would be a team undertaking such a task, perhaps eight people on foot, on bikes and in cars. Overseas, this luxury doesn't usually exist, and agents like Tina have to learn how to do their best while not being spotted; this means compromise and probably incomplete coverage.

On a dull Tuesday, she had followed him as he walked back to his house for lunch and returned an hour later. Knowing he was in the office, it was tempting to knock on his door at home to see who was there, but this would probably be unproductive, and he might have a camera in place. Instead, she walked about and spent two hours in a coffee shop that gave a reasonable view of the office's main entrance. At 5.30pm, he repeated his walk home and stayed there at least until 8.00pm, when she went back to Featherstone.

The next day, she repeated her surveillance, following him on his way to lunch – not at home this time, but to his club. There were plenty of places on the other side of the street and across the junction where she might loiter. By taking photographs over her shoulder, she recorded about a dozen men who entered the club over the next half an hour.

As the members and guests began to leave at the end of their lunch, she made mental notes until Overton bounced down the steps on his way back to the office. She speculated that he would have stayed to pay or sign the ticket, as she had no idea how these clubs worked. His guest, therefore, would have left a few minutes before, unless Overton had been meeting another member, and they would leave together. Three people fitted the bill, and she looked at their photographs as she followed him at a distance back to the office.

In the coffee shop she was using as a base, she stared at the three faces: one was sallow and gaunt with bags under his eyes; one was florid and round; and the last one had a long nose beneath long, black hair parted down the middle. Not surprisingly, she didn't recognise any of them, and, frustratingly, there would be a visitor's book they would have signed inside the club – to which she had no access. Of the three men, the first had walked off briskly in a northerly direction towards the Ritz hotel, the second had jumped into a black taxi, while the third had waited at the kerb for a minute until a dark-green Aston Martin pulled up.

Tina now had the registration number and his face; from this, there was a chance she would be able to identify him later. The other two would take her longer. Whether any of this was progress, she had no idea.

———

It was dark as Tina drove back to Featherstone on that Wednesday evening and parked on Janet's driveway. Inside, an evening meal was awaiting her, and the kitchen windows were steamed up. It was almost as if they were two young sisters again, looking after each other at school. They watched *East-enders* together, but destroying the illusion of the past, two of Janet's children came in to ask about preparations for tomorrow's lessons. The evening passed too quickly.

While she loathed Overton and the way he had punished her after the last fiasco, it was time to concentrate on the other problem: CHOGM and what Overton knew about it.

Using Janet's credit card, she booked a flight one way in economy from London to Paris. The return flight would be a problem for the future, not knowing when and if this would happen.

Her last act before kissing her sister goodbye was to hand her a letter, asking for it to be posted in a week's time if she hadn't returned by then. Janet had been tearful and had tried to dissuade her from leaving, but all to no avail.

By lunchtime on Thursday, 13th March, she had landed in Paris, using her own passport and hoping she had left a sufficiently indirect trail that wouldn't automatically come up if anyone searched. She did not, however, stay in France, but she booked and caught another plane that was flying overnight to Panama City, to connect with a Copa Airlines flight back to Port of Spain.

Here, her normal base, the Hilton hotel, was too expensive. Instead, she stayed in a run-down pension used by roughneck oil workers. It was built of pitted concrete that had been painted a pale orange. All the rooms gave out onto open-sided corridors that overlooked the gardens, which consisted of clumps of scraggly palm trees in roughly mown Java grass.

———

Two days later, she was meeting Hector; this time, it was on the outskirts of Port of Spain in a restaurant that Sheldon had recommended previously for any future liaison with her new contact.

Tina had arrived first and sat at the table she had reserved in the name of Alice Dee. It was purposely early so it wouldn't be busy. In fact, it was empty. She was the first diner to arrive for the evening. There were only a dozen tables, and it could best be described as cosy. The waiter handed her a menu, and she asked for an unopened bottle of water — she didn't want one filled up from the tap. While waiting for Hector, she took in the décor, which was a series of badly painted murals of ancient Rome, mostly featuring columns and steps. Across one corner of the room was a floor-to-ceiling curtain that reminded her of The Green Feathers, and she half-expected — or perhaps wanted — Jess to step out from behind it.

Some music began as Hector came through the door opposite her. He sat down, not looking entirely comfortable.

"Sheldon recommended it," she said before he could speak.

He looked skywards, shaking his head.

The waiter came back out and gave him a menu. Before looking at it, he ordered a beer.

They looked like a couple on their first date, and this was emphasised when the next song was 'Chapel of Love' by The Dixie Cups. On the way back to the kitchen, the waiter — in a dramatic movement — pulled back the curtain to reveal a trio of musicians, who avoided their gaze and played as if the room were full.

"It's OK," she said, "Don't worry. I will kill Sheldon."

For an hour, over a pleasant meal of grilled tilapia, she picked his brains about Guyana.

CHAPTER TWENTY-ONE

The next day — Sunday, 16th March, with CHOGM only nine days away — she flew to Georgetown.

Hector had armed her with as much information as he could, including the names and phone numbers of people who may be able to help her. The relationship between informant and handler was blossoming. While any information he passed on was exchanged for money, anything to do with the threats to Guyana was provided because it also meant something to him and his family members. Tina didn't mind why he was giving her this intel; she simply wanted it to continue.

She was in an isolated and dangerous predicament. Case officers are always ultimately on their own out in the field, especially when meeting people face to face, but usually with a comprehensive back-up system behind them. Now she didn't even have that. Office-based CIA staff were swamped in risk assessments, ranging from the use of boiling water in the coffee machine to holding the handrail while using the stairs. Case officers were mostly free of these; when reduced to basics, everything they did was an unquantifiable risk.

A choice needed to be made, and she hadn't flinched. At whatever cost to her personally, she had to deal with Overton and leave Mike to pursue Eric Fournier, if that's what she chose to do. *Maybe,* Tina wondered, *I could get involved in the project in the future,* although she was having trouble thinking that far ahead.

These were the thoughts going through her head as she caught the bus from City Gate in Port of Spain for the half-hour journey to the airport. It cost $1 US. Shepherding her remaining cash was important, as she had no idea how long she would be away from home and would be unable to use her own credit cards; the latter did, however, remain the option of last resort.

She hadn't wanted to use Janet's credit card; therefore, she needed to buy the plane ticket at Piarco airport by paying in cash. It had cost her $300 US.

The plane was noisy and full of students in tracksuits and trainers. They were on their way to an athletics event taking place the following week. It didn't matter to Tina; the flight only took an hour and a quarter.

When she arrived on the ground and exited the terminal, not being in any rush, she caught the shuttle bus into Georgetown, which took another forty minutes and cost $2 US.

Her scruffy hotel on a road off Heroes Highway was a short walk from the centre of the city and had been recommended by Hector. It was even more basic than the one in Trinidad, but he'd promised there was no in-house band. His sense of humour was coming to the fore now he no longer needed to use an aggressive persona. However, he had failed to mention that the hotel was also missing its back wall, which had collapsed in a storm and was currently being rebuilt with scant regard for the amenity of the guests or indeed the safety of the workforce. The scaffolding appeared to be swaying in the tropical breeze.

It was cheap and well located, which was all Tina needed.

There were no building works at night, and she had slept in worse and more dangerous places.

Not far away, preparations for CHOGM had already started. This was the biggest celebratory event since Guyana's independence from the UK in 1966; it was also possibly the most divisive. Most of the population wanted to leave the Commonwealth, not host the British King and PM. Although these same people didn't want another wave of colonisation and foreign interference from the Chinese.

Many thought history was repeating itself. In 1953, the US vice consul in Trinidad had made repeated visits to Georgetown. The USA saw Guyana as a threat to the Panama Canal, since Russia might be able to obtain a foothold and port facilities there. Now, over seventy years later, the current US President was sabre-rattling again and threatening to take over the canal, Canada and Greenland.

Memories were long, and the treacherous meeting between President John F. Kennedy and PM Harold Macmillan, at Chequers on 30th June 1963, hadn't been forgotten. Kennedy had pressured the British into not giving independence to Guyana, which was, in their eyes, a communist state that rivalled Cuba. They didn't want to see Russian nuclear weapons here or in Havana.

The USA had, via the Agency, poured millions into any political parties in Guyana that were ostensibly anti-communist. Some CIA agents posing as trade unionists had been caught and exposed. And now Guyana was at the centre of world politics again, and the native Guyanese weren't sure if they liked it or not.

Against this backdrop, and through Hector, a meeting had been arranged for Tina with his brother Joseph on Wednesday. This had excited Tina and was her main hope for the visit. Face to face, she could delve into what was happening and, hopefully, be given names.

———

In a coffee bar on the corner of a street not far from her hotel, she was sipping a latte as he entered, dressed in a white polo shirt and dark-blue shorts. He was a fit, good-looking man with his sunglasses pushed up onto his black hair. No one would doubt he had grown up working on boats, and he had a confidence and an awareness of the world that his brother lacked. This was one of the benefits of travelling the world with the super-rich. There was none of the cockiness that his brother somehow felt he needed to display, and he spoke very good English with a slight American accent.

They had air-kissed on both cheeks. He smelt of an expensive, woody scent that had probably been bought duty-free in somewhere like Port Hercule or Porto Cervo.

He sat down and immediately ordered an espresso. There was an intelligence in his eyes and an ease in the way he moved. She wondered how many times and in how many ports he had walked with his crewmates into bars and restaurants, glad to be on dry land and off the boat.

To begin with, she needed to establish what he knew about her and to make sure he understood the restrictions on any conversation in such a public place. He grasped the situation immediately and said only that he'd been so grateful to Hector because he'd been frustrated as a passionate Guyanese having no idea how to pass on his suspicions.

"Who's your boss?"

"Alexei Savin," he replied quietly.

Tina tried not to display any emotion. "What's your boss like?"

"He can charm the parrots down from the trees."

She gave him time to elaborate by taking a long sip of her coffee.

"He's a good boss. He's never in one place for long. Actually, he's never on the boat for long, apart from in the Maldives, where he liked to fish."

"Really?" She was practised in letting her contacts speak.

"He probably only sleeps on board forty nights a year."

Most people would want to know what it was like not having your boss around for over 300 days a year. It sounded like a dream job. This was all background information to Tina. "How often does he come to Guyana?"

"Every year for the last four, he's sent the boat across the Atlantic to here. Obviously, he flies in for a few days and then flies out. It's just a floating hotel to him."

"Does he always go to the Russian Embassy?"

"I've heard that he does. He isn't here for any other reason, I think, and he delivers some crates each time. It was only this last time that I wondered about it."

"Why?"

"Previously, I'd assumed it was alcohol and gifts for the embassy staff. That he'd probably paid someone in Customs, or it had diplomatic immunity in some way. This time, it felt more suspicious, more illegal. I ended up helping to carry a crate ashore that had clearly not been authorised by anybody."

"Were you worried?"

"Yes, but I'm the only Guyanese on board. I could probably talk my way out of trouble. The other crew members were much more frightened. We've never been asked to do anything illegal anywhere else."

Tina had two pressing questions: Who on board organised the clandestine operation? And who collected it once it was ashore?

He answered the second before she could ask. "A pickup was waiting down a track on the banks of the river. There were two Russians. We helped load it into the back."

"Who spoke to them?"

"Ilya; he's one of six Russian speakers on board."

"So you didn't know what was said?"

"No, but this was serious, I could tell. This wasn't some cases of vodka."

"Do you think this has anything to do with CHOGM?"

"I don't know. I hope not. Nobody on board knew what was in the crate."

"Has anyone ever suggested that your boss wanted to kill the King or the British PM? Is he violently anti-British?"

"He has a house in London, I believe. He's a proud Russian and has so much money that I don't think he cares about anything other than his businesses."

Tina went back to something she had forgotten to ask: "Was there anything written on this crate?"

"Not that I saw. It was made of strong planks of wood. It had been stored along with the boxes of spare engine parts we keep for the boat, the ribs, the jet skis and the helicopter. We keep a lot of spares. You can't get them quickly in the Maldives or ..." He shrugged his shoulders, not bothering to list all the out-of-the-way places where the boat sailed. "And the boss doesn't wait for anything."

"Who loaded the crate onto the boat, and where did it happen?"

"I don't know. I'd guess at Cannes, but I don't know. I was ashore for a couple of days on leave."

"Has your boss already flown off?"

"Yes, like I said, I believe he went to the embassy for some meetings and his plane flew him back to Nice – I think that's what I heard. I don't know if it's stopping off to refuel in the USA or the Azores."

"And you've been told you have to be ready to leave Georgetown on Tuesday, the day of the opening ceremony ... and you're part of the crew?"

"Yes, we're taking it across the Atlantic and into the Mediterranean. By June, it will be based in the Maldives for a few months."

Tina frowned slightly. "What do you do all day when you're not sailing?"

"Trust me, there's plenty to do, and there are always guests coming and going. They're the worst, actually."

"Any regulars?"

"Three or four Russians and his English friend, Peter. They fish together everywhere."

"Peter who?"

"Peter Swift."

———

A couple of days later, it was a surprise when Hector called her to say that he himself was going to be in Guyana on Saturday, though he didn't mention he was showing a client around potential development sites. Hector asked if they could meet quickly, suggesting a time when his client was scheduled to be at the British High Commission on a courtesy visit.

They met in the courtyard of the Devonshire Hotel. His friend, Chico, was behind the reception desk as well as, it appeared, acting as the barman. There wasn't much for him to do, as the only other guests – two Russians – got up from the armchairs and walked up to their rooms on the next floor.

In truth, Hector didn't have much more useful information to give her, apart from the names of some local staff who worked at the Russian Embassy. Like most of her new contacts, once he had received his first payment, he was overkeen to show her he was a great source. Over a rum punch, he told her Eric Fournier was back from France and his friend had told him they were now shipping to Europe via Marseille and not Le Havre. This had been a sudden change of arrangements. He had heard no more gossip about Alexei Savin and the Russian Embassy, but he hoped Joseph had proved useful. Hector was looking forward to seeing his brother later – they rarely met in person any more.

When Tina had left Hector, she wasn't to know how excited he was about his life. For him, it was finally falling into place. He was now a paid informant to the UK and was about to introduce a real client to a real development site. Times were looking up.

PART THREE

CHAPTER TWENTY-TWO

It was Sunday, 23rd March, and two days before CHOGM; in London, it was 12.30pm, and in Georgetown, it was 7.30am, and two women were at their wits' end. One believed her friend had been murdered, was desperately trying to find out what had happened and would seek revenge in some way. The other was living a frighteningly risky existence doing everything she could to avoid contacting her friend or indeed anybody who might give Overton an indication of where she was, at least until her job was complete.

In the flat in Ickenham, Mike was shouting and flailing her arms around; frustration had reached an intolerable level, with the need to hit out at everyone and everything. She was wearing her black bandana and waving a carving knife she'd been attempting to dry in a kitchen towel. Wazz had mentioned *Pirates of the Caribbean,* and this hadn't gone down well, on too many levels to specify.

"It was a pretty big place the last time I checked." He was doing his best not to make the situation worse – this being a very likely outcome if he said what he actually thought, which was that she was bonkers.

Mike put the knife in a drawer, picked up a wet saucepan and was twisting it around more like a weapon than as if she were about to use it to cook. "Huh," she said, indicating that a declaration of war might be avoided.

"Where in France are you intending to go?" He was trying to sound reasonable while slicing an onion, his back towards her.

"Provence."

"Well, that's reduced the area a bit." The sarcasm was in no way sanitised.

"Look, Eric Fournier has a farm down there, and Tina probably died down there. Alexei Savin is based in Monaco … so is this Peter Swift, who also lives there and in Cannes."

"And what are you going to actually do? Knock on their doors?"

"I can't stay here and do nothing."

He calmly let the non-sequitur pass – almost. "How come you're so logical when you're sitting at a computer and so illogical the rest of the time?"

"It *is* logical. Where do you expect me to go? China?"

The non-sequiturs were following each other, if that were even possible.

"You'll end up dead."

"I'll be careful."

"And then end up dead?"

He filled the kettle while he thought through the best way to dissuade her from this ridiculous idea. He metaphorically adopted the magician's trick of waving the right hand while using the left to hide the real action. "Why not tell Leonard?"

"Tina said I shouldn't trust anyone at her or my place."

"OK, forget her place, but you trust Leonard, don't you?"

"What's that got to do with anything?"

"Quite a lot, I think. I understand that you don't trust this Overton guy, but surely you can discuss this honestly and openly with Leonard. I think I trust him. I've only met him for two minutes, I know," he said slowly and quietly.

"I'm not sure." She was beginning to calm down.

Wazz had only one objective: he didn't want her going to France or anywhere abroad on some wild goose chase. He'd been involved in two of these already over the last three years, and on both occasions, she had nearly died. "You could show Leonard the three men in the photographs. You don't have to mention that they came from Tina."

"His first question will be 'Where did you get them from?'"

"OK, fair enough; tell him they came from Tina. It's not going to harm her now; she's dead. Where did she take them, by the way?" He should have been a magician.

She hung the cloth back on the chrome rail. Her face was still red from her outburst, and this highlighted her pitted skin, but she had begun to breathe normally. "London, I presume. Actually, I didn't look at the backgrounds, just the faces and the car."

Wazz was truly wasted standing outside a strip club talking to drunks. Perhaps he should have pursued a degree in psychology rather than his current course at the Open University. Like all boxers, he knew how to conserve his energy and when to use his aggression, but, for the most part, how to hide it. He stayed quiet, stared into space and began caramelising the onions in the pan. Mike was certain to react first.

"You've given me an idea. Let me go and check."

She disappeared into the lounge, and he placed both palms on the kitchen work surface, tensing his muscles and staring down at the glittering faux marble surface. He had survived round one; the fight, however, was not over.

———

Tina woke up and turned to her phone. It was 7.30am, and she had slept right through the night. This was despite the noisy, old-fashioned air-conditioning unit that was projecting through the wall, with some tin foil stuffed down the gaps to prevent mosquitoes gaining access. They didn't have to worry as they could fly in through the hole above her, where a rotating fan had been removed, dislodging a chunk of plaster from the ceiling.

Whatever, she had thought to herself, and she'd allowed the rhythmical sounds of the unit to lull her to sleep.

It was Sunday, there were no building works to disturb her, and, apart from the air conditioning, the hotel was relatively quiet.

She shrieked suddenly and pulled back her hand. Without realising it, she had touched a large, dead centipede that lay curled up on the bedside table. This seemed to indicate that a shower might be a good idea, even if the tiles were cracked and had sharp edges, and the curtain had a mind of its own, sticking to itself and allowing the water to spray past it out onto the floor. At least it might wash away some of the black hairs from a previous occupant.

She got up and headed for the bathroom. As the hot water spluttered out of the shower head, she disciplined herself. Today, it was decision time. If she were going to do anything with the knowledge she had gained, it had to be passed on to someone in authority. There was no realistic possibility of her making a direct physical intervention, and in truth, she didn't know the exact details of what anybody was planning.

Any decision making, however, was delayed by her phone buzzing on the bedside table. She got out of the shower, wrapped a towel around her waist, walked across and picked it up. She could see it was Joseph as she answered the call.

"They've killed Hector," he blurted it out, sounding distraught.

"What? Who?"

"In his hotel room yesterday evening. Alice, I'm scared. You must be careful too."

"Are the police involved?"

"They called my father. The police inspector said he'd been shot."

"Who do they suspect?"

"They aren't saying, but I've spoken to Chico who works at the hotel – he's a friend of our family – and he says the only other people around were a pair of Russians."

"They've gone, I'm guessing?"

"They've checked out, and no one knows where they are."

"What was Hector doing in the hotel? Why was he there exactly?"

"He was showing around an investor, he told me, someone called Johnny Boswell who was looking for industrial sites. They flew in together from Trinidad; he runs one of the ammonia plants in Point Lisas apparently."

"Are you on the boat?"

"No, I'm staying with a friend. I'm meant to be back on the boat early tomorrow, ready to sail on Tuesday, but I want to stay with my family." He paused. "What can I do? I feel that really bad things are about to happen."

"Joseph, I'm so sorry about Hector."

"Can't you warn somebody ... you know, at the High Commission?" he cut across her, his voice rising.

"I will. I will," she repeated it, but this was more for her own benefit. "Please be careful and don't mention to anyone on the boat that Hector was your brother."

"Should I sail, or should I stay? I'll be at sea for a month." His voice was breaking.

"There's nothing for you to do here apart from console your family. Think of yourself."

Tina felt guilty saying this, but she reassured herself that having Joseph on that boat was for 'the common good'. This was the phrase she had developed and used to justify her lying and cheating existence; it was so much more preferable to expressions such as 'for king and country'. If she kept everything at a one-to-one, personal level, she would break down emotionally. There needed to be detachment, a separation. It was in everyone's best interests that Joseph stayed on that boat – perhaps apart from Joseph.

When he had asked her if she could warn someone at the British High Commission, he had touched a raw nerve. She wasn't exactly *persona non grata*, but her relationship with the high commissioner, Dame Sylvia d'Oliveira, was very bad, and Tina was more than suspicious of where her loyalties lay.

Dame Sylvia was only interested in one thing: herself. After a distinguished career in the capitals of Europe, she'd been shunted across the Atlantic to end her career, but this was no illustrious career-topping post in Washington, DC. In truth, no one in the FCDO wanted her back in Whitehall chairing committees or setting policy. Her role as high commissioner in Guyana had been sugar-coated by the Foreign Secretary who had personally asked her to handle the build up to CHOGM. She'd been flattered and, after her recent damehood, hadn't seen what was actually happening. Fantasies of a couple of years in a colonial residence in the Caribbean with large grounds full of palm trees and gardeners had tempted her. She had assumed that it was like Jamaica or Barbados, and in this she was to be severely disappointed. She had seen pictures of the large, elegant residence, but she'd failed to notice that it had been sold in 2000 and was now the official residence of the Guyanese PM.

Dreams of hosting the King and the British PM at garden parties in a tropical paradise also vanished as she was told there was no way they were staying a night in Guyana, and the days of the royal yacht were long gone. The destroyer, *HMS Adventure*, would be moored offshore on its way back from the Falklands with a group of special forces personnel on board, but this was for security and communication purposes; it wouldn't be hosting the main dignitaries. The VIPs would be based in Saint Lucia or Barbados, where they would stay in palatial villas or luxury hotels. It was only a ninety-minute flight to Georgetown and "to hell with carbon footprints and COP24". They would be back each day on their terraces, enjoying cocktails before the clapping had died down at the conference.

Over in London, the FCDO and the authorities in charge of protecting the King and ministers were greatly relieved. Despite having expressed enormous reservations at having Guyana as a venue for CHOGM in the first place, they'd been overruled – although not having to worry about security at night was one major headache removed. Of course, dozens of more junior ministers and staff would stay in Georgetown, but these were seen as a low-level risk.

Tina had visited the High Commission on her first trip to Guyana to liaise with the deputy high commissioner; he was the person actually coordinating security and the major logistics. He was a tall Lancastrian called Allan, to whom nothing appeared a problem; a consummate diplomat who had listened to her initial thoughts and offered every help available to him despite being extremely busy.

During Tina's first meeting with him, Dame Sylvia had swanned into the room. She had pooh-poohed Tina's suggestions and made it clear that the Guyanese government was taking the security of CHOGM very seriously as it was *the* showcase for the country on the world stage. Tina had suggested that Russia and China may have other ideas, at which point she'd been dismissed by the high commissioner. After this, a less-than-favourable two-line report on Tina had been sent back to Overton, who hadn't defended Tina and had told her to avoid the High Commission if at all possible. How she was meant to operate in Guyana without the support of the High Commission staff wasn't explained. Overton appeared to have a big problem with Tina.

CHAPTER TWENTY-THREE

Darren Boswell was reflecting on his streak of bad luck. This had nothing to do with his lack of success with his rod at that moment. Fishing out beyond the reef on a Sunday morning was one of the joys of his life.

Nothing seemed to be going his way. He had found the perfect site for a new ammonia plant outside Georgetown and had already fed this information back to his cousin via the family in Essex. Unfortunately, the agent who had introduced him, Hector Candelo, was dead. Even worse, he'd been murdered shortly after Darren had left for the airport to fly back to Trinidad. The Guyanese police had been in contact, having been given his name by the hotel. There was little he could do to help the police inspector as he had seen nothing.

It was only a temporary setback. It wouldn't take long to find the site owners and begin negotiations directly. Looking on the bright side, he would no longer need to pay the introduction fee to Hector, not that this was a large sum.

"Relax, I'll look for an industrial unit near this new site you've found in Guyana." It was as if Eric could read his thoughts and was gently winding him up.

Darren lifted his rod skywards and reeled in the lure a little. "Even if we buy it, we're three or four years away from producing ammonia there."

"I know, I know, but it'll take the pressure off our factory here in Trinidad and give us an alternative source should the authorities take an interest in our operation here."

This wasn't the conversation Darren needed at this precise second. He was trying to forget that he was still supplying Eric, with anhydrous ammonia. A discussion about the tying of flies or the colour of the dyed feathers on the lures would be more to his liking.

The water was calm, and there was a mirage that made a tanker on the horizon look as if it were flying at 500 feet. The sky graded from peach to duck-egg blue, but the wind must have veered because the international flights were now over the sea coming into land at the airport, and the change in their engine noise as they approached broke up the general tranquillity. Some terns began diving in a specific spot, which might indicate that the bigger fish were feeding.

"I'm going to cast over there," Darren said.

"Good idea. I'll leave mine here. It's good to cover all the bases."

Darren had a feeling that the conversation hadn't moved on and perhaps this was a metaphor for his life. There seemed to be no escape. If he were caught by his cousin, he would be killed, and if he stopped supplying, Eric he would probably die even more painfully.

The silence was broken by Eric, who was reaching down into the cooler box to pull out a bottle. All of the more-distant sounds appeared to stop, with only the sea lapping gently against the side of the boat.

"*Mon cher*, I'd like to buy more product from you. The demand for meth is going through the roof in Europe. We can't produce it fast enough."

"Eric, please don't ask that. I'm already risking my life selling it to you."

"Why are you bothered if it's one tonne or two? We are a legitimate company buying it as a raw material. Who's going to know? Who's going to ask anything?"

"It will get out, I know."

"Not if you keep quiet and say nothing." Eric paused. "Nobody in your organisation suspects, do they?" He was under pressure himself since the hijack in Bourges. His Moroccan masters wanted to know who had informed the Dutch or whoever they were. Someone had told them which consignment of fire extinguishers contained the drug. They wanted Eric to ramp up production and send it via a different port, where it would be given an armed escort.

Neither man knew it was a worker called LoverBoy at Eric's factory who had tipped off Hector, who had himself sold the information onwards. LoverBoy's simple action was a perfect illustration of Edward Lorenz's chaos theory – a butterfly flaps its wings in the Caribbean and causes a storm in Europe.

"We need to ramp up production. I need another load tomorrow at the latest," Eric demanded.

Darren stared down into the water, knowing he had no alternative but to arrange it. Privately, he'd been thinking about the safety of his family; he couldn't contemplate something happening to his children or wife, and this must surely come next. In dark moments, he thought the only way out was to quit his job and go back to Essex. He would think up some lame reason why he couldn't hack it any longer and fall on the mercy of his cousin, who wasn't likely to be happy. Whatever the outcome, it would be better than living in Tobago, constantly looking over his shoulder, and at the beck and call of Eric and the cartel behind him.

A fish they had caught a few minutes ago managed one last flap in the box next to Johnny before dying in the Caribbean sun. Its shiny eye was fixed on him. He lifted the lid back on top to hide it from view, but he had made up his mind. He was leaving Trinidad and Tobago for good.

———

Wazz had learnt it was impossible to stop Mike; there were no brakes, and her foot was permanently on the accelerator. She could, however, be diverted or distracted.

When he left for work on that Sunday afternoon, she was sitting in his lounge, checking the location of where the three photographs had been taken. Throughout the night, as he froze on the doorstep of the club, he would sincerely be hoping that she would still be there when he emerged from his bed about 10.30am for his brunch and she hadn't headed off to France or some other place without any plan. Whether this happened or not was touch and go.

As the door to the flat closed behind him on his way out, she was adjusting the laptop on her knees. With a new focus, she was examining every pixel of the pictures Tina had sent her, ignoring the three men's faces and concentrating on the backgrounds. To begin with, she made the decision to assume these were taken in London. If she failed in her first attempts, she would widen her search, but thinking about this was too daunting. She'd been to Bristol, Bath and Edinburgh, and she guessed there were very many British towns and cities with Georgian terraces.

In one, she managed to convince herself that the man walking away in the distance was Overton, but seeing what one wants is always the danger if one stares at an image for too long.

In the first photograph, she could make out the word 'place' on a road sign and that there were perhaps eight letters in the first word, which was a good start. The terrace of buildings had grand entrances up steps and basements behind railings and gates. She couldn't read any of the names or numbers on the pillars.

In the second one, she could discern what she thought was a gentleman's outfitters shop window. Inside, behind small panes of glass, there were what looked like black suits on headless mannequins with perhaps pale-grey waistcoats underneath. The name of the company on a beige-coloured sign was out of focus, but she could roughly count the number of words and letters. This was also an upmarket establishment that would only be found in certain parts of the capital; the scale of the buildings in the Georgian terrace appeared to confirm this.

A search for bespoke male tailoring in Central London came up with seventy potential results. She parked this part of the search while wondering if Tina had filmed the three leaving this shop specifically and if the business was relevant.

In the third photograph, a temporary notice was affixed to a 'no through road' sign. No matter how much she zoomed in, she couldn't make out the name of the London Borough.

There was nothing else to glean, so she returned to the list of bespoke tailors. How many had an address ending in the word 'place'? It turned out only four fitted the bill and only one had eight letters in the first word – the photographs were taken in or just outside Longford Place, St James's, in the City of Westminster, which was part of the West End of London. The name of the outfitters, the font and the beige background of the sign matched perfectly.

She rubbed her eyes. It was so easy to spend hours and hours staring at the screen without taking a minute to focus on something else. It took all her self-discipline to stand up, get a drink and open a new packet of biscuits.

While the outfitters featured in two of the photographs, she needed to check out the other houses and businesses in Longford Place. This didn't take long as there were only two commercial enterprises, and they were both private clubs. The remainder of the addresses were private residences, and although these three men could have been visiting a house, she felt intuitively that they were in Longford Place to go to one of the clubs, but which?

The first was established in 1825 by artists and actors. The second had been established by members of the East India Company on returning to London and requiring a meeting place. It had evolved into a club for diplomats and civil servants involved in international affairs and was now called the Overseas and Commonwealth Club.

Mike didn't bother to look further; she was convinced this was the place these individuals had been visiting. It was too much of a coincidence that this was an international club and Tina was looking for someone up to no good, probably in the Caribbean.

Next, she wanted to check the biographies and any gossip about the three men, but this didn't happen as her Sunday afternoon was disturbed by the phone buzzing. She answered it.

"I need you here in the office tomorrow morning ... early." This didn't sound like the usual Leonard.

"Sure, I was intending to come in anyway. What's the panic?"

"No panic. Have you heard from Tina?"

"No, she's dead, isn't she? Why? Do you think she's alive?"

"No, I meant had you received any communication from her?"

Mike looked around the flat as if there were hidden cameras on the curtain rails or microphones in the table lamp. How did Leonard know she had received the note and photographs?

"No. Have you heard anything else about her? How was she killed? You know I won't let it drop."

"Overton has told me nothing. Let's speak tomorrow, say 9.00am in my office?"

"Sure. This sounds like I'm being called into the principal's study for a detention?"

"Since when did you ever listen to your teachers? See you tomorrow."

He rang off, and she remained on the sofa, trying to gauge his tone. Was he friendly or annoyed? She couldn't decide.

———

It was Sunday lunchtime in the Caribbean.

The royal party was the first to fly in aboard an RAF Voyager, and the King and Queen were whisked away from the airport in Saint Lucia to a group of three villas in the hills overlooking the Pitons – the iconic or, perhaps more accurately, conic volcanic plugs – which are the mountains that define the south-western coastline.

The Queen already had a welcome cocktail in her hand and was gazing out from the elevated balcony at the exact time when an Airbus A321 carrying the British PM and his entourage flew into Grantley Adams airport in Barbados, where they were driven west to Saint James and a small hotel that had been taken over by the party of thirty-five. The accompanying press pack were particularly happy; they had recently been to far-worse countries with much-less-salubrious accommodation.

British special forces had arrived on both islands the week previously to check out and monitor the locations. The King and the PM had been made aware of the unspecified threats, but this wasn't a rare occurrence on such trips; they'd been advised what they should and shouldn't do. The actual time to be spent in Georgetown had been reduced to the absolute minimum without causing offence to the host nation, the Commonwealth members or the Secretariat.

On both islands, the finishing touches to the two main speeches were being made and coordinated. While climate change was to be the key headline, all the writers' effort was being expended on weasel words that addressed the slavery reparations issue without committing to an actual sum. A recent report commissioned by the University of the West Indies, and former International Court of Justice jurist Patrick Robinson, estimated that the UK should pay over £19 trillion.

While it had been possible to keep the matter off the formal agenda, nothing could be done to stop groups of countries meeting on the side and raising the issue. If it had been a hot topic on the other side of the world in Samoa in 2024, it would be an even hotter topic in the Caribbean where slavery perhaps had its biggest impact. The fifteen CARICOM countries had already met in anticipation of the CHOGM in Guyana. Tensions and expectations were high.

During a very restricted meeting in London, the advisers to the British delegation had discussed whether finding some excuse for the King and the PM not to attend CHOGM might be worth exploring. They had leapt on the reports that there were unspecified threats. A privileged few even speculated whether the threats were self-generated, given how wonderfully convenient they were.

Whatever the truth, the British parties had arrived in the Caribbean.

———

Some people, however, were departing.

Darren Boswell had booked his family on the Sunday evening flight out of Piarco airport in Trinidad. He had made up some story but, in reality, neither his wife nor his children had taken much persuading; they were missing Essex.

They had kept a house just outside Brightlingsea, which was currently being renovated, but there were enough rooms untouched that they could move in immediately. A bigger problem came from what to do with the villa, furniture and cars in Tobago. Would he ever come back? Probably not. From the second the plane left Trinidadian soil, he was a dead man if he returned.

He had given all his keys to Malcolm, a friend unconnected with any other part of his life – especially Eric and the factories in Point Lisas. Darren had given him a few thousand dollars and clear instructions on what to do and when to do it. Malcolm was the only person who knew he was leaving the Caribbean for good. Even the actual manager and team at the ammonia plant were under the impression that he was going back on holiday. It wasn't a problem to them; he wasn't exactly a hands-on director, and they often went weeks without seeing him face to face.

His heart was tinged with sadness as the plane flew over Toco at the eastern end of the Northern Range, and he could see Tobago in the distance. He would miss the fishing – it wasn't the same, sitting by a lake near Burnham-on-Crouch on a grey, wet Tuesday in February – but it was better to be alive in England than dead in Tobago.

CHAPTER TWENTY-FOUR

Deciding what to wear on her head usually took no time at all. There were always more important things to worry about, but if Mike stopped to consider it, she would dither and overthink.

Before leaving the flat very early on Monday morning, the choice she had made was probably significant. For the first time in over three months, she had put on her jet-black, cropped Cleopatra wig. Standing outside Leonard's office door, she adjusted it unnecessarily, reflecting on whether it had been the right choice. Was this regression? Insecurity?

Unusually, she was left waiting before he called her in and invited her to sit down. As Mike entered, she became aware of the quiet, but perhaps there had always been silence in his office and she had simply never noticed it before. For all she knew, never having thought about it, the room was probably lead-lined and triple glazed, but it was certainly not disturbed by any outside noise from Central London.

He waved a hand at the chair in front of his large desk without saying anything. She saw him in a slightly different light, not as an overweight buffoon but as what he was: the very experienced CIA head of station.

"Mike, we have a problem."

She rocked on her chair but remained silent.

"I've been asked by the Brits to suspend you ..."

She started to speak, but he raised a hand.

"Please don't say anything until you hear everything I have to say. A few hours ago" – he looked up at one of the two clocks on his wall, which showed the time in Washington, DC, and London – "the King and the PM arrived in the Caribbean. You get the picture that the Brits are real nervous."

Mike, like when she was a young girl, shuffled to sit on her hands as a way to suppress her desire to interrupt. Something told her to not express any opinion.

"They have big security issues, mostly trying to keep the delegation safe. They tell me that, apparently, what Tina had been doing wasn't helpful. They're involved in a delicate operation, and, no, I'm not telling you about it."

She couldn't hold it in any longer, so she asked in a normal voice, "What's it got to do with me? I've only been trying to find out where she is or who killed her."

"Perhaps they know who killed her but can't get into that right now." He looked directly at her, weighing up how to proceed. "Mike, we have triggers in place, you know this. Brent Cromer had no choice, and I should do exactly the same as him. They're in place for a reason, and it's not for an individual in any organisation to question it. That's how it works ... for all of us."

Mike was never comfortable in wishy-washy greyness – she needed to get out into the sunshine. Today, she was in a cloying, thick fog. She was disorientated. "But what have I done? What did she do?"

"You both began poking the hornet's nest. It doesn't matter if you did it intentionally or unintentionally; the effect is the same. People get stung. You're jeopardising something really important, and I can't tell you which nest, otherwise you'll go on poking, and the situation will be made worse. It's easier to remove you until the issue passes. I'm sorry Tina got caught up in it all."

"And Zara."

"Possibly."

She stared at him with a little menace, but she didn't verbalise what was passing through her mind. Zara's death was a battle for another day. Instead, she said, "All this is because Tina and/or I got close by accident to someone who was on the Red List?"

"Let's forget anyone on the Red List."

"So that's a yes?"

"Mike," he pleaded, "help me not put you on garden leave for two months ... please."

She leant forwards and released her hands, waving them around to indicate that she was at a loss. "Can we meet halfway?" This was as reasonable as she had ever sounded.

"Where exactly in the garden is that?"

"How about in your summerhouse, but I don't need internet access? Tell me the name, and I promise not to search for it."

"Summerhouse? This is London – I don't even have a yard."

There was a very long pause before he asked in a serious voice, "Now think very carefully before you answer. Has Tina been in contact in any way since she disappeared?" He was staring straight at her.

"Well, not directly."

"Let's start with indirectly, and don't leave anything out. I'm not interested in clever word games." This was from a man who liked to use anagrams of his name as aliases.

"There has been nothing – no calls, no messages, no emails. Nothing. Just a note and three photographs she posted to me at my house in Wiltshire. I got them two days ago." He was looking at her with a furrowed brow, so she decided to come clean: "She posted them to my pub. I wasn't expecting anything; it was a complete surprise."

"What did the note say? Do you still have it?"

"I burnt it. It said she would be completely out of contact and was going abroad and not to trust anybody at her place or here. She said she had no idea if the men in the three photographs were relevant or not. It was a very short note."

"What did she ask you to do?"

"Nothing, really. I think she was letting me know in case something bad happened ... which it obviously did."

"That was it? She didn't mention any names or places?"

Mike had now to make one of the most important decisions of her life: whether to mention Tina's concerns about Gordon Overton or not. Leonard probably already had suspicions about him anyway. If she were caught out in a direct lie, it would all be over. She watched Leonard's face before responding. "She didn't mention specific names in the note, but I've been checking, obviously."

There was no way Mike would mention what had been written on the bottom of the coffee machine when Tina had stayed with her before disappearing. Mike hoped her apparent honesty would win him over. Yes, it was a technical detail that Tina hadn't mentioned Gordon Overton specifically in the note, but Leonard would have seen this as a clever word game.

He pushed one of his chins up towards his mouth and began squeezing his cheeks. She was expecting him to say that some name she had searched for was on the Red List, and if she did this again, she would be out of the Agency for good. However, he surprised her by changing tack. "Who were the three men in the photographs. You still have them?"

"Um, yes, I do. I've only positively identified two. One is a sports presenter on TV called Edward Bunting and the other is someone called Peter Swift who lives in Monaco and Cannes ... and Essex. He's a billionaire who runs a mineral and chemical conglomerate."

Either side of his large desk sat two people: Mike in her

white blouse and black wig, facing Leonard slumped back in his chair, his wispy, ginger hair thinning by the day.

"I'm going to offer you a choice, and there will be no negotiating. You choose one or the other. Understood?"

She nodded.

"Either I call one of the friendly commanders I know here in the Met and have them arrest you for some misdemeanour. I bet you've ridden your bike through a few red lights or something. I'm sure they'll find some reason to lock you up for forty-eight hours" – he paused to let this sink in – "or you promise me you won't search for anyone and, in particular, the three men in the photographs, whoever they are. If you do – and we'll be monitoring you – I'll have you shipped back to Washington as express freight where the FBI will be waiting, and you'll be locked up for a lot, lot longer than forty-eight hours. Understand?"

"Yes."

"So you accept option two? You sit at your desk and track the drug cartel – you know, do what you're actually paid to be doing."

"I do, and thank you." She knew that, if it were Cromer or any other director opposite her, she would already be on the plane and probably in handcuffs. Unfortunately for Leonard, she was already thinking of all the things he had said and not said in the conversation.

Mike needed to keep Leonard on side, so she began by saying, "Before she disappeared, Tina passed back through the system the name of Eric Fournier, a Frenchman who's likely to be behind the production of a lot of meth in the Caribbean that's sent to the USA and Europe. I'm in the middle of tracking him."

"Good. This is what I need to hear. Where does it enter the USA and Europe?"

"Galveston and Le Havre ... in fire extinguishers."

"Great. Keep me in the loop."

"When, in twenty-four hours or whenever this panic is over, will I be allowed to find out what happened to Tina?"

He breathed out heavily. "When, and I repeat, when this is over, I'll get the details from the Brits, and I promise I'll tell you, OK?"

"Thank you. You know I can't let it rest forever. I have to know what happened to her."

"I don't think you'll have to wait too long. Occupy yourself with the drug shipments. That'll be a big win for us."

The meeting was over, and she had survived. Mike stood up and made for the door, but she stopped. "Can I ask you one question before I go?"

He nodded.

"Do you trust Overton?"

He hesitated one second too long before he said, "Yes."

———

Joseph didn't know what to do for the best.

He was making his way back to his friend's house that he was using before he rejoined the boat in a few hours' time – or perhaps, at the last minute, he might decide not to rejoin it. As he walked along next to the sea, the waves were breaking far out beyond a beach scattered with rocks. There were uncollected piles of rubbish on the sand under palm trees struggling to survive.

He still hadn't made a decision about his future, and grief wasn't helping him to choose. The seabirds above him were also disorientated as they were buffeted by the erratic winds.

During their last conversation, Hector had happened to mention the name of one of his friends, Troy, who worked as a driver at the Russian Embassy. Whether this could prove useful or not, he had no idea, and Joseph wouldn't ordinarily have followed this up had his brother not been killed. He didn't know

Troy personally, but he had met his sister previously. Guyana has a very small population, and no one is far removed from anyone else.

Immediately, Joseph had arranged to meet Troy on his lunchbreak not far from the embassy, in the area of Georgetown known as Kitty. Troy had been shocked to hear that Hector had been murdered in the Devonshire Hotel and probably by Russians.

Sitting on an uncomfortable concrete bench above a low sea wall with a little shade from a stunted fig tree, they had chatted freely, and Troy had answered all Joseph's questions as best he could. There was no one in earshot, and they looked like any other couple of young men chilling while gazing out to sea.

Troy had said he was aware of the wooden crate that had been delivered from Savin's boat, but not what was inside. It had been unloaded from the truck in the compound and taken to a secure store to which the native workforce had no access. It could have been opened inside at any time by Russian members of staff.

Whatever happened inside the store, he'd been instructed to drive the planks and waste packaging away in the embassy pickup truck. He was frustrated he couldn't add anything further that might be useful, but he confessed to not paying attention. However, he did say this wasn't the only wood and cardboard that had to be taken to the Haags Bosch landfill site less than five miles away along Heroes Way. Several other crates and packing cases had been delivered in the weeks before. These were generally longer and wider. As a consequence, the truck had been piled high and filled to its maximum, with everything secured by ropes.

Joseph was asking questions not knowing what was important, but he was trying to anticipate what would be useful to Alice Dee, as he knew her. He tried to imagine her in front of him in case this might trigger some ideas. Troy was also keen to help, but he admitted that he worked pretty much on automatic pilot and hadn't seen anything suspicious.

However, it was a throwaway remark that piqued Joseph's interest. In the embassy compound, sheets of galvanised metal or similar had appeared, presumably from some of the crates and boxes. These sheets had been welded together by two locals into rectangular-section air-conditioning or extraction ducting. Everyone had thought these were to be used in the refectory or the consular buildings, but this wasn't the case. He'd been asked to drive into the centre of town and help to unload them at the back of a takeaway restaurant. He had made a total of three trips in the end.

"Why is the Russian Embassy assembling ventilation ducts?" Joseph had asked, completely puzzled.

Troy didn't have the slightest idea, but he had noticed that the restaurant was closed for refurbishment. In the past, they had both eaten burgers there many times.

"Who actually owns the restaurant? Are they Russians?"

"No idea. There were only contractors in the building when I dropped the ductwork off."

"I need to check."

"They needed me to help carry the longest section up the stairs to a room on the top floor where the ceiling had been removed."

Troy went on to say that there were two Russians at the embassy who had arrived a week before. They were different from most of the others, whom he called bean counters or drunks or both. He had driven these two men in an official Mercedes-Benz down to a car park just behind the restaurant and waited for about an hour before driving them back.

The two men were still at the embassy, staying in a flat within the compound, but they didn't generally mix with the other Russians or venture outside the walls.

Joseph needed to call Alice Dee.

CHAPTER TWENTY-FIVE

Mike spent the time in the office behaving herself, but as soon as Leonard left the building at 4.40pm, she made for the door.

Nevertheless, the time hadn't been wasted. She'd been investigating the company Pyrandox, looking for a connection to meth and its distribution. She'd been imagining different scenarios, but had settled on the most obvious: the meth was being hidden in fire extinguishers. Hacking into the company computer system in Nice had been surprisingly easy, and she began scanning through the shipments from Port of Spain and their destinations. She was looking for patterns or where a routine had been disrupted. It had taken her most of the day, but she eventually stumbled on to something odd. The next shipment from Trinidad to France would go to Marseille, not Le Havre; this was a last-minute change within the previous twenty-four hours. They could be purposely varying the route to make it harder for the authorities to spot, or there could be a raft of other reasons.

She looked for changes in policy or policing at Le Havre, but she couldn't see anything that would cause Pyrandox to change ports. It was while she was checking if there had been any problems with the last delivery that she found a link to the murder of a Serbian lorry driver, who had been transporting a container of fire extinguishers from Le Havre to Clermont Ferrand when he'd been hijacked near Bourges on Saturday, two days previously.

Early reports concentrated mostly on the murder and the fact that the lorry had yet to be found by the French police. The fact that the cargo was fire extinguishers didn't take up too many lines in the mainstream press or on social media.

This was the point Mike had reached when Leonard had stuck his head around the door to say goodnight, perhaps confirming that she was still sitting at her desk. If he had checked what she'd been working on, he would have seen she had stuck to their agreement. This, however, would soon change.

———

Wazz was running a Dyson over the carpet in the lounge when she came through the front door of the flat. The relief on his face came from the fact that she hadn't gone on some mad trip to France or any other place where she would end up getting killed. He turned the Dyson off and folded it up. He didn't work on Mondays and Tuesdays, so that was when he did his domestic chores and went to bed late if he wanted to.

"Hi, honey, how was your day?" He was purposely keeping it light until he could evaluate her mood.

"Sandra in Accounts has gone on maternity leave."

"About time. She's been pregnant for three years."

He felt that the pressure had eased, although obviously not yet for the mythical Sandra.

"Leonard didn't suspend me."

"That's good to hear." Wazz wondered whether he'd perhaps been premature, unlike the mythical Sandra.

"He made me an offer I couldn't refuse."

Wazz managed to control his emotions and continued

putting the Dyson back behind the sofa where he kept it. The only cupboard was full of suitcases, the exercise bike and the ironing board.

"He was very reasonable." She was virtually unrecognisable; therefore, he knew something was up. "He said he wouldn't suspend me if I didn't search for certain names."

"And you agreed to this arrangement?" Wazz merely needed reassurance; the details would mean nothing to him.

"I did ... well, sort of ..."

He sat down on the sofa, waiting for the nuclear bomb.

But she continued in a surprisingly calm manner, "I behaved at work, and he didn't suspend me."

"Um ... do you mind if we go back to Sandra and her pregnancy because all this is beginning to hurt my brain?"

"The big conference is happening tomorrow in the Caribbean. As long as I don't do anything that might derail it, I'm in the clear."

"And you aren't doing anything that might derail it, are you?"

"Of course not; I agreed with Leonard that I wouldn't search certain things at work ... which I didn't."

He put his head in his hands. "Therefore, you're going to do it at home, I'm guessing."

"I'm going to take a couple of days' holiday – it's long overdue."

"A bit like Sandra?"

"Yes, but at least she'll probably have a job to go back to."

He looked at her, but, thankfully, she was smiling and not flying to France to confront drug barons and contract killers or anyone vaguely like this. In the flat, he could protect her – just possibly.

Twenty minutes later, she was in the kitchen on her laptop, eating cheese and biscuits while scooping the remains of some chutney from a pot. Wazz was serving his own food, and he carried it into the lounge, where he needed to complete his revision. To say that it had been a long and tortuous journey would be an understatement. More importantly to him, it represented how he had turned his life around.

Mike breathed in and took stock; she needed to get real. She was beginning to smell a rat – actually, rats in the plural; in fact, she was overrun with the critters.

This is where the gifted analyst comes into their own. Exploring every lead wasn't an option, so where and how was she to prioritise? Did she start with Gordon Overton, the three men or the locations in Longford Place? With a little more thought, she ditched the unknown first man in the photographs. If he turned out to be the key to all this, she was doomed to failure anyway. Every database and AI search facility had been used, and there were no useful matches; he remained Mr X and had been wholly relegated to the pending tray.

Edward Bunting, the sports presenter, was tempting, but she was struggling to see how he might fit into the broader picture. He could also waste hours of her time with a very low likelihood of any return. There were so many stories about his indiscretions on social media, but were these really relevant?

She had already superficially researched Peter Swift; he remained firmly on the radar, and it was tempting to start with him.

Top of the list was always going to be Gordon Overton, for three reasons: firstly, she hated him; secondly, Tina had written his name on her coffee machine, having told her not to trust him; and, thirdly, because he was so patently central to whatever was happening. There was, however, a huge problem in checking him out further. His job meant that he lived a purposely clandestine life, and he knew how to hide any wrongdoing. In addition, any searches could trigger alarms, which was something she desperately needed to avoid.

This left Longford Place. Why were the three men, and possibly Overton, there and being photographed by Tina?

She could also spend hours and days hacking into the two clubs' and the bespoke outfitter's computer systems, but she didn't have the luxury of endless time. Alternatively, she could make clear assumptions based on likelihood and pursue the reasoning for these men to meet in pairs or a group.

Dismissing the tailors and the arty private club, she settled on the more obvious international club. Now she had to make a decision: Was Overton a member? Was he at the lunch/meeting? And with whom?

She guessed it was a lunch from the angle of the sun casting shadows in the pictures, and she put the most money on it being Overton and Peter Swift. This would be her starting point: trying to find a connection between the two of them.

This could be their first meeting, or they could be old friends or acquaintances. She couldn't check much if it were the former, but could search a few places if they had history together. Playing the percentages and staying focused, she started with Overton's schools, saving the names as she went. Mike had got this absolutely right, but she was missing one vital piece of the jigsaw: Peter Swift wasn't Peter Swift. This name didn't appear on the lists of pupils and students at any of Overton's schools or university.

———

While Mike was being given the ultimatum on that Monday morning by Leonard, Darren Boswell and his family were arriving on the overnight flight from Port of Spain. London Gatwick was busy, and the queues at passport control were very long. Everyone was bleary-eyed after broken or uncomfortable periods of sleep during the night, and the sound of babies screaming echoed throughout the hall.

A minivan was waiting to drive the family and their suitcases around the M25 and over the Queen Elizabeth II Bridge to Essex. The children slept for most of the two-hour journey.

The relief that Darren felt on walking through his own front door was immeasurable, and the fact that half the house was a building site was irrelevant in the scheme of things. Sally, a cousin, had prepared everything as best she could, including stocking the fridge. She had put both of the children's beds in one room and removed all the contractor's tools and materials from the kitchen.

Darren's wife made tea as a first act, while he opened the dozen or so letters, which were mostly flyers. The children went straight to the garden, where there was a trampoline and a treehouse.

On hearing that they had arrived home, Sally came around immediately to welcome them. Everyone began to relax, and the volume of laughter increased; that is, everyone except for Darren, who still had one more hurdle to cross, but that was for another day.

Any relief he felt was, however, short-lived. While the children were in the garden and his wife was upstairs making sure the immersion heater was turned on, Sally passed on the message that his cousin was flying back from Nice that afternoon to see him. The blood drained from his face.

"He said that he'd be here by 4.00pm," she said.

"Great. No problem. We have a lot to catch up on. Thanks, Sally."

"He was only here on Thursday. That's not like him. Must be important."

"Well, our return was a bit sudden, so I expect there's lots he wants to talk about."

"It's brill to have you all back. We've missed you." She hugged him, but his mind was elsewhere. "Relax, it'll take a few days to settle back in. We should have a party. We could make it

Caribbean fancy dress!" Her gravelly voice was breaking into a cackle, but she managed to add, "Nice tan, by the way."

The fact that he wouldn't see the sun every day from his villa in Tobago depressed him. His tan would soon fade – if he lived that long.

———

The previous day, Peter Swift had completed a meal in his favourite restaurant in Cannes, La Brouette de Grand Mère – The Grandmother's Wheelbarrow. It was unique and the complete antidote to the sameness of the international cuisine of the five-star hotels on La Croisette. He had eaten quail in a rich, creamy, red sauce after a board of rough-cut charcuterie. Stroma had never been sure about the restaurant, but the choice of eating place wasn't up to her. She was simply glad one of her better clients was back after his travels.

The meal had put him in a good mood, which was a huge improvement, given how irritable he'd been after his return from England a few days ago. This often seemed to happen, and she wondered why he kept flying back there – although he never spoke about the trips much, apart from mentioning some family bickering.

Once back at his villa high up above Cannes, they had spent a relaxed evening and night together; he had a lot of tension that he needed to release.

He had bought the villa from the estate of a British-born Hollywood movie producer. Having visited it many times for parties, he knew it had the best views and was as secure as any place could be, with its high walls, tortuous access and alarm systems. The gardens were mature, and the palms and Lombardy poplars provided a perfect frame to the Mediterranean Sea. He loved it all so much that he'd bought it with all the furniture and fittings from the previous owner. The signed photographs of actors and politicians were still on the mantlepiece.

Stroma was no fool and took pride in working out her clients in minutes, but she struggled with Peter. He didn't obviously fit into the Riviera crowd and had, in effect, bought a life in Monaco and Cannes. His hairstyle made him look bohemian, yet he was extremely conservative. The toiletries in his bathroom had to be positioned exactly as he left them and his pyjamas folded in a particular way on his bed.

He was a mass of contradictions: talking constantly about Essex but choosing not to live there, loving his family but hating the idea of marriage and children, and purporting to be from a working-class background yet speaking with a public-school accent. Monaco was his tax base, but whenever he went there, he spent the day on some boat, fishing, not in his apartment.

She also wondered about his friends. Apart from a handful of wealthy men who shared his love of fishing, he didn't appear to have any. The party scene left him cold, but he always managed to turn up and make small talk, coming back to her in the evening.

One of his friends was a Russian oligarch who was beginning to pay her increasing attention. She was extremely picky about her clients, and Alexei Savin gave her the creeps. He kept mentioning his superyacht, which was the biggest in the Mediterranean or some such meaningless claim. There was no way she was going on it without Peter; this was one of her golden rules. On a boat, she was trapped and had no control, even with a crew around. The first and probably second meeting always took place in a well-known restaurant or hotel. If she wished to proceed, they could book a room in the hotel. Only after these tests would she venture to their homes. Boats were only acceptable after she was completely happy that she understood them and had established some manner of control over them.

When alone with Peter, it was pleasant, and he treated her with the right amount of respect. Unfortunately, he was never around for any length of time before his phone rang, and he jumped on a private jet.

At his villa, he was relaxing after eating his favourite dish at his favourite restaurant, although she had never worked out why it was called The Grandmother's Wheelbarrow. They'd been sitting on a sofa with the curtains wide open, staring out at the night sky and the lights of ships on the Mediterranean below them.

As happened so frequently, he leapt up to take a call out of her earshot on the other side of the room. She didn't need to speak to him as his face had darkened. He immediately called Louise and asked her to arrange a jet to Stanstead for early tomorrow, Monday, afternoon. He was flying back to Essex.

CHAPTER TWENTY-SIX

The sooner he was on the flight back, with Paris out of the right-hand window, the better. Thursday, when he had flown back last week, seemed like a year ago. Sitting two seats in front of him, Louise was on the phone, confirming the pickup time with his uncle Jimmy.

He'd been in two Zoom meetings after midday with senior staff at the ammonia plant in Point Lisas to ensure that they had no immediate problems nor needed anything from him. In fact, the second call had in effect been an online interview with the deputy manager, who was the prime candidate to replace his unreliable relative.

After the last bust-up about supplying anhydrous ammonia to some illegal drug producers, he thought he had made his position clear. His cousin hadn't even got the balls to ring him but had rather sent an email to say he was having a nervous breakdown and was flying the family back to Essex. He was sorry, but he couldn't take the pressure any longer.

After initially wanting to kill him, Peter had calmed down enough to accept that he needed someone reliable running the plant. This required him to fly back to Brightlingsea to talk it through with his cousin so he understood what the new manager would face from the drug gangs. The matter was meant to have been dealt with immediately after their last meeting, but apparently it had not.

Therefore, he was in a Gulfstream heading for Stanstead, sipping a gin and tonic with no ice but with a slice of cucumber. He was loudly munching snacks while thinking things through and having to dust bits of food from his lemon-coloured shirt with its button-down collar. Louise was still busily confirming arrangements.

For separate reasons, it wasn't a convenient time. Other matters in his life were at a delicate stage of negotiations, and he would have preferred to have stayed in France or Monaco. UK Border Force at Stanstead would log his arrival, and he knew exactly what they would do with this information.

———

Two months earlier, something very strange had happened while he was at the villa in Cannes, where he had received a call on his private phone out of the blue.

The voice was distinctive, and it had triggered something in his memory. The caller had asked for Johnny Boswell not Peter Swift, and this had bothered him.

"Hello, Johnny. This is a voice from the past."

He hadn't been able to place it despite racking his brains. "Sorry, who is this?"

"Gordon, Gordon Overton." He had paused before adding, "From school ... Cheddings."

"Oh yes, hello ... well, this is a surprise." The real surprise was that he had obtained this phone number, which was known by only a handful of people.

"Johnny, I'll cut to the chase; I work for the old Foreign and Commonwealth Office ... the FCDO as it's now called. I was wondering if we could meet the next time you're back in London? I'd rather not go into too many details now, if that's all right?"

Gordon Overton had always been a self-righteous and universally loathed individual at school, and Johnny needed to be careful. When Gordon had left Cheddings, he had only just got into university by the skin of his teeth – Keele or Warwick, as far as he could remember – to study history and politics or something like that. He would trust him as far as he could throw him – which would be off a cliff, given the chance. If Gordon had managed to climb up the greasy pole and genuinely worked for the FCDO, he may well know how much Johnny was worth and possibly may have worked out that he was masquerading under a different name as far as the tax authorities were concerned.

On the other hand, he might have been given the number by a mutual friend and was ringing him up to wish him happy birthday.

"Great to hear from you, but I have to be honest and say that I don't come back to the UK much these days. I live abroad."

"So I understand, but perhaps you'd like to be able to come back any time you liked?" Overton had left a long silence to let his meaning be digested.

"I can come back any time I want now."

"Sadly not, although that might depend on which passport you're using."

"I'm not sure I understand you."

"Johnny, this is a once-in-a-lifetime opportunity. Trust me, not many people are offered a deal like this."

"I live in the Caribbean and come back perhaps three times a year. I don't need any deal, thanks."

"Which would be true if you lived in the Caribbean and came back three times a year … but you don't."

"You've lost me."

"Sadly, I haven't lost you. You're sitting in your villa in Cannes, as we speak."

"Gordon, have you been on the magic mushrooms again?"

"No," he replied, but there was just a hint that this reminder of his schooldays might have irked him.

"What's the real reason for this call?"

"To make you an offer."

"Fire away. I'm always interested in offers."

"At the moment, this is unofficial – just between you and me. If we can't agree a way forwards, it'll become official, and by that, I mean with the involvement of the Home Office and HM Treasury. You understand the implications?"

"Why do I have the feeling that I'm about to be blackmailed?"

"No, no, Johnny; nothing like that. It's true that I need something from you, but not money, even though I know you have it coming out of your ears."

"What do you need?"

"Help with something that you're in a great position to deliver, but I don't want to talk about it on the phone. Walls have ears and all that, and I should know."

"Hypothetically, what do I get if I were to deliver this service to you?"

"Well, nobody else has noticed what you've been up to for the last seven years, and who's to say anyone else ever will, if you're careful."

There had been no comment from the other end of the line.

Therefore, Gordon had continued, "There's absolutely no record of any of this. I've been extremely careful, and it can stay this way, but if you'd prefer – and it's your choice – I could explore negotiations with HMRC and immunity from prosecution over the ... shall we call it 'passport issue'?"

Gordon had seemed to know too much already, but Johnny

had needed to be careful in case this was a trap and the call being recorded.

"It would be good to see you again anyway, after all this time, Gordon." Saying this particularly had stuck in his throat as he had always hated the man.

"I'd like to meet you at my club in London at your earliest convenience." He had pronounced 'convenience' as if it were a word from an obscure language that required precise articulation.

"How about, for our first meeting, you come out here, say?" Johnny hadn't fancied being arrested at Stanstead airport and spending the next ten years in jail.

Overton had appeared to have read his mind. "You don't have to worry about me recording our meeting or having you arrested. I shall be breaking the rules as well."

"I'm not worried about you recording anything. I've done nothing wrong and won't even admit to breaking a speed limit."

"Johnny, that's unlikely – you don't drive."

"Why don't we meet in Paris? You could fly or catch the Eurostar?"

Gordon had taken a few seconds to think about this. "OK, let's meet, but this needs to be very soon, like tomorrow. If I fly to Nice, can you send a driver? I'll fly on to Germany in the evening."

"No problem. Send me your arrival time. My driver will be there."

———

Two months later, on Monday, 24th March, Johnny was in a leased Gulfstream on the approach into Stanstead and wondering what had happened to his life in the intervening period. Had he won or had he lost?

First things first, he must get to Brightlingsea and sort out his weak and dangerous cousin.

———

While Johnny was walking down the steps of the Gulfstream at Stanstead, Mike was in the flat, checking on Gordon Overton's university colleagues at Keele and his fellow golf club members. She could find no Peter Swift and was cursing that she couldn't look up Overton in *Who's Who*. Obviously, he was banned from having an entry by his employers, but she would bet he would be in it like a shot if he could. His vanity might be his downfall.

Needing a change of approach, she turned her attention to Peter Swift. Looking at some of the photographs, he appeared distinctly odd to her eyes. Did all billionaires look weird? Mike thought he resembled her when she was wearing the black Cleopatra wig. What was that all about? Perhaps he had grown long hair as a teen and stuck with it. She searched for earlier photographs.

Despite persisting, there were none of him anywhere before about seven or eight years previously. This was when he went from anonymous rich to mega-rich. His biography was also a bit vague. She delved deeper, looking for his parents, his birth certificate, his driving licence, etc. and anything about his early life.

She found Peter Swift's birth certificate, but his parents were dead. There was nothing about schools and no criminal convictions. It wasn't until she called up his driving licence that her attention was grabbed. She blew up the grainy photograph on her screen of when Peter Swift was eighteen and had just passed his driving test. The first thing she noticed was that he was blond, and the second was that his nose was a completely different shape. Was she mixing up two Peter Swifts?

Deep in thought, she had bitten a nail on her left hand to the point that it hurt. There was no newer driving licence, so he must have let it expire. However, this had given her a route to find out his National Insurance number, and she discovered that he hadn't submitted a tax return for years and years. In all the searches, Peter Swift had given his address as a house in Brightlingsea, despite obviously living abroad.

Mike wondered how often he came back to the UK and whether he ever visited his Essex house. Little did she know that he had just arrived, having been driven there by his uncle Jimmy in the Aston Martin.

She was hungry, having forgotten to eat, as usual. By wandering into the lounge, she was hoping to provoke Wazz into cooking something, but he was wearing headphones and revising. His exam was soon, and it was on a significant date to him. It would be the anniversary of his release from prison.

He lifted one side of his headphones and checked what she wanted.

"Nothing," she had replied, and she went back into the kitchen to take the biscuit tin out of the cupboard. Needs must.

She didn't suffer from claustrophobia, but there were times when her obsessive tendencies led her further away from the surface where she had started and down ever-narrower branches of a cave system until she felt her shoulders being pinched by both walls. It was probably time to back herself out.

Somewhere deep in her stomach, she knew Peter Swift was key to all this, but she couldn't make any meaningful connection from him to Gordon Overton or to Tina. Was she disappearing down a rabbit hole *again*?

She put the lid back on the biscuit tin with a loud click, as if to signify that it was only a passing fad and unlikely to occur again.

Back to basics. Always go back to basics. For some reason, Tina had sent a picture of the billionaire Peter Swift, suggesting that it might be relevant. The photograph was probably outside a London club frequented by diplomats, and Overton was probably walking away in the distance. Even if it weren't him, Tina had written his name on the bottom of her 'lifesaver' and she'd done this at some critical moment while visiting Rodbourne before she disappeared for good.

Another starting point was that Peter Swift owned the ammonia plant in Trinidad. How could this be remotely connected and of use to her and her searching?

She went back to what she had discovered from Sheldon's and Hector's phone records; scrolling through the list of names and possibilities, these ranged from Eric Fournier and LoverBoy to Johnny Boswell, who was the Caribbean director. Everything needed to be cross-referenced.

MELD-ORE was the AI-driven piece of software she used to do this. All the names from the lists, phone records and sources were cross-referenced and checked (it even allowed for typing mistakes or other unintentional variations). It took less than two seconds, and she had the results.

Needing a distraction and time to think, she reopened the biscuit tin.

What? She read that the director of the ammonia plant in Trinidad, Johnny Boswell, went to the same private school as Gordon Overton. This wasn't what she was expecting, and she couldn't immediately think what it meant. Surely Tina's boss wasn't involved in meth production? Even Mike, who revelled in not excluding any possibility, was struggling with this idea.

She saw one possibility that Tina had come across this connection while in the Caribbean and had confronted him. Perhaps this had led to him or his mates killing her? Tina had tried to warn Mike about him.

Mike began to suspect that one or more of the men in the photographs was involved in the operation, and her task was to find out which. They could all be old classmates, although she struggled to imagine the anonymous blond man in the first picture up to no good. As to the sports presenter, this also appeared extremely unlikely, which really only left the very wealthy Peter Swift. Mike wondered if this was how he had made his millions in the first place. It looked as if he had 'swum upstream', as it's described in the business world, taking over his suppliers, distributors and anyone critical to the operation.

It was 8.30pm, and there was only so much that she could do until morning.

CHAPTER TWENTY-SEVEN

When Gordon Overton had walked out of Nice airport arrivals hall, he'd been met by a driver holding up an iPad displaying the name "Gobbo", his nickname at Cheddings School. Johnny Boswell couldn't resist, and the thought that someone with a nickname for being talkative and untrustworthy had ended up at the FCDO beggared belief. Gordon really did work there, and not just ordering paperclips, a mutual friend had confirmed.

Johnny had needed to be cautious, however much he hated the man. Gordon was in a position to completely ruin all his hard work. No one apart from extremely close family and one overpaid accountant who had set it all up knew what Johnny had done.

And he now regretted that decision.

He had always been hot-headed – quick to explode, quick to calm down. However, he really should have considered the future. Not paying £50 million in tax and being able to visit Essex whenever he wanted had seemed like a no-brainer. Darren, his cousin, had been more than happy to play the role, and there didn't seem to be a downside. Yet after only a few years, £50 million meant nothing to him and ninety-one days a year in

Brightlingsea was more than enough. He rather enjoyed Cannes and floating in a superyacht around the Maldives and the Seychelles, fishing.

Metaphorically, what he'd done was to create a virus. He would love to buy his way out of the problem, and there might be a very limited window in which he could do this. Once out of the bottle, it would spread like contagion.

When Gordon had first phoned, Johnny had been incandescent and wanted to pay to have him chopped up into little pieces, but after an hour, he had realised this would only potentially compound his problem, raising the stakes and the consequences. Whatever Gobbo wanted, as long as it compromised him as well, it made him part of the conspiracy and might even lead to another unexpected layer of protection.

With that in mind, Johnny had waited in an extremely exclusive restaurant up in the hills of Provence, sitting at a table under a canopy of leaves that provided some screening from the sun. He had found himself wondering if Gobbo still had that annoying quiff, which he constantly brushed away from his eyes. It was the first thing he had seen as Gordon Overton had walked across the patio accompanied by the maître d'.

"Gobbo." Johnny had stood up and extended a hand.

"Tonto."

Neither had been called by these names for over twenty-five years. They had both smiled, and to anyone nearby, they were long-lost friends.

Johnny had waved a hand, inviting his guest to take a seat. "When we were at school, this wasn't how I thought we might meet again twenty plus years later." He kept it polite.

"Too true; you've done incredibly well, but I think we always knew you would." Gordon had looked around the open-sided restaurant with its views down to the coast and, more importantly, at the widely spaced tables and the fact that the one nearest to them had no place settings but was reserved. Johnny had arranged that they would have privacy, whatever the cost.

"I hear that you've risen through the ranks as well."

Gordon had looked downwards in fake humility. He had needed to flick his quiff out of the way on raising his gaze back to Johnny. "I've also been lucky, and we were both fortunate that we went to a good school and made good friends."

Johnny, for his part, thought the school was distinctly average and he had never gained a penny from knowing anyone there. "Do I have to assume that this lunch is being recorded and filmed?"

"You can imagine whatever you want to imagine, but I said to you that I'd also break the rules so we were in it together, so to speak."

"In what?"

A waiter had brought over some seafood canapés with black caviar on top. He had poured Gordon a glass of white wine, topped up Johnny's glass and left.

"For the sake of this lunch, may we assume that I know what you've been doing for the last decade? You don't need to confirm or concede anything. However, if my understanding of your situation is correct, you might benefit from any help I might be able to give you" – Gordon had hesitated to let every word sink in – "Let's not waste time; as I said on the phone, this help will come at a cost, but not a financial cost."

Johnny had been beginning to think that financial blackmail might be easier to deal with, although having the bastard put through a car crusher had been looking ever-more tempting. "I'm fascinated to hear how I might help you."

Gordon had put a canapé in his mouth and swallowed it. "It's not really helping me, although it well might; it's for the benefit of king and country. Now you may be able to see that, in return, king and country might like to help you ... regularise your affairs."

They had both sipped from their glasses of wine. Johnny had a few more lines around his eyes, and Overton had put on a few pounds, which made his face rounder, but, otherwise, they hadn't changed much from school. Neither had altered their hair style, although Johnny's was looking increasingly bizarre as he aged.

"I'm always happy to help king and country."

"Good man. May we just lay down some ground rules? Neither you nor I tell anyone – that's *anyone* – about what we're discussing or what either of us might do. Nothing gets written down or recorded."

"Fine." Johnny had taken another sip. "If nothing's written down, how do I know your side of any bargain is being implemented?"

"You don't. Cards on the table" – Overton had paused for effect – "you're fucked. You either do what I propose and trust me, or you'll never return to the UK and will have to base yourself pronto in a country without an extradition treaty – and that's a very short list. Currently, Algeria looks your best bet, assuming you don't fancy North Korea or Somalia."

They had stared at each other before Gordon had started his pitch. "Cutting a long story short" – he had begun, and Johnny had expected a ten-minute monologue, but this didn't happen – "I'm interested in one of your acquaintances, and I want you to cultivate him for me."

Johnny hadn't been able to stop wondering why Gordon didn't ask for £10 million like any normal person, given what he clearly knew, but he obviously had a different agenda.

"Who?"

"Your fishing partner, Alexei Savin."

Johnny had digested this request, having not expected that name. "Really?"

"How much do you know about him? Has he ever explained where his money comes from?"

"Gordon, we don't talk about money. I have plenty; he has plenty. It's not relevant. We talk about fishing, food, drink, the pain of living in Monaco, and, occasionally, about oil and gas in the Caribbean, which we're both interested in – that's about it."

'I have plenty; he has plenty" was the understatement of the century, but it perhaps explained a reality that's incomprehensible to most of us. Money just wasn't an issue. They both did what they wanted, when they wanted to. What anything cost was irrelevant – absolutely irrelevant.

"Where do you usually meet?"

"It could be in Monaco at a restaurant, in Cannes at my villa, or on his boat, normally when it's somewhere in the Indian Ocean."

"When are you seeing him next?"

"I'm flying out to Malé in two weeks. The boat is in the Maldives for a month."

"Now, Johnny, this is where I cross the line by telling you why His Majesty's Government – the good old HMG – is interested and what I want you to find out, all without frightening the horses. This is beyond top secret, as one might say. Your friend is one of the main money launderers for the Russian President, for which he's paid handsomely; this is how he has a $400-million boat. He also undertakes certain projects for the Russian President so that they're sufficiently deniable."

The waiter had begun to walk over with some menus, but Johnny had waved him away politely, allowing the key part of the conversation to be completed. Food wasn't the priority.

Gordon had continued, "These projects are often in the Caribbean. For the last two years, the focus has been on Guyana, the old British colony. However, we're getting intelligence that Savin might be organising a major disruption of the world order by organising an attack at the big event planned in Georgetown in a couple of months: CHOGM. You know what CHOGM is?"

"I do."

"Does he ever mention Guyana?"

"He flies there a few times a year, I think. The Russians are interested in the minerals – aren't we all, including the Americans and the Chinese?"

"What are you interested in?"

"Making anhydrous ammonia from any natural gas. Like I do in Trinidad."

"We'd like to know when he's going there again and anything he mentions about what he's up to with the embassy there."

"He won't be shooting anyone. I've seen him firing a gun off the back of his boat; he couldn't hit a Boeing 747 at a hundred yards."

"No, we know he isn't the sniper or bomber, but we believe he must be the enabler."

"If I were to discover something, how do I let you know, and how do I know it has benefitted me?"

"I'll give you a number to call. You're the only person who has access, and there's no record. Call it day or night, and only I will answer. As to you benefitting, I'm not a lover of those who don't pay their taxes, Johnny, but I am pragmatic, and if you help HMG with intelligence on such matters as Guyana, I really can't get excited about your misdemeanours. If neither the King nor the PM is shot, bombed or poisoned at CHOGM, I'll begin discussions with HMRC, the Home Office, etc. – if this is what you want. It's probably time to come in from the cold, as we say in my world."

"What's your world, Gordon?" Johnny had spent his life striking deals, as had his grandfather, and he knew when he had the upper hand and when he didn't. On this day, he definitely didn't, but knowing the position of your adversary could only help.

"I've always been a patriot, and I'll do all I can to protect British interests, whether that's the King, the PM or anything at risk."

Johnny had managed to breathe in and let the view distract him for a few seconds. Wasn't it Gobbo who had orchestrated a line of classmates to drop their pants and moon at the Queen on her way to Ascot? He was as obnoxious now as he was then. "Why me?"

"Well, the planets have aligned, don't you think? I'm in charge of finding out about threats to our sovereign in Guyana, you're best mates with the main suspect, and you and I know each other of old. What are the chances of that happening?"

"I can't ask him outright if he's intending to shoot the King. What do you want me to do in reality?"

"You were always smart, and he won't suspect you, so the odds are in your favour. Anything you find out is useful. Please pass it on to me."

Johnny had taken out his phone and tapped a few buttons. "After the Maldives, his boat, the *Bellis Mare*, is going to Cannes for one of the festivals and then on to Georgetown for 13th March, according to his private log. Does that help?"

Gordon had smiled. "If you and I are clever, this could all turn out to be beyond our wildest dreams."

The waiter had stepped out of the shadows but remained at a discreet distance, a few paces out of earshot. Johnny had called him over so they might order some food. After the discussion so far, it was probably time to eat.

Gordon had opened the large menu and was blown away by the choice. There were no prices on his copy, which was a good thing, as his meal would cost more than he earnt in a week.

———

In Guyana, it was still twenty-four hours until CHOGM.

On that Monday morning, it was bright and sunny in Georgetown. Tina had decided to wander down to the Mahaica Convention Centre, or at least to the point where the public was already prohibited access by metal barriers across the road. Helicopters were in the air, and there was a frisson caused mainly by the growing sense that this was a very big day for Guyana.

As expected, she could only walk so far, but she could see the façade of the fast-food outlet ahead of her; it was boarded up at ground level with posters of the President and PM trying to distract from the ugliness of the panels of chipboard. The extraction ductwork could be seen projecting from the roof at a high level, but it wasn't a surprise that there was no smoke or steam coming from it. On the street below, the press were bagging their positions on the temporary grandstand, which had been built from scaffolding poles and planks. One interview was already being filmed, while men from other companies were dragging cables everywhere and camera mounts were being clamped in position. All this was under the watchful eye of half a dozen police and two ministry officials.

She didn't want to draw attention to herself; therefore, she turned around, walked down a side road and immediately went right behind the row of shops. Several of the TV broadcast vehicles were parked here as it would be the nearest point to the action tomorrow.

It didn't take her long to spot the back of the takeaway; there were two large food-waste bins. Old metal grilles covered the lower windows as if the contents of the building warranted protection from theft. Perhaps food was considered worth all this effort. She walked down an alleyway and across to a car park. It felt like she was in a different world, without international meetings and the attention of the world's media.

Having burnt her bridges, Tina now had choices to make about how she used the information she had gathered, incomplete though it was, and whom she should share it with.

Life was never straightforward.

CHAPTER TWENTY-EIGHT

Mike Kingdom was up very early on Tuesday morning, checking out the director of the ammonia plant in Trinidad. She had woken with a thought that had subconsciously been bothering her overnight: Johnny Boswell and Gordon Overton went to the same private school. This was too much of a coincidence and too important. Everything else could wait. She was checking this out before breakfast, trying as hard as possible not to disturb Wazz, who was having a lie-in on his day off.

She was being very careful in her searching, but she was worried she was triggering every alarm bell at work. It didn't matter, as Mike couldn't stop herself.

Someone called Peter Swift was the billionaire owner of the ammonia plant and had met Gordon Overton in London. Someone called Johnny Boswell was the director of the plant and went to school with Gordon Overton. She needed to keep her focus from wandering.

Cheddings School helpfully produced a yearbook that was available online; it was a good marketing tool – probably. It highlighted some of the minor sporting celebrities and business leaders who were among the alumni. Mike clicked on the group photographs for the appropriate years and had no trouble finding Gordon Overton, who was always near the centre of the image next to the masters, his blond quiff being distinctive. She struggled to find Johnny Boswell, so she blew up the image and panned across the rows. She couldn't find him, but she did spot the unmistakeable Peter Swift with his longish, black hair parted down the middle.

"*What the ...?*" she mouthed, utterly confused. A walk around the cramped kitchen didn't do much to help her resolve the conundrum.

Wazz came out of the bedroom, rubbing his eyes. He couldn't sleep either, knowing that today was a big day. Unusually, she didn't speak first. "Careful, you'll wear out the tiles. They're not cheap – they came from B&Q."

"I'll vary my route around the table, but it's a bit difficult in this tiny kitchen."

"Good morning." He gave her a kiss.

"Good morning." She smiled back. "I'm confused and light-headed."

"That's because you constantly go around the table clockwise. You need to vary it."

"Huh."

"You're confused ... by what?"

"Can I show you something?" She leant over the laptop and called up the school photograph next to a scanned version of Peter Swift taken in Longford Place by Tina. "This is Johnny Boswell at school, and this is Peter Swift in London a few days ago." She reminded him of some details of their roles in her investigation.

"Looks like the same person to me. If the Johnny Boswell in Tina's photograph has changed his name, who's impersonating him in Trinidad?"

"Well, whoever it is, he's doing it with the real Johnny's blessing. Remember that the real Johnny owns the company, and whoever the impersonator is, they're a director out there."

"Have you searched for this director?"

"No, I haven't yet. I never questioned it. Why would anyone? I'm on that next. Are you making breakfast?"

"Scrambled eggs?"

"You're wonderful. Where did I find you?"

"By the bins at the Yellands' villa in Spain, if I remember correctly."

She looked up at him affectionately. "Where did the years go?"

"Doing my degree mostly ... which I hope will be over soon."

"You're going to do fine. You're a genius."

"I'm not sure about that."

They both concentrated, him on the cooking and her at the laptop. He beat eggs in a bowl and put bread in the toaster. She resumed her searching, occasionally swearing or updating him.

"Well, our director has been called Johnny Boswell since he was in the Caribbean. Hey!" she shouted, "His UK address is in Brightlingsea in Essex. That's where Peter Swift lists his UK address. What are they up to?"

"No good?"

By the time she had eaten the scrambled eggs and Wazz had gone for a shower, she had found a photograph in the *Essex Gazette* of Johnny Boswell's parents' wedding anniversary. It was a lavish bash at some country house hotel. She also found photographs of Johnny and Darren Boswell, as teenagers, winning fishing competitions.

There was no doubt that Johnny Boswell was the long-haired billionaire now known as Peter Swift and Darren Boswell was the director now using his cousin's name.

When she explained this to Wazz as he emerged from the bathroom with a towel around his waist, his first question was, "Why?"

"And what has this got to do with Tina?" he added, drying himself.

"No idea, but I have one more bit of checking to do before I go to the office. Leonard has cracked the whip and wants me in all day. He doesn't trust me not to get up to no good ... like those cousins."

"Wise man."

―――――

In the four weeks following their first meeting at the restaurant up in the hills above Cannes, Gordon Overton and his old school mate Johnny Boswell had met several more times, but always on neutral ground outside the UK. The first meeting had been in Lille at the Museum of Illusions, a somewhat apt location, and the second had been in Bruges at some three-Michelin-star restaurant that had dark oak-panelled walls and low lighting, but with discreet service and beyond exquisite food.

It had suited Gordon Overton to jump on the Eurostar, meet for lunch and be back in London early evening. Johnny Boswell had been happy to fly up to northern France or Belgium to meet Gordon while he established whether the offer that had been made originally was for real.

On the superyacht, the *Bellis Mare*, a couple of weeks after that first lunch in Provence, Johnny had looked at Alexei in a new light. He had never thought the man was an angel, and no billionaire Russian keeps their fortune without having strong links to the Russian President, but Gordon had opened Johnny's eyes. While sitting in the upper lounge of the boat, they'd been chatting to the captain, who happened to be a youthful-looking Englishman or, as he liked to describe himself, a Cornishman from Calstock who had grown up gig racing on the river Tamar.

The conversation with the captain had been about the long-standing ban on helicopters in the Maldives and the impact on the superyachts, where owners and guests had to come ashore by launch. When alone, the two billionaires had chatted freely about fishing and the Indian Ocean. The conversation had meandered randomly to the Chinese influence in the region, the fact that Russians could fly freely to the Maldives, and rising sea levels.

Alexei didn't drink spirits or beer; he drank wine and only French wine. This was another subject where they could chat away for hours, consuming bottles that may have cost a small fortune but didn't benefit from the rolling of the ship; decanting the reds was an absolute necessity, even though the bottles were stored in boxes hanging on gimbals, which removed much of the movement of the sea.

Over a fine Bordeaux, they had begun talking about tax-friendly jurisdictions for their businesses and flags of convenience for boats – subjects never far from the thoughts of the mega-rich. Alexei had mentioned his interests in the Caribbean and, in particular, Guyana with its rich, untapped mineral resources. Johnny hadn't needed to probe very vigorously for his host to begin pontificating on the subject of the Chinese influence in Nicaragua, Panama and Guyana.

Unusually, Johnny had held back on the wine and let Alexei sink into a relaxed and happy state in which he chattered on about subjects central to his life. He had mentioned that the crew were about to take the boat back through the Mediterranean Sea and across the Atlantic to Georgetown. It would be there for an important meeting of heads of government, and he would use it as a base and fly in and out.

It had been so easy for Johnny to ask, "Are you there for the meeting?"

"No, I'll fly home before it starts."

"Are some heads of state using the boat?"

"No, but maybe that's a good idea." Alexei had laughed and,

in his broken English, asked, "I have some business in Guyana. Why you not have ammonia plant there?"

"I'm busy looking for one, trust me."

"You want to use boat? It's there for two weeks, I think."

"No thanks; it's my director who's looking for sites there and all over the Caribbean."

"Guyana is best opportunity. Many minerals ... and much oil and gas offshore."

"Are you interested in the minerals?"

"I'm interested in bauxite for my aluminium factory, but Chinese are ..." Alexei had searched for the word in English.

"Buying their way in?"

"Big problem. Americans and Brits are OK. Chinese, they buy whole country."

A pair of white-tailed tropicbirds had been chattering overhead while flying back to their island. The sun had been setting between towering golden clouds, and the sea had been oily and calm.

———

It was 9.00am on Tuesday, 25th March, and Mike was already sitting at her desk, having learnt from Morag that Leonard had arrived over an hour earlier.

He had made it clear he wanted her in the office all day while CHOGM was happening 4,500 miles away across the Atlantic. To make a point of it, he put his head around the door of the large room she shared with five others, including her friend Chuck.

"Good, you're all here. Mike, can you give me the heads-up on your project?" He turned without waiting for a response and went back to his office.

She logged out of the network and made her way after him,

past the faces all wondering why she had been singled out for special attention during the last few weeks.

When she arrived at his office, the door was left open for her to enter. Unusually, he had two laptops on his desk, both apparently being used. He was swaying gently in his seat as he glanced from screen to screen. Whether it was through excitement or a medical complaint, she didn't ask or comment – best not to speculate.

He tapped a few keys with his podgy figures and turned to her. "Tell me about your project. What have you been doing?"

Here, she was in a dilemma. She could waffle about Eric Fournier and fire extinguishers, or she could mention what she had really found, which was the possible connection between him and the man she now knew to be Darren Boswell, the cousin of Johnny Boswell in Cannes, and that the real Johnny Boswell was one of the three men Tina had photographed. A man who had gone to school with Gordon Overton.

"I've been going through the background of the director of the ammonia plant in Trinidad. Something isn't right." She watched his face for any reaction, but there was none.

"Has the next shipment left for Europe or the USA?"

"According to Pyrandox's system, it left yesterday for Marseille and another ship leaves for Galveston tomorrow."

"Hey, that's great. Is it time for our guys at Galveston to check out the cargo?"

"Only if we can coordinate it with the Trinidadians. We need to catch Fournier and this shady director."

He gave her the power to suggest the point in time when this should happen, plus the name of the new CIA man in Langley who would authorise it.

"Any more mysterious letters and photographs from Tina Persad?" He could sound so disinterested and benign.

"No, nothing. Why would I have? She's dead, isn't she? Why do you keep on about her?"

"Look, I can only go on what the Brits tell me. They think she's incompetent and has gone rogue. She begins poking her nose in where she shouldn't, then she disappears completely. She's probably dead, but that could be a smokescreen while she rains on our parade ... or at least the Brits' parade."

He was sounding so reasonable that Mike didn't explode, but she began to digest what he had just said. Had she let her dislike of Overton cloud her judgement? Had Tina been playing her all along? She looked down at her hands. "She's a friend ... was a friend."

"That makes it doubly tough. Trust is the most difficult thing in our business. That's why it sucks when we're betrayed by a friend or colleague."

Sitting before her was the only person, apart from Wazz, whom she trusted. Her eyes began to well up, but she managed to keep it in check. What if he were right? She let this sink in, and once she started to view the recent past through a different lens, it began to fall into place. Tina had subtly directed Mike's anger and attention onto Overton and was perhaps trying to compromise him with the three photographs. After a silence, which Leonard allowed to dominate the room, she said quietly, "Is that why she flew to Paris on her own passport? I told you I found this out; she didn't tell me."

"Possibly? Tell me again how you found out."

She told him the details of this and how she had gone to Janet's house in Featherstone. "I also found out that an unidentified woman's body had been found in the Siagne River near Cannes. I put two and two together."

"That's always tempting, but very dangerous. I once tried double veggie burgers with double fries ... biggest con since they started bottling tap water." He stopped for a second. "For what it's worth, I don't think she's dead."

This should have been the best news that Mike had heard for years, but she felt oddly flat. "Where is she?"

"I don't know, but I think she'll turn up very soon." His eyes dipped across to one of his screens.

Mike had crossed a bridge, and there was no going back, so she began telling Leonard everything: "Please don't fire me, but I've been doing my own research." She added as a defence, "It's related to my project."

"Mike, I won't fire you, but please, we're in the last minute of the game. The clock's ticking down."

"The director at the ammonia plant is masquerading as Johnny Boswell – I don't know why. His real name is Darren Boswell, but he seems to have adopted his cousin's name when he went out to the Caribbean. The real Johnny Boswell is the long-haired man in one of Tina's photographs. He's a billionaire who lives in Cannes and Monaco, but he's masquerading as someone called Peter Swift. I don't know why this is either." She paused to look at his face, but all she saw was a bored history teacher listening to a schoolchild describing the Battle of Agincourt, which he had heard a hundred times before and the outcome never changed.

"This long-haired billionaire met Gordon Overton at his club in Longford Place," she continued, now in full flow, "and one last thing: Tina left Gordon Overton's name written on the bottom of my coffee machine. In her letter, she told me to look there and not to trust that name. There, that's it."

He rocked backed in his chair. "Thank you, that makes a few things a bit clearer. You have been busy."

"Sorry."

"We need to find her before she does something stupid ... again, like on that other project."

Mike liked the sound of the word 'we'.

CHAPTER TWENTY-NINE

It was the morning of CHOGM, and so many flights were arriving at Cheddi Jagan airport that they were parked out on the apron and the passengers were being transferred in buses, which meant they spent long periods queuing in front of the two-storey buildings with their bright-blue roofs. The additional security demanded by so many world leaders slowed down the process. Despite sizeable investment and planning, it was a logistical nightmare.

The rains began, and a blanket of grey cloud swept in from the east.

The British High Commission staff were being tested to the limit, mostly by coordinating the arrival of the two planes: one carrying the King and Queen, and another with the PM and his entourage. Four black Range Rovers and two Discoveries had previously been shipped out, but there was a general shortage of vehicles; it was decided that it would be easier if the planes landed two and a half hours apart.

The flight from Grantley Adams airport in Barbados arrived first, and after a series of pointless formalities on the sopping-wet red carpet, the British PM escaped beneath large, black umbrellas to a convoy of vehicles heading north to the centre of Georgetown. He had two important meetings arranged at the convention centre before the conference started in earnest.

The first was with the PM of Mauritius to discuss the aftermath from signing a ninety-nine-year lease on the Chagos Islands. This ensured their continued use by the US and British air forces and navies together with GCHQ on Five Eyes' joint behalf. This was yet another example of the West playing catchup as China quietly flexed its muscles. It would cost the UK £100 million a year to keep them from establishing a base in the southern Indian Ocean and depriving the UK and the USA of a critical military foothold. The handful of buildings and fuel tanks now occupied some of the most expensive real estate on the planet.

The second was with India, Pakistan, Bangladesh and Sri Lanka about undersea internet cables. As with the first meeting, this was as much about keeping China at arm's length and making sure that the subcontinent remained linked to the West and not to the other countries in the BRICS group such as Russia and, again, China.

As these side meetings were concluding, the King and Queen had arrived, having flown from Hewanorra airport in Saint Lucia. The heavens opened, and there was no way the military band could play outside or indeed that anyone could stand on the red carpet, which was now covered with a sheet of water. The Queen was holding on to her hat and pulling her coat tightly closed as an aide tried to hold a large, black umbrella over her head. After a perfunctory, formal welcome in a small room used for VIP jet arrivals, they made their way to the waiting vehicles.

Irritatingly, the rain then eased, and the clouds broke up. To the sound of the tyres spraying water, they were driven directly towards the Mahaica Convention Centre. Here, they were to be met on the steps by the Guyanese President and PM.

———

As she walked away from a busy crossroads in the centre of Georgetown, Tina had been surprised to receive a call on her burner phone. She was staring at the City Hall, a neo-Gothic building straight out of an Addams Family film – albeit that had been painted in white and pale blue, possibly to avoid frightening the residents.

It was Joseph who was keen to update her, as he'd been speaking to a group of his friends. His brother's murder had energised him beyond words. His one objective now was to find out what was happening at CHOGM and how it was connected to Hector's death. "Can we speak?"

"Better to meet up; where are you?"

"At a friend's in Georgetown. Where are you?"

"By the City Hall."

He did some mental gymnastics, told her the name of the nearest café and suggested they met there in fifteen minutes. She set off, under a cheap umbrella she had hastily bought, to the background noise of police sirens, which were now the norm in a city on edge, and found the café without difficulty on the corner of a two-storey wooden block in the colonial style prevalent throughout the capital.

She was drinking an americano when he walked in, wiping the sweat and rain from his forehead.

"It's a hot one." He pulled out a very narrow wooden chair that didn't look comfortable and found out that, indeed, it was not; he perched on it as if it were a kid's tricycle.

"And a wet one. The city is buzzing. Get yourself something to drink."

He jumped up, went to the counter, and came back with a bottle and a chocolate bar. "I've been busy," he said.

She waited for him to continue, holding her cup in both hands.

"It's about the takeaway restaurant. My friends say it was sold two months ago to a man from Suriname, but he's not Dutch – he's Russian or half-Russian."

Tina paused to take this in. She knew Suriname used to be known as Dutch Guiana and it bordered the old British Guiana. "That's strange. Why would he buy a business like that?"

"I don't know; it could be legitimate. Guyana is a great place to invest in for the future, but I think it's connected to CHOGM. Do you think they're going to use it as a base for an assault, perhaps as a place for a shooter or somewhere to put a bomb? In fact, as you know, it's quite a narrow street outside the convention centre, so a bomb would be effective."

Tina was staring at him. "What would replacing all that ventilation ductwork be for?"

"Apart from the obvious, I have no idea. Why would the Russian Embassy be involved? It must be important. It's not like it's next to the US Embassy or anything. It's just a burger bar in a busy street."

Tina wiped some coffee from her upper lip and stared out of the window as a small bunch of people walked by carrying flags and banners despite the rainy squalls. Joseph stood up, saying that he needed to use the toilets at the back, and disappeared through a white door with the silhouette of a cowboy on it.

She suddenly felt lonely. This was a culmination of many things, but mostly because she had no one close with whom to discuss anything. Her confidence had taken a battering when she had made several bad calls on her last big project with Mike. It turned out that the person she'd been trying to recruit was part of a Russian honey trap into which she had fallen headfirst. All the progress that had been made by teams from several countries was very nearly jeopardised. She'd been reprimanded, given a formal warning and put on a retraining course at some old military camp in Dorset. After three weeks, she had very nearly jacked the whole thing in and returned to forensic police work, but Gordon Overton had offered her a second chance to work in the Caribbean. Tina had jumped at the opportunity, even though she still hated the man.

Controllers were the same the world over: constantly casting you out into the unknown and then reeling you back in, praising and chiding you in equal measure. They were as much sadists as field officers were masochists.

Her daydream was broken by Joseph returning to the table.

"Should I ring the police? I can do it anonymously." He looked as if he had reached the end of his tether.

"No, no ... there's no need. I'll ring it in now. I'm just thinking about what to say. I wanted to wait until I was certain what was happening."

"We don't have any more time."

She gave him an odd look, which he couldn't read.

"I'll make the call now. Thanks for everything. Stay in touch." She stood up and left the coffee bar, remembering to collect her umbrella on the way out.

———

Thirteen days previously, and unaware that Tina was hiding nearby, the final meeting between Gordon Overton and Johnny Boswell had taken place over lunchtime in London at the Commonwealth and Overseas Club in Longford Square. This had been a big move for Johnny, not meeting on neutral ground, and he had half been expecting that the police would come bursting through the door to arrest him. He had delivered what he'd been asked for, and in return, Gordon had compromised himself by passing back confidential and, in some cases, top-secret information of great value to Johnny.

It was when they were in Bruges weeks before that Gordon had given Johnny the details on Eric Fournier and his relationship with Darren, his cousin. Tina had discovered the link and passed it back via Oscar. This was the point when Johnny had genuinely believed he and Gordon were in this together to their mutual benefit.

This information had made him boil inside. He had flown back to Essex to meet his cousin and to tell him to end the relationship with Fournier. Johnny knew that not only was he risking the whole business empire but also he, albeit unwittingly, was risking the legitimisation process that was well underway with HMRC via Gordon.

It was while he was back in London that he had met Gordon in the private club. It was symbolic. He was Johnny Boswell again, and it felt good. Peter Swift was dead and buried – well, that was true on so many levels. He also had some more information that would interest his old school friend.

Inside, the club looked authentic, but whether it was like the old broom where the head and handle had been replaced three times was unclear. It smelt of cigars, even though no one was allowed to smoke them, and the red leather chairs weren't worn in any way. It rather contrasted with Cheddings School, where all the furniture and decoration was tired and dirty.

They had found it easier to talk freely at a corner table in the dining room, where the waiters in white gloves did their best to conjure up a past that, in reality, may never have existed. The menu was, however, purposely like at the private schools of so many of the members. For the two of them, the thought of steak and kidney pudding with a suet crust and thick gravy had been too hard to resist.

Over a glass of the club claret, Johnny had opened up. "I've seen our friend with the boat again. It's going to arrive over there on Monday, 13th March, and stay until Tuesday, 25th. He's flying in on the Monday and sleeping on the boat for two or three nights. Then he flies back to Monaco." Johnny had taken a sip for effect and continued, "He's in London on that Tuesday, 25th – we've agreed to have dinner in his favourite restaurant, which is called The Macedon. Eating out in London is a luxury that wasn't entirely open to us before."

"Thank you, that's helpful. I'm sorry I can't tell you why it's helpful, but I'm sure you understand." Gordon could still manage to sound pompous and patronising whatever he was saying, but he had some good news: "I understand that your accountants and HMRC have had several useful meetings and agreed a provisional sum."

"I believe so, and thank you." Saying thank you continued to gall, but it would have to be continued for a few more weeks yet.

"Hopefully, we can have a lot more lunches here in the future without the pressure that has been on you."

Over my dead body, was the thought that had run through Johnny's head, but he had said something banal and appeasing instead.

CHAPTER THIRTY

"Have you called it in to head office yet? We need to make this all about the USA and seize that container of fire extinguishers at Galveston." Leonard was trying to keep Mike focused on her central task.

"Yes, I have." She looked around his office while her mind was moving on to the main thing preoccupying her. "We have to stop her; I honestly believe she's going to do something stupid. I feel it in my waters."

"Which reminds me, I need to take a leak," he said, getting up out of his chair.

"What do you think she's doing?" Mike was still coming to terms with the fact that her friend was probably a traitor.

"If I knew where she was, I might be able to work that out."

"Well, she got off a plane in Paris" – she did a quick calculation – "twelve days ago. She could be anywhere on the planet, including back in London."

"My gut feeling is that she's disappearing up her own ass or chasing her own shadow. She's not the sharpest knife in the drawer. Send me any updates on Galveston." He escorted her to the door, which he closed with a reassuring solid 'clump' sound behind him.

She was wondering what he meant about Tina as she walked back to her office. Thinking like her might be a good starting point. There was nothing more to do on the meth project, and her thoughts were roaming elsewhere anyway. She was going to find the woman she had thought of as a friend.

Once back at her desk, it dawned on her that Tina wasn't likely to have stayed in France for twelve days, and the most probable place for her to go was the Caribbean and, specifically, Guyana. It didn't take her long, with free access to the full CIA system, to find where Tina's passport had last been used. In minutes, she had the details of Tina's flight to Port of Spain via Panama. It had never occurred to Mike that her friend had purposely bought a flight to Paris just to deceive her into thinking she was going somewhere in France. Tina had been so cunning.

Moving on to the question of why she had flown to Port of Spain, Mike decided to start with Sheldon and Hector. She rechecked their phones, looking at everything from a fresh perspective. Would Tina have contacted them or used them on this secret visit? It was laborious, but she eventually spotted one message on Hector's phone referring to someone identified as "AD". It came to her in a flash that this was Alice Dee.

If Tina were involved in some way with the meth production or distribution, she wouldn't have told Mike about Eric Fournier; she would have hidden this information. It became patently obvious to Mike that she was involved in the sabotage of CHOGM in Guyana. Hector was Guyanese, and it was likely that she went there next.

An hour later, she had found Tina's flight to Georgetown and that she had paid cash for it, presumably to avoid using credit cards. Mike tried to keep calm, but she couldn't avoid trying to understand Tina's motives and actions. Time was pressing. It was 5.00am in Guyana, and CHOGM would begin in six hours.

Checking the hotels in Georgetown for the previous week would take days and was unlikely to be productive. If Tina wanted to disappear, this wouldn't be difficult – especially if she paid cash, as there would be no searchable record. A thought went through her head, *She might be being offered accommodation and sheltered by* ... here, Mike struggled. Who was Tina working for? The Chinese? The Russians? The Guyanese? Private interests?

Her blood pressure began to rise, and she needed to calm down. How could Tina betray her friends? Mike was having trouble controlling her emotions, and she couldn't resist replaying conversations and meet-ups in her head, looking for any indication of what Tina's motivation to swap sides might be, unless she had always been a double agent.

Had she wangled her way onto the CHOGM project so she could derail it? Like Kim Philby rising to head of counterintelligence, she would be in the perfect position to tip off her controllers about what the UK (and the USA) knew about any planned covert actions, to act like a cuckoo and gradually to evict genuine personnel such as Overton from the nest.

Here, Mike felt a twinge of guilt. While he wasn't her type, Overton had been trying to deal with a difficult situation. What could he do once Tina had triggered an alarm? Perhaps this was when his fears were confirmed. Mike felt a second twinge when she remembered that she had withheld the information about Tina's visit to Janet and her flight to Paris. If only she had told him.

Mike was chastising herself. Her inability to separate or isolate her personal emotions made her useless as an operative. Her dislike of Overton, the man, had immediately clouded her judgement, as had her friendship with Tina. She had got them the wrong way round. Sitting at a desk as an analyst was where she should be.

Her last thought before she resumed searching was that she must treat the individuals in the photographs in a different light, supposing Tina was trying to compromise them or Overton. It was very likely they were red herrings purposely dangled in front of Mike to lead her away from the truth and waste her time. Checking out the three men further, however, was for another day.

———

The sniper was restless. He'd been stretched out in the ventilation duct for three hours, not able to take the risk that plans might change and his target would arrive early. He knew the pattern of the blobs of solder at the joints of the galvanised panels intimately, having nothing else to look at.

To make his position more bearable, he had collected cardboard from the upper storeroom and used a dozen pieces to make a crude bed beneath him to lie on. His hip had made a depression in it, which made the wait more comfortable. When it came time for him to lock on to the target and fire, he would be resting on his front, with one hand holding the stock of the rifle on its small tripod and a finger of the other hand ready to pull the trigger. His ear protectors and glasses would never be more necessary as he was about to fire in such a confined space.

Cleverly, the installers from the embassy had put a grille on the outside of the duct with the vanes angled downwards. It gave him the perfect angle to aim at the steps of the convention centre below.

He would be glad to leave his hellhole where he had lived for thirty-six long hours, making the minimum of movement and noise in case there were listening devices in place or next door was being used by the security forces. He was conscious of every new sound, especially throughout the night when there were long periods of silence.

Through an earpiece, he was being given snippets of information. Communication was reduced to an absolute minimum, but it came as a welcome relief from the boredom and tension.

He'd been told that his target should appear on the centre steps in less than ten minutes. There were several spotters from the Russian Embassy who were distributed around the city and feeding back information to the ambassador. One man had been watching for the convoy of black Range Rovers behind two police cars and four police motorbikes that was travelling to Georgetown from the airport, bringing the King and Queen to the opening ceremony.

The royal party was on its way.

It was the first visit for the Queen, but the then Prince Charles had visited twenty-five years ago when he became interested in the Iwokrama International Centre for Rain Forest Conservation and Development, a project in which he had remained involved. He had retained an affection for Guyana and was said to be pleased it was hosting CHOGM.

At that moment, he was pointing out to the Queen the muddy, brown Demerara River flowing alongside them and explaining its significance. Having seen a roadside advertisement, they had previously been discussing the growing of cacao, given her penchant for bitter dark chocolate. She had said that she would die for some.

———

Tina had left the café and walked across to a bench. She couldn't sit down as it was wet; therefore, she stood next to it, collapsing the umbrella. Her mind was made up. She didn't need any more information, and her options were limited. Having been compromised by the Russian honeytrap during the last project, her life had changed. They'd done their research well, and she had fallen hook, line and sinker for a man she thought was American.

Her rehabilitation course (or punishment, as she liked to think of it) near Portland was the last straw. There was a certain irony, she felt, that she was a mile from Portland in Dorset at the time when her friend, Mike, was on holiday back in Portland, Oregon, with her parents.

The sun was now out and reflecting into her eyes from the water on the white bench. She looked at her watch. After all the years in the secret-squirrel world, it had come down to this. She dialled the one number available to her.

Her heart was pounding, and she could feel her pulse with the phone pressed against her ear. An inordinate amount of time passed as it rang and rang before finally cutting off, not giving her the option to leave a voice message. Tina wanted to scream and explain how her life had led up to this point, this phone call. She had no idea how to get him to call her back urgently or whatever was more urgent than urgently.

She dropped her hands to her sides and allowed the wave of frustration to pass over her. Tina was out of her depth, and she knew it. This was the end.

There wasn't time if the necessary actions had to take place. Why hadn't he taken her call? With her head bowed, she accepted that there was only one possibility left to her. She lifted the phone back up and dialled.

"Hello?"

"It's Tina; don't speak, just listen. The Russians are intending to shoot the King or the PM at CHOGM. They're in the roof of a takeaway restaurant called Harpy's Burgers opposite the Mahaica Convention Centre. I've tried to contact the High Commission, but I'm *persona non grata*. Tell somebody you trust, but not Overton."

"Tina? Tina? What are you talking about?" Mike was completely thrown.

"Mike, I'm sorry. If you don't pass this message on, I don't know what will happen, but I'm guessing the King will be shot in a matter of minutes."

"What the fuck have you been doing?"

"That's for a discussion over a drink one day in The Green Feathers. Please tell somebody what I have just told you; there's no time to explain. I'm going to try to stop it myself."

Tina ended the call and walked away from the café.

———

In London, an already tense Mike shook her head from side to side and tried to reflect. She failed. Her head was completely scrambled. What sort of mind games were these? For absolutely no obvious reason, her eyes were drawn to the automatic sprinkler system on the ceiling of the office. This had never registered with her before, but she desperately needed a pointless distraction for a minute to allow her brain to come to terms with what she had just heard.

Irrespective of the fine details of any fire suppression system, it didn't take Mike long to realise that there was only one person to talk to, and not thinking it through any further, she sent him a message, rang his PA and ran up the stairs to his office. If necessary, she would hammer on his door. He would probably guess who it was.

"You can go in," Lana, the woman outside Leonard's door, said, smiling. He had given her the green light.

"I'm guessing this is good news," he said as she entered, with the solid door closing behind her.

"Tina's just called me."

"*Holy moly*, where is she?"

"Guyana, probably. She said that the Russians are going to shoot the King or the PM from a takeaway restaurant called Harpy's Burgers across from the convention centre."

"Why ring you?"

"What? Because she said she's *persona non grata* at the British High Commission and can't get through." While Leonard was thinking, she added, "She told me not to tell Overton."

Squeezing his eyes together, he pinched his nose high up on the bridge, deep in thought. "OK, leave it with me. I'll deal with it."

CHAPTER THIRTY-ONE

As a woman climbed over the barriers and fell to the floor, she was shouting a warning that there was a gunman in the burger bar. In case this was a diversion, four or five of the Guyanese security contingent moved forwards to grab her before she could detonate her suicide vest or pull out a knife. The policeman nearest to her had both hands outstretched, pointing his gun at her.

Two shots rang out.

Up in the metal duct, it provided the perfect echo chamber and funnelled the ear-splitting bangs down towards the crowds. The narrowness of the street further channelled the sound, creating panic everywhere. The watching crowd had no idea where the shots were coming from and had nowhere to run. They compounded the situation by trying to push each other out of the way. People were trampled in the chaos.

Secret service officers and police grabbed the VIPs and hauled them away or formed huddles so as not to provide a line of sight to the sniper. Everyone was waiting for the next shots. The world's media also cowered, but they somehow managed to keep all the cameras running and the microphones recording.

Outside the convention centre, a body was sprawled on the steps, hidden from view by the security teams. To the right, two black Range Rovers and a Discovery discharged some protection officers and began reversing.

Inside the convention centre was no different – it was pandemonium. News of what was happening outside came from multiple phone conversations. Was it safer to stay in the hall and perhaps lie on the floor between the seats, or to begin to leave by the fire exits? The noise generated by over a thousand frightened guests was reaching a crescendo. There was confusion as to whether one or two people had been shot.

The master of ceremonies, in a black suit and tie, came to the microphone on the stage and asked everyone to stay calm and to stay put while the police and emergency services dealt with the incident on the front steps. He repeated that there was no threat to anyone in the room, but his source of this information wasn't revealed.

The British delegation was standing near the front in a huddle. Everyone had a phone pressed to an ear. There was much waving of hands and voices were raised.

The Commonwealth Secretary-General walked out onto the stage, wearing a colourful dress and headscarf. She looked calm and lowered the microphone on its stand. The noise in the room reduced considerably as she informed everyone that the incident was now under control and an ambulance was on its way to the hospital. There was no cause for alarm. She asked everyone to stay in the hall while the police swept the area and added, rather unnecessarily, that the morning session would be cancelled. Everyone would be told over lunch what the new timetable would be. She stressed that threats to the Commonwealth wouldn't prevail and the meetings over the next few days would continue as close to the planned timetable as was possible.

The sound of sirens could be heard all over the city as the

ambulance headed for Georgetown Public Hospital. It was in a convoy of police cars racing away at high speed.

This was unnecessary. The patient inside was dead.

———

Out to sea, beyond Point Lisas, the clouds were forming in a long line, mushrooming upwards. As if mimicking their rhythm, a row of tankers was moored offshore, ready to be loaded the following day when the docks were free.

A mile inland, one man in a Rastafari hat and dark glasses with black frames was walking past a turquoise house with metal grilles on the balcony and windows. Another man, who remained at the wheel of the car, was bald, but he, too, was wearing shades.

As the first man approached the factory entrance, the driver started the engine and pulled past before turning around in a gateway. He drove slowly back the way he had come, watching in his rearview mirror and monitoring his friend, who had opened the outer door to the building.

Not a word was said in the small office as he raised a gun and shot the three people inside. After moving to the inner door of the warehouse, he pushed his way in and shot two more. There was no one left alive. On the way back out through the office, he took out two large bottles of petrol from his jacket pockets and doused the stud walls, desks and chairs. His last act before leaving and closing the outer door was to throw in a match.

He walked casually across the small car park, opened the passenger door and slid in before his friend drove off. As they made their way to Port of Spain, they never saw the fire nor the billowing black smoke that blocked out the sea view for the residents of California in Point Lisas.

They also didn't appreciate the irony of a fire-extinguisher factory burning down.

It would take days before the autopsies revealed that the staff inside had been shot, and the fire was now seen as arson. Apart from the three much-loved locals, one of the dead was identified as a chemist from Martinique and a second as Eric Fournier, a director of Pyrandox from France. A statement issued by the company expressed sadness and stated that it didn't intend to replace the factory and would be undertaking a rigorous examination of its existing facility in Costa Rica.

Eric's was the hundredth killing in Trinidad and Tobago that year, and it was only March.

Nobody in the Caribbean made any connection between the arson attack and a drug cartel turf war that was reaching fever pitch in France and Holland. Hector, by passing on information to a Dutchman for $1,000, had caused mayhem among the drug cartels across Europe.

He had also led unwittingly to the death of his friend LoverBoy at the hands of a local hit squad paid for by the Moroccan cartel.

———

"Zeppo has left us. Groucho and Harpo are safe, and so is Chico." This message came through to Marston House from Allan, the deputy high commissioner, and it triggered an extensive series of operations on both sides of the Atlantic.

In Guyana, two fast rigid-hulled inflatable boats, or RHIBs, from the Coast Guard sped across the surface of the water towards the *Bellis Mare*; they'd been anchored in the mouth of the Demerara River awaiting any trouble. Also steaming towards the superyacht was a $500-million white US Coastguard cutter with its red helicopter having taken off from the aft platform. The cutter was on one of its trips down to Argentina from its home port of Cape Canaveral in Florida. It had its 2.2-inch gun trained on the *Bellis Mare* in case it was stupid enough to try to make it out into international waters.

The Cornish captain of the superyacht was expecting a man to board before setting off across the Atlantic to the Mediterranean. However, he would never turn up, and the *Bellis Mare* wouldn't leave Georgetown, as it was being impounded and the captain arrested pending investigations. He would be released three days later, but only after he'd been accompanied on board by several members of the Guyana Defence Force, who took control of the boat.

None of this affected Joseph, who wasn't on board. He had made the decision to stay in Guyana and help his family come to terms with the death of Hector. Two months later, he was in the Bahamas on an even larger boat, this time owned by a Greek billionaire.

———

In London, behind the high walls of a detached Georgian villa near Regent's Park, another arrest was about to take place. On a low table in the upstairs lounge were the remains of half a dozen oysters next to a silver wine cooler draped in a white linen napkin. It had struck him as bizarre that oysters had achieved such a status in London and New York when, back 200 or 300 years, they were the food of the poor in both cities. London was full of oyster shell mounds, and the Big Apple should really be called the Big Oyster as the shells were many feet deep in places.

His own father had supplemented the family's meagre evening meals by catching sturgeon in the Irtysh River. To him, it was the most basic of foods, whereas today, in the restaurants of Europe, it was a luxury. How things change.

This was his private lounge where he did what he wanted, even if this meant the curtains and sofas reeked of smoke. He had open on his lap a boat brochure, while he was enjoying the favourite ciga-rettes of his youth: Belomorkanal. They were unusual in that they had an empty cardboard tube packed with strong tobacco at the end and had been created in 1932 to commemorate the construc-tion of the White Sea to Baltic canal; he was addicted to them.

A member of staff knocked and entered before advising him that he had visitors who had been let in through the front gate and weren't yet at the front door. It was the police.

Alexei Savin was surprised to come down the grand staircase to be greeted by six of them armed and with weapons drawn. Despite his protestations and saying that his friend the Russian ambassador would be on the phone to the FCDO within minutes, he was read his rights. The chief inspector pointed out to him that the Foreign Secretary had already been informed, part of his team would remain with a search warrant, and his helicopter and Gulfstream had been impounded.

He was bundled out of the front door and taken to a secure police station in Central London.

Alexei Savin never made it to dinner at The Macedon with Johnny Boswell.

CHAPTER THIRTY-TWO

The assassination of the Guyanese PM caused shock and consternation around the world.

Decisions needed to be made. The Deputy PM of Guyana met quickly with the Commonwealth Secretary-General to decide on an immediate course of action. It was agreed that the PM would have wanted CHOGM to go ahead and to maximise the opportunity for the fifty-six countries and states to meet. This was untrue – he had hated the Commonwealth – but it sounded believable. A reduced opening ceremony would be put back until the afternoon.

The King had made it clear that he wouldn't allow terrorists to win and would officiate at 2.30pm. The lunchtime airwaves were full of world leaders condemning the assassination and praising the heads of government for continuing with the conference and meetings. Out of respect, all social and recreational events were cancelled.

The Russian President, speaking from Moscow, condemned the action of the gunman, whom he described as a lone terrorist. He wanted to emphasise the close links between Russia and Guyana and that all help would be provided to the investigating authorities. The sniper, whom the local news networks were saying had been killed by the Guyanese police after a tip-off from the public, had been identified as a Georgian national.

This wasn't completely true.

There had been no tip-off from a member of the public. Tina had failed to get through to Allan, the deputy high commissioner, because he was going back and forth to the airport and was more than busy. He was using a dedicated phone for the duration of the conference, which is why Tina couldn't get through to him or leave a voice message. However, in London, Mike had told Leonard. Reassuringly, he had said that he would pass the intelligence about the possible assassination on to Gordon Overton.

This he did, but not immediately.

It was members of the British special forces masquerading as the Royal Protection officers who had approached the back of the takeaway and waited for the sniper to exit the building after coming down the stairs. It was one of this team who had shot the gunman, but only after he himself had successfully fired at and killed the Guyanese PM. Timing had been everything. The Russian died falling backwards over the food bins and collapsing on the greasy, stained tarmac.

It was Allan who had suggested this to the SAS sergeant, such that the sniper was only to be killed as he left the building. These instructions were never written down. Allan and Gordon Overton were almost the only ones who knew the Russians were planning to kill the Chinese-leaning PM, and they were tacitly allowing this to happen.

It had taken Gordon Overton months of planning, beginning with his cultivating of – if that's the right term – his old school-mate Johnny 'Tonto' Boswell. He'd been fed enough intel about the Russian operation that he knew the objective was the Guyanese PM. His death wouldn't be unwelcome to the British Government, but they had to be beyond arm's length away from such action. Over the last few weeks, the plan had been adjusted so the so-called 'Royal Protection' team could be seen as the good guys taking out the Russian or Russians. The killing would seem like spontaneous action by the team once the assassination had happened.

No one outside a very tight circle would know that the King and Queen weren't in either of the blacked-out Range Rovers arriving to be formally greeted by the Guyanese PM, as that would have been too risky. They were in a separate Range Rover a mile away. The British PM and delegation were also already safely inside the hall. None of the British contingent was at risk from the sniper.

Months earlier, Gordon Overton had, however, needed to be seen to be trying to investigate whether there were plots and threats to CHOGM, so he had sent Tina Persad – whom he regarded as a pretty incompetent case officer – to the Caribbean. She had practically cocked up a previous job, but on this one, she had begun to get too close, and he had tried to warn her off. However, instead of taking his instructions, she had disappeared from the face of the earth; that is, until she had phoned Mike Kingdom minutes before the assassination.

Gordon had also tried to get Mike Kingdom removed from investigating where Tina had gone. He hadn't wanted Tina found, unless it was by him and a very small, dedicated team. However, Mike had proved to be tenacious, and it was fortunate that Leonard de Vries had been able to keep things under control. US interests completely aligned with the UK on this matter, and the US President was content to be even more distanced from the action. Plausible deniability was all that the Brits and Americans wanted.

With CHOGM back on track, the biggest problem for the Brits was deciding who stayed for the funeral after the meetings had ended. That unlucky card was pulled by the British Deputy

PM, who was flown out immediately after the rest of the delegation had flown back to the UK.

———

"Well done on the drug project. I knew you'd crack it. That's Trinidad and Costa Rica crossed off the list, and no more imports of meth through Galveston, Le Havre or Marseille. Langley will be pleased, and the French are pretty happy too. That makes a change – I mean the French being happy." Leonard was walking with Mike along one of the sandy paths used for horse riding through Green Park, next to Constitution Hill in London. They couldn't see Buckingham Palace through the plane trees a couple of hundred yards away to the south or the Commonwealth and Overseas Club in Longford Place the same distance to the east, beyond Lancaster House and St James's Palace.

She was incredibly annoyed and confused. Leonard had decided that it was better to talk to her outside, one-to-one, rather than in his office. They had walked further than he intended, but him being out of breath merely added to the charade.

"The gang war isn't over," she said.

"Yeah, but they've lost a big source of meth, and they're killing each other, which makes me happy because it doesn't involve us in anything risky, and they tend to make mistakes, which is also good for business. C'mon, cheer up. You were great."

She didn't feel great.

They were avoiding the main subject, but they were now hundreds of yards from anyone else.

Leonard took the lead: "Speaking of shootings, don't beat yourself up. Guyana worked out well for us all. Well, not for their PM, obviously, and not for the Chinese ... or the Russkies who take all the blame. That's a slam dunk in my playbook."

"You could have told me." She sounded twenty years younger.

"C'mon, Mike, it was too sensitive. Sometimes, we're here to stop things, and other times, we let things happen. It's a tough call. We got this one right, but only a handful of people have worked it out even now."

"Did you really pass on my message from Tina to Overton?"

"Yeah, of course. It was just a bit too late. Shame about that." He was failing to say that, yes, he did pass on the message to cover his own back, but only when it would be too late for the information to be seen as usable. He knew full well what the Brits were intending, but if they were formally told that the Guyanese PM was likely to be shot, they became complicit. He waited until the information would be seen to be too late to act upon. They were both protected by a credible cover story and sequence of events.

Mike had failed to make all the connections and, like the rest of the world, was still mostly in the dark. "What did Overton have against Tina?"

"Instead of sticking to being a case officer, she had started to get nosy and began playing at being an analyst. You lot never stay in your boxes."

She looked across at him from under the peak of her khaki cap.

"What?" he asked in mock horror.

"You've never known the difference."

"What? It's one of my skills. Do you know, I think that I'm growing into this job."

He had avoided mentioning that Overton thought Tina was, in his words, "a shit agent". Better not to antagonise Mike, who was surprisingly subdued, but she referred back to the project they had all done together through Five Eyes. "That's unfair. She only made one mistake."

"Becoming an agent, you mean? She should have stayed in the lab."

"I didn't mean that ... and you make her sound like a virus."

"Viruses have worldwide impacts."

"Huh." She paused briefly and continued, "We could have stopped the assassination. An innocent man got killed."

"I wouldn't call him innocent. The pockets of his pants were so full of Chinese money that they were around his ankles. He was selling out his country. Mike, when the game goes your way and you win, don't beat yourself up that your tactics weren't followed to the letter. You won. Period."

She was, at heart, a details person not a strategic thinker. Mike would never accept the sacrifice of a pawn in chess, despite it being the best option overall. She would fight to keep them all – and probably lose the game.

Leonard was pleased with the way the conversation had gone and how he had handled Mike; it was a walk in the park – literally.

"Oscar told me Tina's been fired." Mike was moving on.

He bit his tongue and kept quiet, rather than saying she had nearly got herself shot. It was better to let Mike say everything that she needed to so as to get it out of her system.

"I'm sure she knows she broke all the rules and shouldn't have disappeared for all that time, but I think Overton's been a bit of an asshole," she added.

"Her intentions were good, but her execution was crap. Sorry. There's no way back for her, but at least she's not dead like you thought for so long. Although she nearly got herself killed."

"Did Overton have to tell me she was probably dead?"

"He was trying to stop you looking for her. He knew your reputation. He didn't want her found until after CHOGM, and that's dead or alive."

"I hate him, but I suppose he's like a dog with three tails –

the Guyanese PM killed, the Russians blamed and Savin arrested in London?"

"True ... and Savin, that was a great catch."

"He might have acknowledged that Tina gave him that name."

Leonard, to use one of his favourite expressions, didn't want to rain on her parade or her friend's parade. "It may have come from several sources."

"Do you mean Zara?"

"She was one of them, and before you ask, her death was an accident. A tragic accident."

There was a silence before she spoke again. "I think I need some time off. I'm finding it all a bit tough."

"Sure. Take a week off. Send me a postcard."

"I was thinking of two weeks. I'm going to Wiltshire. They only have postcards of Stonehenge and Salisbury Cathedral. Which do you want?"

"Salisbury Cathedral. Every time I stare at it, I'll be reminded that we got even and stuffed the Russkies."

———

All the way as she was riding down to Rodbourne, she was wondering about that word 'we'.

———

On the anniversary of his release from prison, Wazz felt that he had reached a significant milestone, he had celebrated by going out and buying a beaten-up used van, which he christened Denzil after misreading the registration plate. It was a Fiat Fiorino in silver with 20,000 miles on the clock.

It was Friday, and he was picking it up in the afternoon and driving it down to Rodbourne, after which he and Mike were going to take a couple of weeks' holiday. Meanwhile, Mike had roared off on the motorbike, with her large rucksack and both panniers full.

The journey down in perfect weather had felt liberating. For the first time in months, she wasn't agitated or traumatised.

A familiar musty smell welcomed her as she opened the back door of the house. It was probably the age of the building, but it could be a rotting mouse or dove in the roof space. Why she had bought a house in a thatched terrace still mystified her. Perhaps it was her dream about living in a typical chocolate-box English village. Whatever the reason, she was now faced with the upkeep of a 200-year-old house with a roof made of thatch – whatever that was.

Unlocking the back door, she had to be careful to step over the piles of peacock shit. What did those birds eat?

After ten minutes of unpacking her clothes and the food she had bought, she would sit in her lounge relaxing with a coffee and some chocolates. She had no new project to worry about and, currently, no missing or dead friends.

Her tasks completed, she slumped back in an armchair with her coffee remaining untouched as she fell into an untroubled sleep. Wazz would be down at about 8.00pm, and they could look forward to spending some time together, not burdened by their work or unsocial hours.

She was woken up by a rat-tat-tat at her front door. It startled her, and the fact it was dark outside told her how long she'd been asleep. Memories of Cromer's men came flooding back. What now?

Mike opened the door to find Tina standing there clutching an overnight bag.

They fell into each other's arms and burst into tears.

The next hour was spent filling each other in on their versions of what had happened. They moaned about everyone, but mostly Gordon Overton and Leonard de Vries. They concluded they'd been badly treated by their bosses, although they were blissfully ignorant of what had really taken place and how the two of them had nearly ruined the British and US plans. They had both almost breached the wall of plausible deniability, behind which the two countries could hide while joining the worldwide condemnation of Russia. Since CHOGM, the Deputy PM of Guyana had already announced a more pro-Western stance, which was music to ears in Washington and London.

Mike left a note for Wazz to say that they were in the pub and for him to join them.

With linked arms, they walked the short distance to the High Street and approached The Green Feathers with its sign rusted solid at a jaunty angle. Mike opened the door, and the bell tinkled. They entered to the usual chatter and grabbed a table with four unmatching chairs. The glassy-eyed green woodpecker in its domed case paid them no attention.

Jess came out from behind the curtain and ambled across, ignoring a series of orders and requests as she passed through the tables.

Vic was sitting in his seat, smiling at everyone and silently encouraging tolerance. He would act as go-between once Jess had disappeared back behind the curtain, for which he might be rewarded with a pint of beer. "Did they Mormons come back an' pester thee, as well?" he asked Mike as she passed by.

"No, I was in London."

"I spoke to the silly beggars for hours. Nice folk."

"They don't drink alcohol, Vic."

"Oh bugger."

The two women pulled out their chairs and sat down.

"Jess, you remember Tina. Can we have a large Pinot Grigio and a pint of beer?"

"There's £1.50 excess postage to pay on that letter. You forgot to put on enough stamps."

It was good to be home.

ACKNOWLEDGMENTS

I would like to begin by declaring my debt to the late Gerald Pollinger who, with his father, was agent to Graham Greene among others. He represented me in the late 1990s and his support and advice were invaluable, particularly as I began to write the Mike Kingdom series; he never lived to see *The Tip of the Iceberg* completed.

Further thanks go to my wife, Natasha, my sister, Angela, and my friend, Amber, who have shouldered the burden of reading my first draft. Paul and Mandy have also given me great encouragement.

All five of the Mike Kingdom thrillers have been edited by Lindsay Corten and she still has not changed her name and moved abroad. I hear her voice in my ear even as I write this. She has been the most wonderful critical friend.

Jem Butcher has produced the stunning covers for the series picking up on all of the subtleties as only a gifted designer can.

My thanks go to Adrian Hobart and Rebecca Collins at Hobeck Books whose advice, support and friendship are what every writer needs. It only took me twenty-nine years to find them.

Finally, a big thank you to the reviewers and bloggers who have all been so generous and who have, unwittingly, given me the strength to follow Mike Kingdom wherever she takes me.

DAVID JARVIS

ABOUT THE AUTHOR

David Jarvis went to art college, and then ran his design and planning practice for forty years, working all over the world. He ended up planning countries. His canvases just got bigger and bigger.

HOBECK BOOKS – THE HOME OF GREAT STORIES

We hope you've enjoyed reading this novel by David Jarvis. To keep up to date on David's fiction writing please do follow him on Twitter/X, Bluesky or Instagram.

Hobeck Books offers a number of short stories and novellas, free for subscribers in the compilation *Crime Bites*.

- *Echo Rock* by Robert Daws
- *Old Dogs, Old Tricks* by AB Morgan
- *The Silence of the Rabbit* by Wendy Turbin
- *Never Mind the Baubles: An Anthology of Twisted Winter Tales* by the Hobeck Team (including many of the Hobeck authors and Hobeck's two publishers)
- *The Clarice Cliff Vase* by Linda Huber
- *Here She Lies* by Kerena Swan
- *The Macnab Principle* by R.D. Nixon
- *Fatal Beginnings* by Brian Price
- *A Defining Moment* by Lin Le Versha
- *Saviour* by Jennie Ensor
- *You Can't Trust Anyone These Days* by Maureen Myant

Also please visit the Hobeck Books website for details of our other superb authors and their books, and if you would like to get in touch, we would love to hear from you.

Hobeck Books also presents a weekly podcast, the Hobcast, where founders Adrian Hobart and Rebecca Collins discuss all things book related, key issues from each week, including the ups and downs of running a creative business. Each episode includes an interview with one of the people who make Hobeck possible: the editors, the authors, the cover designers. These are the people who help Hobeck bring great stories to life. Without them, Hobeck wouldn't exist. The Hobcast can be listened to from all the usual platforms but it can also be found on the Hobeck website: **www.hobeck.net/hobcast**.

ALSO BY DAVID JARVIS

The Mike Kingdom Thrillers
The Tip of the Iceberg
This Is Not a Pipe
The Violin and Candlestick
The Mongoose and the Cobra
The Green Feathers

The Collation Unit

Buy online, from your local bookshop or from the Hobeck
Books website.